BOONE

A DEEP SERIES PREQUEL

NICK SULLIVAN

Cover design by Shayne Rutherford of Wicked Good Book Covers

Cover photo by Mihtiander/DepositPhotos.com

Interior Title Page Artwork by AArows/Shutterstock.com

Copy editing by Marsha Zinberg of The Write Touch

Proofreading by Gretchen Tannert Douglas and Forest Olivier

Original maps of Bonaire, Curaçao, & ABC Islands by Rainer Lesniewski/Shutterstock.com

ISBN: 978-0-9978132-9-6

Published by Wild Yonder Press

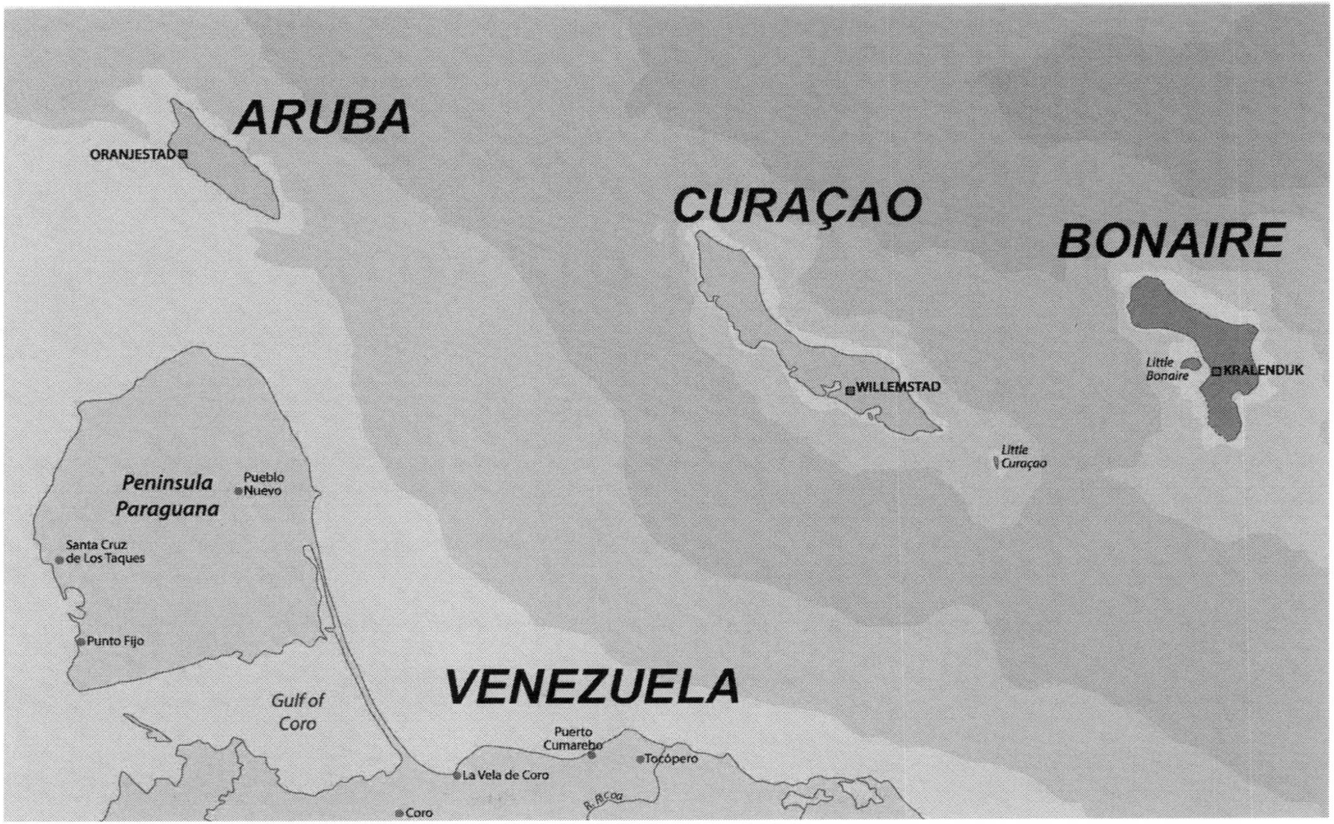
ARUBA
ORANJESTAD
CURAÇAO
WILLEMSTAD
Little Curaçao
BONAIRE
Little Bonaire
KRALENDIJK
Peninsula Paraguana
Pueblo Nuevo
Santa Cruz de Los Taques
Punto Fijo
Gulf of Coro
VENEZUELA
Puerto Cumarebo
Tocópero
La Vela de Coro
Coro

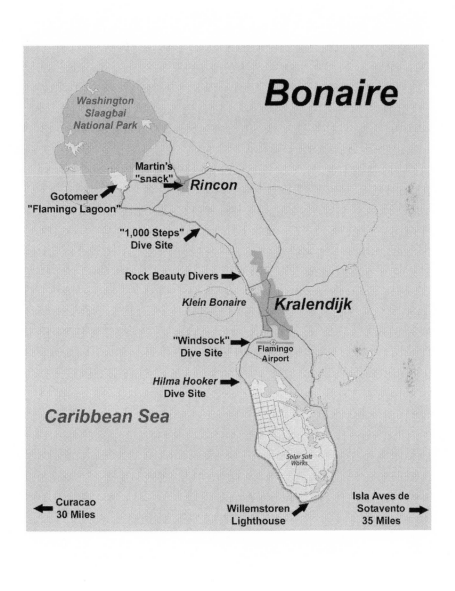

For Mom. Thank you for supporting me in all my childhood endeavors. The person I became owes everything to you for the hobbies you encouraged, the places we visited, and the lessons you taught me.

AUTHOR'S NOTE

If you're reading this, there's a good chance you've read other books in The Deep Series. Full disclosure, when I call this book a prequel, I mean it. We've all heard the adage, "life is a journey." I'll go further to add that it's all the stops along that journey that make us who we are. Many prequels consist of a short adventure that takes place before the first book in a series, but I wanted to do something different. I wanted to explore what makes Boone tick. What are some of the experiences that created the Boone we meet in *Deep Shadow*? This is that story.

The journey of a thousand miles begins with a single step.

Lao Tzu

PART ONE

ONE

"You're nuts."

Eleven-year-old Boone Fischer turned to find his best friend sitting astride his bicycle on the walking trail. Boone's own bike lay on its side in the grass beside the shore of the Clinch River.

Boone shrugged his bony shoulders. "I go snorkeling in the Clinch all the time."

Eugene Shelton rolled his eyes. "I know that. I'm talking about the rocks I saw you put in your pockets!" The smaller boy walked his slim bicycle closer and set it down beside Boone's knobby-wheeled dirt bike. Eugene's glasses slipped forward on his face as he bent over, and he quickly slid them back into place. "You ever hear the phrase 'sink like a stone'?"

"That's the idea," Boone replied, scanning the bank of 58 Landing Park for another right-sized river rock. This area of the Clinch River had less boat traffic than the Watts Barr Reservoir farther to the south, and Boone was planning on a brief under-water adventure.

3

"I don't get it. Don't you have to breathe?"

"Eventually." Boone spotted a smooth rock the size of his fist and added it to his right pocket, where it clacked against the current occupant. His left already bulged with a similar pair, and he had to snug the swimsuit's drawstring tighter to keep it from slipping on his slim frame. "See, when you hold your breath, the air in your lungs makes you buoyant. But I wanna hang out on the bottom, and the rocks'll help. A local fisherman taught me this trick when my mom took me to Aruba last year."

"That's where you're going this weekend?"

"Yeah. This'll be my fourth time."

"That must be expensive..."

"Probably. But my mom loves it there. It's where she met my dad."

"I haven't seen him in a while," Eugene offered hesitantly.

"Yeah... me neither," Boone muttered. "Mom's been missing him. But he's gonna meet us there. Dad's at sea a lot."

"He's Dutch, right?"

"Yeah."

"Does he wear those little wooden shoes?"

Boone snorted. "Don't let him hear you say that. He's in the Royal Netherlands Navy."

"Right, I remember. You know, the Dutch used to have a big navy and lots of colonies."

"Yeah, I learned about that playing a video game with pirates."

"Reading books is another way to learn," Eugene teased.

"Not nearly as fun." Boone went to his backpack, which held a cheap mask, snorkel, and fins he'd picked up at a store in nearby Oak Ridge.

"So... does that make *you* Dutch, then?" Eugene ventured.

"Half, I guess." Boone sat at the edge of the water and grunted as he tried to pull on one of the full-foot fins.

"You're gonna need new flippers," Eugene observed.

"Fins," Boone corrected. "One time, I called 'em flippers on a snorkel trip and the guide asked me if I was a manatee. Scuba divers call them fins."

"Oh, so you're a diver now."

"I will be." With a supreme effort, Boone managed to cram his foot into the fin. "Dang. These fit fine last time."

Eugene laughed. "Better quit growing then, Bigfoot."

Boone grinned and waggled a finned foot at his nerdy friend. It was true; he'd had a bit of a growth spurt. Boone had already been the tallest kid in his class, but he seemed to have added an inch in just the last month or two.

"So, why would a fisherman want to sink to the bottom?" Eugene asked. "Don't they just sit on a boat with a fishing pole?"

"This guy had a boat, but he liked to spearfish. He wore weights on a belt, but told me he used the trick with the pocket rocks when he was a boy. Said he was a freediver. Could hold his breath a long, long time."

"How long?"

"Several minutes at least. I've been practicing. I'm up to two minutes."

"No you're not," Eugene scoffed. "No way."

"Wanna bet?"

"No. But I want to see you do it. I'll time you. My watch has a stopwatch function." He raised a skinny wrist.

Boone nodded and stripped off his shirt, tossing it to Eugene. "Dump that on my bike, wouldja?" He picked up his mask and spit in it, rubbing the saliva into the lenses.

"Nasty." Eugene grimaced.

"Keeps it from fogging. Hey, how'd you know I was here?"

"I didn't." He pointed across the street at the hill above, where the Kingston Public Library sat, overlooking the riverside park. "I was biking up to the library and saw you down here."

Boone smiled. His friend spent a lot of time at the cozy little library. Satisfied with his mask, he snugged it onto his face.

Eugene came down beside him and examined the shoreside rocks himself, searching for a flat stone to skip. "You looking for anything in particular down there?"

"Nah. Can't see more than a few feet, anyway. I just wanna get ready for Aruba." Boone sat in the shallows and floated on his back, giving himself a moment to adjust to the shock of the cold water. "If you're gonna skip rocks, aim 'em away from me."

"Naturally," Eugene said, turning sideways and attempting a throw. The rock hit the water like a lead balloon with nary a skip. "What if a boat comes in?" he asked, gesturing toward the concrete slip at the southern end of the park. "You don't want to get diced up by a propeller."

"I'll hear 'em. And I'm not going that far out." Boone turned and kicked a few times, then ducked his head. "Can't see shi... can't see anything," he quickly corrected. His mother had been on him recently for some of his language. Eugene never cursed, but some of the other kids Boone hung out with could cuss up a storm, twanging away in their strong East Tennessee accents.

Like Boone, Eugene didn't have much of an accent, and Boone hung out with the bookish boy a lot; partly because the Sheltons lived just two houses down, but also because Eugene was an encyclopedia of knowledge, from plants and animals to the stars in the sky, probably due in part to his father being a bigwig scientist over at the Oak Ridge National Laboratory.

Boone thought Eugene was rubbing off on him a little. Since his friend had moved into the neighborhood, Boone's grades had gone up. Not because Eugene was doing his homework for him or anything like that, but Boone found himself reading more, and his internet searches had transitioned from video game strategies to islands, marine life, and freediving.

"You ready?" Eugene called out when Boone had gone about ten yards from shore.

"One sec. Trying to find something." The tips of Boone's fins could touch the bottom, but when he ducked his mask under the surface, he couldn't make them out. "Be right back."

Boone jackknifed and dove for the bottom, the slight pull of the four river rocks giving him a minor assist. *It was around here somewhere... there!* Boone spotted the object he was searching for on the bottom and ascended, placing a fin against it to hold position when he broke the surface. "Found it!"

"What? Pirate treasure?"

"I wish. Naw, just an old tire I found one time. Gonna hold onto it to help the rocks out. They won't be enough for a long breath hold."

"I'm ready!" Eugene held up his watch.

"I'm not!" Boone laughed. "I gotta relax and focus. I'm supposed to make my exhales longer than my inhales... that slows down the heart rate."

"What, like those Shaolin monks can do?"

"No idea. Shut up and let me chill. When I'm ready, I'm just going to sink, so have your finger on the timer."

Boone emptied his mind and began the breathing preparation he'd been reading about. After a few minutes, his body felt ready. He bent his knees and brought his fins back, slipping beneath the surface and gently dropping toward the bottom.

Even with the pocket rocks, his air-filled lungs wanted to pop him back up, so he reached out with a skinny arm and found the inside of the tire. Carefully, he grabbed hold, pulled himself down, and relaxed atop it.

Normally, this was when Boone would start counting one-Mississippi, two-Mississippi, but with his friend handling the timing, he could truly empty his mind and relax. In short order, he lost track of time, with the only jump in mental activity occurring when a curious catfish approached his mask before angling away into the murk. Eventually, his body let him know his time was nearly up. Gripping the tire tightly, Boone pressed his fins against the silty bottom and focused, willing himself to stay down a little longer. At the first sign of true discomfort, he shoved off from the bottom and shot to the surface, sucking in a glorious lungful of air.

Eugene stood on the shore, his watch-bearing wrist held aloft, staring at Boone with his mouth agape.

"So...?" Boone gasped. "How'd... how'd I do?"

"Holy crap, Boone," Eugene said, shifting his eyes back to the watch. "Two minutes, twenty-nine seconds!"

"Nice," Boone said, kicking back to shore. "So that's the record I gotta beat next time." He removed his fins at the water's edge.

"You see any sturgeon?"

Boone cocked his head. "Nah, just a big catfish. There aren't any sturgeon in here."

"They're endangered, but there are probably still a few around," Eugene said. "And there are going to be a *lot* more pretty soon. They're reintroducing them starting next year. The Tennessee Aquarium down in Chattanooga is helping."

"That place is awesome," Boone said. "When I grow up, I wanna work there as a diver."

"I hear someone's building a new aquarium in Gatlinburg," Eugene said. "I think it's the Ripley's Believe It or Not company. They've got one out in Myrtle Beach."

"Cool!" Boone loved visiting Gatlinburg, a tourist town in the foothills of the Smoky Mountains, especially during the holidays. His mother was less of a fan, since she was the one who had to drive in the hellacious traffic. That being said, his mother didn't hesitate to visit nearby Dollywood around Christmastime to enjoy the festive displays of lights.

Boone tossed his fins onto the grass alongside the shore and dumped the rocks from his pockets next to a piece of driftwood.

"So, what time do you have to leave for McGhee Tyson?" Eugene asked, referring to the Knoxville airport.

"Too early. First, we gotta fly to Miami, then on to Aruba."

"Guess you can't join me at Big Ed's, then? My mom's taking me to meet my dad there."

"Aw, man, why you gotta torture me?" The Oak Ridge pizzeria was a local institution and Boone would ordinarily jump at the chance. "I can't. Have to finish packing, and Mom said she's bringing dinner home when she gets off work."

Boone pulled a plastic bag out of his backpack and stuffed his wet snorkel gear inside before shoving the bag into the pack. He zipped up the sides, leaving the tips of the fins protruding out the top.

Eugene picked up his bike. "I guess I'll see you when you get back. Hey, bring me some Aruban coins! I'm a numismatist."

Boone laughed, lifting his own bike from the grass. "If you want me to bring you some coins, you have to tell me what a new-miss-mat-whatever is."

"It means coin collector. Some Aruban coins are square and I want some!"

"Okay, I'll do my best. And I'll send you a postcard."

"It'll arrive after you get back," Eugene said with a laugh. "Just bring me the coins."

Boone biked home along shady Euclid Avenue, beside Bethel Cemetery on the rise to his right. He took the steep lane that cut through the cemetery and his legs were burning by the time he reached the top. Eugene had often urged him to get a bike with gears, but Boone's old dirt bike was still perfectly functional, and his mother wasn't exactly swimming in cash.

Boone coasted down the hill to Church Street and pumped the pedals up another hill before the white picket fence of his little house came into view. The carport was empty, and Boone glanced up at the sun. His mother got off work at four and he guessed it was about that time, but she would be grabbing takeout from somewhere. He still had time to dry off his snorkel gear and get some packing done.

Boone went around back and put his bike into the shed by the fence. In the neighbor's yard, a flurry of barks and whines greeted his ear. Boone approached the adjoining fence and opened a gate the two families had installed. He was nearly bowled over by an overjoyed mutt, its wagging tail a blur.

"Hey, Shingles! How you doing, boy? You have a good time with Mrs. Cable's dogs?" Shingles pawed at Boone's legs, and he treated the eager pooch to an abbreviated game of fetch. Shingles was an excitable young dog composed of at least three breeds, and had earned his moniker when Boone's mother had to replace the roof. A puppy at the time, the dog had discovered that discarded shingles made excellent playthings. Those impromptu dog toys had long since been obliterated; a tennis ball would have to do.

Boone spotted one of his neighbors watering a potted fern on her back porch. The Cables were retired and provided a second home for Shingles when Boone was at school and his mother was at work.

"Hi, Mrs. Cable! Did Shingles behave for you?"

"Oh, hello, Boone! Yes, he was a dear... Beasty and Beauty were the rowdy ones. Although Shingles did eat some of Beauty's food, so there was a bit of growling and tussling."

"Oh, sorry about that."

"No problem at all—dogs will be dogs. And honestly, we're looking forward to watching Shingles while you and your mother are away for... two weeks, was it?"

"Yes, ma'am."

"Well, I hope you have a wonderful vacation. You're seeing your father there, is that right?"

"Yes'm."

Mrs. Cable nodded and started to say something, then shook her head and smiled. "You take care of your mother, Boone."

Boone thanked her and turned away from the fence. When a slobber-covered ball dropped at his feet, he snatched it up and tossed it toward the back of the yard. Mrs. Cable seemed... concerned? *Maybe she hates to fly or doesn't swim,* he thought, as he headed for the house.

He entered by the kitchen door, leaving it ajar while Shingles continued to cavort in the backyard. After pausing to drink from the tap, Boone took his backpack into the bathroom and toweled off his mask, snorkel, and fins. Then he grabbed a fresh towel and dried the interior of his backpack, since he intended to use it as a carry-on. Gathering up everything, he headed for his bedroom at the end of the carpeted hall.

His mother had left his suitcase at the foot of the bed; he thumped it down on the mattress and unzipped it. Inside was a handy-dandy packing list his mother had scrawled on a piece of paper. Smiling, Boone placed his fins in the bottom of the suitcase, then set about grabbing items of clothing from various drawers, as well as a few from the floor. Then he spotted something atop the bureau that wasn't on the list.

Alongside a model ship of the USS *Olympia* that he'd painstakingly constructed last year lay a small, flat stone. On one side of the rock was an eye, painted in red, yellow, and black. Boone placed it in the palm of his hand and locked eyes with the painted image.

Many years ago, when Boone was very young—and during one of the few stretches of time when his father had spent several months with them in Tennessee—his dad had taken him into one of the wealthier neighborhoods to a house with a backyard pool. The owners offered swimming lessons to kids in the area, and the "graduation test" involved holding your breath with your eyes open and swimming to the bottom. The teacher had laid out several painted stones there, and if you came up with a stone, you passed. As an added bonus, you got to keep the stone.

Most of Boone's memories from that early age were hazy, but he remembered that particular summer day with absolute clarity. His father had been so proud of him, telling him to hang on to that rock for luck. As a reward, he'd taken Boone for ice cream in the neighboring town of Oak Ridge. His mother had been at work that day, and Boone remembered how happy he had been to have his dad all to himself during the drive out and back. Two days later, his father had left Tennessee for the

Netherlands to return to active duty. He'd been back from time to time in the years since, but never for as long as that distant summer.

But I'll see him tomorrow, Boone thought, gripping the eye-stone in a tight fist. Turning, he tossed the rock across the room into his suitcase. After a moment's thought, he went over and retrieved it, then slipped it into a pocket of his backpack.

TWO

"You want the window?" his mother asked.

"Yeah!" Boone scooted across the intervening seats and tucked his backpack by his feet. During the early-morning flight from Knoxville, Boone had slept in a middle seat, leaning on his mother's arm. But for the Miami-Aruba leg, he wanted to see the ocean below.

His mother put her carry-on in the overhead compartment, then joined Boone in the row. Across the aisle, a man was speaking loudly into a cell phone. It was a bit smaller than most of the ones Boone had seen before; a tiny antenna waggled in the air as the man berated someone on the other end.

"I'm telling you, sell it! Sell it all! Tech's in a bubble, I just feel it! Listen, I'm about to take off, so you're going to have to handle it!" He paused, red-faced. "What do you mean you don't have authorization? I signed it last night!"

"Mom, why don't you have a cell phone?"

She leaned into him and spoke quietly. "Because I don't

want one, dear. I mean... look at that man. Does he look happy to have it?"

"I guess not." Boone knew of a few families in Kingston that had cell phones and figured cost was the main reason his mom hadn't gotten one.

The plane took off on time, and in moments the sparkling water of the Atlantic appeared outside Boone's window. He grabbed his backpack and pulled out a map of the Caribbean he'd printed out on MapQuest. "The flight from Miami to Aruba is three hours," he said, tracing a line between the two points. "Do we fly over Cuba?"

"I don't know, Boone. We can ask a flight attendant."

Boone nodded, looking at the map. Aruba was all the way down by Venezuela, and to the east of it lay two other islands, Curaçao and Bonaire. "You think maybe we can go to one of the other ABC Islands this time?" he asked.

"ABC...? Oh, the other two. I don't know. We'll have to ask your father."

"They're Dutch, too. And the guidebook says they have flights between them."

"Well, we'll see. I haven't seen your father in a long while, Boone. We need to make the most of our time together."

Boone continued to look at the map, but his mind was focused on other parts of the world. "Mom...? How come we've never visited Dad in the Netherlands?"

When his mother didn't answer, Boone glanced up at her. She was looking at the back of the seat in front of her, a sheen of moisture in her eyes. Then she smiled. "Maybe this Christmas."

Boone looked out the window, remembering the year his mother thought they would be going to Amsterdam over the holidays. His father's parents were dead, and he had no siblings

—that was the reason Dad gave when he'd canceled those plans; the holidays in Holland were too painful, he'd said. But that Christmas hadn't exactly been a picnic for Boone and his mother, either. After the holiday meet-up was canceled, she had stayed in her room for several days, and Boone had decorated the tree all by himself.

Three hours later, the island of Aruba came into view. Flat and arid, it didn't look like Hollywood's idea of a tropical paradise, but the turquoise waters that surrounded it were the most beautiful shade of blue that Boone had ever seen. As the plane began its descent, more and more white sand beaches came into view. A few minutes later, they touched down and taxied toward the main terminal of Queen Beatrix International Airport.

Boone looked out the window and watched as a set of airstairs was maneuvered toward the plane. Soon, they made their way down the steps, the tropical heat slamming into them as they exited the air-conditioned cabin. Following the flow of passengers along the apron, they headed for customs.

"Can I have my passport?" Boone asked, once they reached the line.

"Sure, one second." His mother fished in a pocket of her carry-on and handed him his passport, the Customs Declaration Form tucked inside it like a bookmark.

Boone looked through it, examining the various stamps from previous trips to Aruba. *One of these days, I'm gonna fill this with stamps from all over the world!*

"There he is," Boone's mother whispered as they exited the terminal. "My dear Dirk."

Boone squinted in the bright sunshine, spotting his father in seconds. The Dutch people had the distinction of having the tallest average height in the world, and Boone's dad was no exception. Over six and a half feet tall, it was easy to spot him beyond the crowd of taxi drivers and resort staff that clustered near the exit from the airport, awaiting passengers from the flight from Miami.

Dirk Fischer was a strikingly handsome man. Trim, fit, and tanned, his brown hair was longer than Boone remembered. Normally it was buzzed close to the scalp in a military cut, but it was thick and wind-tossed today. Boone looked to his mother; she was beaming, her face radiant. Jennifer Fischer was a stunningly beautiful woman—even more so when she was happy... and not exhausted from a long workweek.

"Look, Dad has a cell phone," Boone remarked. Dirk was speaking on a stubby black phone and hadn't yet spotted them. "C'mon!" He started forward, but his mother stopped him with a gentle grip on his shoulder.

"Let's see if he spots us."

Dirk continued speaking on the cell, smiling and laughing at one point. Then his gaze caught the pair of them and he spoke quickly into the phone before pocketing it and striding toward them.

"Jenny, *mijn liefje!*" He scooped up Boone's mother, holding her off the ground for a long hug before lowering her to her feet and kissing her deeply. He turned to Boone and tousled his hair. "And Boone... look how much you've grown! You're taller than your mother!"

"He had a bit of a growth spurt," Jennifer said.

"Pretty soon you'll be as tall as me!" Dirk proclaimed, grabbing hold of both of their suitcases. "Come! I'm sure you'd like to get to the resort. I rented a car. This way!"

He led them into the parking lot, turning back over his shoulder to say, "I spoke to a friend of mine who knows this airport. He said they are going to expand it... add jetways so planes can offload directly into the gate. Very unusual for the Caribbean. And this whole parking area? They are going to cover it with solar panels!"

"That's a great idea," Boone said. "Clean energy for the island and shade for the cars."

"Smart boy!" Dirk caught Jennifer's eye. "He gets that from you."

She blushed, then said, "Boone's grades have been much better this year."

"Yes, you mentioned that on the phone... because of his clever friend, yes? What was his name...?"

"Eugene," Boone supplied. "I just saw him yesterday. I was practicing my breath hold in the river and he timed me."

"You were doing *what*?" his mother asked, her voice pitching up.

"It's all right, Jennifer," Dirk reassured her. "Boys will be boys, *ja*?" Rolling the suitcases to a stop beside a white Jeep, he turned to Boone. "How long?" his father asked with interest.

"Two minutes and twenty-nine seconds!" Boone declared.

"*Dat is goed!* Very good!" He grabbed Boone's shoulder and squeezed. "I am proud of you."

Boone grinned, basking in the approval. "I want to do a lot of snorkeling this trip," he announced. "And if I see something cool on the bottom, I can stay down there with it for a real long time."

A crafty smile crept onto Dirk's face as he opened the tailgate of the Jeep and loaded the suitcases into the back. "You know... there is a way to stay on the bottom even longer."

"I don't know, Dirk... he's so young!"

"It's perfectly safe," Dirk reassured her. "I learned to dive at twelve. And the governing body for recreational diving safety just changed the rules last year. PADI's Junior Open Water Diver course now allows kids as young as ten to take it."

"And I'm almost eleven and a half, Mom."

"A shame you aren't twelve yet," his dad teased. "You can only dive to forty feet right now. But next time you'll be allowed to go to sixty."

The trio was sitting in an outdoor restaurant near the resort Boone's mother had booked. It was a beautiful, mid-range property—not too pricy, not too cheap—located on the northwest coast of Aruba. She had splurged for an oceanfront, and their two-bedroom suite overlooked the white sands of Palm Beach. The nearby open-air restaurant they sat in was just across from the Hadicurari Fishermen's Pier. Dirk and Jennifer held menus, but Boone's eyes were buried in the PADI manual his father had given him.

"The dive boat operates right from there," Dirk added, jerking a thumb over his shoulder at the pier.

"But I start in the pool, right?" Boone asked.

"*Ja*. Before they throw you in the ocean, you'll train in the swimming pool—they call those Confined Water dives—and then, there's classroom work. There will be some quizzes to take. Sorry to make you do homework during your summer break."

Boone laughed, riffling the pages of the manual. "This kind of homework, I'm okay with!"

His mother took the book from him and looked at the cover. "What does PADI stand for?"

"Professional Association of Diving Instructors," Dirk answered. "The resort has a deal with a local dive shop. The instructor will come right to us, and the Confined Water lessons will happen in one of the resort pools."

"Cool!" Boone exclaimed.

"Don't get too excited. Those classes happen at six thirty in the morning, so the guests can have their pool back by eight. And after the instructor thinks you're ready, there will be four Open Water dives where you'll complete your training."

"When do I start?"

"Day after tomorrow," Dirk replied.

"Hey, Mom... *you* should take the class, too!"

"No, no... that's not for me. I just want to lie on the beach and read a book and sip a tropical drink." She returned the PADI manual to Boone and locked eyes with Dirk. "And spend time with you."

"There will be plenty of time for that, *mijn liefje,*" he reassured her with a crooked smile. "I'll go with Boone on some of his dives, though."

"How long will these classes take?" she asked.

"Depends on how well Boone does. So, study hard!" he urged, tapping the manual. Then, catching Jennifer's eye, he slid the book away from Boone. "But not at the dinner table. Study the menu instead."

THREE

The PADI instructor—a long-haired American nicknamed Divemaster Dave—was patient and thorough. The class started with just two, but the other student—a ten-year-old boy from Arizona—stopped halfway through the first pool session and announced he didn't want to do it. The kid had panicked when asked to swim underwater across the pool without a mask, popping up wild-eyed only halfway across. The instructor tried to get him to relax and try again, but the boy was having none of it. Boone had the distinct feeling the classes had been more for the kid's dad than the kid himself. The father had sulked as the mother led the boy away to go play on the beach.

Now, with just one-on-one instruction, Boone breezed through the class. Swimming across the pool without a mask was a cakewalk, particularly since Boone had been doing that in the Clinch River for years. And although Boone wasn't typically a show-off, he couldn't help himself when he reached the far side of the pool, spinning around and pushing off to go back the entire length of the pool to where he started.

"Where'd you learn to swim?" Dave asked.

"Neighborhood pool, and also a big community one the next town over," Boone said, gripping the edge of the resort pool. "And the river. And I watch how they do it in the Olympics. And I've been practicing my breath-holding. I coulda gone back and forth one more time."

"Impressive," Dave said, nodding but not smiling. "And if you become a freediver someday, that'll come in handy... but once you've got a scuba tank on, it's a whole different ball game. What did we learn in class?"

"Never hold your breath when breathing compressed air."

"Bingo. Because?"

"Um... the air you're breathing expands when you ascend... so if you come up while you're holding a breath... you could hurt your lungs. A pulma... um..."

"Pulmonary embolism. That's a rupture in the lung. And anything else?"

"Yeah, you can get nitrogen gas bubbles in your blood vessels. And you can get... um... I forget the whole name, but it's like the word 'age.'"

"Correct... an Ay-Gee-Ee. Arterial Gas Embolism."

"And that can kill you?" Boone asked with a touch of concern.

"Yes. But *you* won't get one. Because when you're diving, you won't...?" Dave prompted.

"...hold my breath," Boone finished with a smile. Then he furrowed his brow. "But freedivers... they hold their breath when they come up. How come *they* don't get hurt?"

"Well, they *do* get hurt from time to time, but they don't have the same problem as a diver. Why is that?"

Boone shrugged a bony shoulder. "I dunno."

"What happens to air at depth?"

"It gets compressed," Boone answered quickly. "Another atmosphere every thirty-three feet."

"Right. It's one atmosphere of pressure at the surface and two at thirty-three feet of depth. So... at sixty-six feet... if you filled a balloon with a liter of air from your tank and ascended to the surface...?"

Boone was decent at math and answered quickly, "When you got to the surface, that liter would expand to, like... three liters?"

"Right. Pop goes the balloon. So, why doesn't that happen to a freediver?" Dave asked.

Boone chewed his lip for a moment, then slapped a wet palm down on the tile at the pool's edge. "Because the air the freediver has in his lungs came from the surface! It won't expand any more than when he started."

Divemaster Dave smiled and tapped his nose.

"How is he doing?" a Dutch-accented voice called out.

Boone spotted his father approaching from the direction of the beach, a local Balashi beer in hand. "Hey, Dad!"

"Mr. Fischer, your son is one smart cookie."

The Dutchman raised an eyebrow. "I assume that is a good thing?"

"Oh yeah, definitely. And he's an amazing swimmer. He's ready for the scuba gear. Pool first... ocean soon."

The following week, Boone sat on a bench aboard the dive boat *Dushi Diver*, a name that gave Boone the giggles. Apparently, *dushi* was a Papiamento term of endearment, but for an

English-speaker, it sounded like what it sounded like. He'd already performed a checkout dive alongside the fishermen's pier, but this would be his first from a boat.

The *Dushi Diver* had a group of five divers from Canada aboard—two men and three women—along with a divemaster for that group. Dave and Dirk sat on either side of Boone, listening to the other divemaster give the briefing for the site called Pedernales. This was a wreck dive, of sorts... but not of an entire ship. The *Pedernales* was a British steam tanker that had been torpedoed amidships by a U-boat in World War II. The hapless vessel was towed into port, where the damaged portion was removed, the bow and stern were welded together, and the now-stubbier ship sailed to the United States to be rebuilt.

The orphaned midsection of the ship was used for target practice by the Dutch Navy before being sunk as an artificial reef offshore from Hadicurari Beach, in view of Boone's resort. The site was roughly mapped out on a whiteboard that the divemaster held as he explained the dive profile. Once he finished, the Canadians began suiting up.

"Aruba is known for its wreck dives, and Pedernales is perfect for a beginner," Dave explained. "Most of the site is shallow at just twenty feet... deepest part is thirty-three feet. And there's almost no current."

"Are there any sharks down there?" Boone asked eagerly.

Divemaster Dave laughed. "Maybe a nurse shark, if you're lucky. But this site is known for a bunch of large groupers that hang out by the wreck."

"Cool! Should I get ready?" Boone asked.

"Hang on a sec. First, watch the members of this dive group. See how they gear up. We'll follow once they're all in the water."

Boone observed the Canadians as they suited up. Most of them seemed to be experienced, their movements methodical, but one young woman on the bench opposite them was a bit slower than the others. Her companions were already making their way to the swim platform at the stern of the dive boat while she continued to check her gear. She looked up and smiled at Boone, then her eyes flicked to the side, and she smiled again as she struggled with a strap. Boone glanced to his right and saw his father grinning back at her. Dirk rose and crossed to her bench.

"May I assist?"

The woman looked up at him with a shy smile on her face. "It's been a while," she said with a gentle laugh. "Diving, I mean," she added quickly, blushing a little.

Dirk chuckled, then helped her into her buoyancy control vest. Boone spotted the Canadian group's divemaster watching the exchange while he suited up. He nodded to Dave, who leaned over to Boone.

"Chrissy is the least experienced, and their group has an odd number, so their divemaster will buddy up with her."

Boone nodded, watching his dad take Chrissy by the hand and walk her to the stern; his father towered over the young woman, who was dressed in a one-piece swimsuit that seemed out of place with her tank and gear. Dirk said something that Boone couldn't make out over the lapping of the waves, and she laughed heartily before putting her regulator in her mouth and plunging into the ocean. The divemaster followed, and the Canadian divers descended as one. Dirk turned back to Dave and Boone and fired off an "OK" sign.

Dave clapped his hands together. "All right, Boone, let's hit it. Is your air on?"

"Yeah," Boone said, as he double-checked the valve knob

and gave the purge button on the regulator a quick pulse with his thumb. He held up the pressure gauge. "3100 psi."

"Great. Pool's open! Gear up!"

Boone put on his weight belt and sat in front of his tank and BCD. When his father reached over to help him into it, Dave intervened.

"Let him do it, Mr. Fischer."

"Oh, of course. Sorry."

"I got it, Dad." Boone quickly slid into the vest and adjusted the straps.

"Lookin' good," Dave said. "And we can adjust the weight on your belt if we need to. Remember, you're more buoyant in salt water than you are in a pool."

"Or a freshwater river," Boone added.

"Right. And if you get a wetsuit, you'll need to add even more weight to the belt."

Boone was diving in his swim trunks and a long-sleeved rash guard his father had bought for him. He had secretly hoped his dad might buy him a wetsuit from the dive shop, but Dirk had explained the water was warm enough that he wouldn't need one. "Besides," his father had added, "at the rate you're growing, it wouldn't fit you next summer." And Boone had to admit, the rash guard was pretty cool, with a sea turtle on the back and the Aruban flag on the breast.

"We've got some defogger," Dave said, when Boone spit in his mask and rubbed the lenses.

"Spit works."

"Fair enough," Dave said, spritzing his own mask with a spray bottle.

"What's in that?" Boone's father asked, as he shrugged into his own BCD.

"Water with a little dish soap. Want some?"

"*Ja, bedankt,*" Dirk said, offering his mask.

In minutes, the trio was geared up and made their way to the stern. Boone stepped to the edge and looked into the sparkling water. "Giant stride?"

"Yep," Dave replied. "We'll test your backward roll entry later, but a giant stride is what you'll use on most dive boats. You'll want to extend one leg far forward and follow after it. If you just dropped straight in, you might smash your tank against the platform. Now... what do you do with your hands when you step in?"

Boone answered by inserting the reg mouthpiece and pressing the base of his palm against it and his fingers against his mask, holding both in place. With his other hand, he gathered the hoses of his gauges and secondary "octopus" regulator against his midriff, pressing against the buckle on his weight belt.

"Bingo. Although, if the water isn't calm like today and the boat is rocking and rolling, you can use that 'hose hand' to keep a grip on the boat until you step off." He turned to Boone's father. "Mr. Fischer, if you want to go ahead and enter... just descend to the bottom and join the Canadian divers, we'll be along shortly."

"See you below, son!"

After he entered the water, Boone took a deep breath as he watched his father's bubbles.

"Your turn," Dave prompted. "You ready?"

Boone looked at the turquoise water below him and grinned. *I've never been more ready for anything in all my life.* He stepped into space and entered another world.

FOUR

Boone's mother looked out from under her floppy sunhat as her son came tearing across the beach, sand flying from his bare feet. She swung her legs off the beach chaise and stood to greet him.

"So? How was it?"

"Oh my God, Mom, it was *amazing*! I've never... it was like *flying*! And there were these groupers that followed us around. They were *huge*! And Dave—that's my divemaster—Dave blew this bubble of air and made a big ring that floated up and he stuck his head in it like a halo, and Dad tried to make one, but he couldn't. Oh! And there was this big green moray—that's a type of eel, Mom—and it was *gigantic*!"

Boone's mother nearly staggered back from the breathless onslaught of enthusiasm erupting from her son. "Sounds like you had a lot of fun," she said, laughing.

"It was so much more than fun, Mom. I can't wait to go out there again!"

Jennifer grinned and gave her son a hug, her eyes searching the beach behind Boone. "Where's your father?"

"He's still at the shop. We were rinsing our gear—it's real important, Mom... salt water is super corrosive—and he said he would finish up, and I should come find you and figure out what we're doing for dinner."

"Oh, that's sweet. I'm thinking we should try this local place that serves some of the Creole food I've been wanting to try. But you should be washing your *own* gear, right? This is all part of your training, isn't it?"

"I suppose..."

"Run back and help your father; then we'll get cleaned up for dinner."

"Okay!"

Boone dashed away, heading back to the little dive shack that was on the periphery of the resort. As the rinse tanks came into view, he spotted his father leaning against the wall of the drying room where divers kept their gear. The Canadian girl, Chrissy, was standing beside him, laughing at something he'd said as she scribbled on a scrap of paper. She handed it to him, waggled her fingers playfully in a goodbye gesture, then walked away in the direction of the resort, tossing a parting smile over her shoulder.

Dirk smiled back and shook the piece of paper at her; then he caught sight of Boone and his smile ratcheted up a notch.

"There he is—my son, the adventurer! I finished up with the gear. It's all hung up to dry."

"What did she give you?"

"Hmm? Oh, this? I asked if she knew any good restaurants and she recommended one."

"Mom already picked one."

"Well, then... whatever your mother says is where we'll go!"

29

He slipped the paper in his pocket and started toward their resort room. "We need to shower, *ja*? Come!"

As his father strode ahead of him, Boone followed, a frown on his face. He knew in his gut that his father had just lied to him.

The days swept by, and Boone finished the PADI courses, passing every test with flying colors. After the final dive, Divemaster Dave asked Boone to meet him in the office, where he presented him with his certification card.

"Here you go, Boone. You're now a certified Junior Open Water Diver. And once you hit fifteen, that will become a regular open water certification."

Boone didn't speak as he stared at the card and ran a thumb across it. Finally, he looked up. "Thank you. This means a lot."

"More than you know, I bet," Dave said with a grin. "I have a feeling you'll be using that a lot. I don't say this lightly, but... I think diving's in your blood."

"Maybe I can do what *you* do!" Boone blurted.

Dave chuckled. "Not something I'd normally suggest to an eleven-year-old, but... yeah... you could, one day."

"We'll probably be back again next year," Boone said, thinking aloud. "Maybe I can dive with you again!"

"You could... but why not try out a different island?"

Boone shrugged. "Mom loves it here. It's her and Dad's special place."

"Well... next year... you'll be allowed to dive to sixty feet," Dave noted, "and there will be a lot more dive sites you can try!"

Boone thanked him and dashed off to find his parents. He

found his mother in her usual patch of beach and proudly presented his brand-new certification card. "Check it out, Mom! I graduated! I'm a diver!"

"Boone, that's wonderful!"

"My teacher said, if we come back next year, I can dive even deeper!"

His mother beamed at her son. "And what did your father say to that?"

Boone cocked his head. "Well... nothing. He wasn't there."

"I see... was he cleaning the gear again?"

"No... I did that myself. I only dove with Divemaster Dave today."

His mother's smile faltered as she sat up in the chaise. "But... this was your last dive of the class. Your father said he was going to be diving with you."

"I thought..." Boone trailed off, stopping himself from saying he'd thought that his father was spending the day with her. "I think... I think he wanted me to finish the class myself. You know... like... not helping me or anything."

"Oh. Yes, I suppose that makes sense."

"Maybe he had to do some navy stuff," Boone quickly added. "Hey, can we go get some ice cream? I keep forgetting to find some of those square Aruban coins for Eugene; maybe we can get some in change."

"Of course," his mother said absently.

Boone reached out a hand to tug his mom to her feet and the two of them made their way across the sand. His dad had indeed told Boone he thought he should sit the last dive out, so Boone had boarded the boat with Divemaster Dave, a second divemaster, the boat's captain, and the Canadian divers. Well... *most* of the Canadians. Chrissy hadn't been on the boat either. Boone looked up at his mother as she pressed her sunhat to her head, battling the stiff Aruban trade winds. After a moment, he looked down at his bare feet as they traversed the sand, choosing to keep his thoughts to himself.

───────

That night, Boone couldn't sleep. After a while he sat up in bed, staring at the bedside alarm clock that announced it was two in the morning. Once he'd stood and padded across the cold tile floor to the main living area and kitchen, he stepped out on the balcony and stared up at the night sky, keeping an eye out for any shooting stars. Eugene—who counted astronomy as one of his many areas of interest—had told Boone that the Perseid meteor shower would be nearing its peak while he was in Aruba. Not spotting any shooting stars, he went back inside to grab something to drink from the fridge. On the way, he spotted his PADI instruction manual on the kitchen island countertop, a pen lying beside it.

I left that on the end table by the couch, didn't I?

Boone went over to the book and picked it up. Opening the manual, he spotted words scrawled on the title page. The glow of the moon spilling in from the balcony would be enough to read by, so he stepped closer to the light to see what was written.

Boone,
You did it! You're a scuba diver now. A whole new world has opened its doors to you. I'm very proud of you, my son.
Love, Dirk Vader

Boone grinned, equal parts touched and amused. Rather than sign it "Dad" or "Dirk Fischer," his father had followed his given name with *Vader*, the Dutch word for father, repeating a private joke between the two of them after they'd watched a *Star Wars* movie together. The word was pronounced differently, but it still looked funny on paper. That had been many years ago, during one of Dad's brief visits. Boone's smile slipped as he remembered why he'd spent the last few hours staring at the ceiling. Why had his father lied to him? And to his mother? And what else had he been lying about?

On the end table beside the couch, he set the PADI manual down beside his father's cell phone, which was plugged into a wall outlet to charge overnight.

Curious, Boone detached the phone from the black charging cord and examined the buttons. One of the rich kids in school had his own phone and had let Boone check it out one time. The layout of the buttons was similar. He pressed one of the arrow keys and a number came up, along with a time-and-date stamp from today. Boone knew about area codes, and this one had some additional numbers that he knew to be a country code. His mother used one to call Dad, but she always did the dialing, so Boone wasn't sure what the code for the Netherlands was.

I wonder if this one's for Canada? he thought. He slid open the balcony door and stepped outside. The moon shone brightly, leaving a pearlescent road across the ocean. Boone gazed at the otherworldly sight for a long moment, then returned his eyes to the phone.

He thumbed through more calls over the last few days. There were several different numbers, but one came up over and over. Boone suddenly realized that his heart was racing and he knew why. He had already made a decision... and he acted on it. With the recurring number on the screen, he pressed the green button.

There was a click, followed by a single ring, and then the style of dial tone changed to a series of pairs of short rings. After a moment, a woman's voice answered.

"Diederik? Het is erg laat op de avond voor jou. Waarom bel je?"

Boone knew that some Canadians spoke French, but this wasn't that. He recognized it immediately. He'd heard his father speaking Dutch on many occasions, and Dirk had taught Boone a few words. That country code must be for the Netherlands. He opened his mouth to say "sorry, wrong number," but his brain reminded him he was calling from his father's phone. So, instead, he remained silent. In addition to the woman's voice, another sound was audible in the background... a baby crying. The woman made some shushing sounds, then she returned to the line.

"Diederik? Ben je daar? Is alles goed, mijn liefje?"

Boone swallowed. "Diederik" was Dirk's full given name. And Boone recognized those last two words. He'd heard them often enough, from his father to his mother. *Mijn liefje* meant "my darling."

Then another voice came over the phone, also in the background, competing with the crying child. This one sounded like a young boy, asking in Dutch, *"Is dat Vader?"*

Boone mashed the red hang-up button and raised the phone over his head to hurl it into the swimming pool below. After a moment, his arm dropped to his side, where he clutched the phone for several minutes, breathing heavily. When his breathing had slowed, he turned and went back inside, reconnected the phone to the charging cord, then shuffled back to the balcony to stare at the ocean. If there were shooting stars in the night sky above, Boone did not see them.

PART TWO

FIVE

TWO YEARS LATER

Boone stood at the shore of the Clinch River, bouncing a river rock in his hand. The smooth stone might have been one he'd put in his pockets the day before that final trip to Aruba. After a moment, he cocked his arm and whipped it sidearm, scything the rock into the river. Even with its rounded shape, it skipped across the surface three times before disappearing into the water.

Boone glanced over his shoulder to check on Shingles. The mutt was snuffling around, investigating every smell he could detect within the reach of his extendable leash, the handle of which Boone had affixed to a hefty chunk of driftwood. He had taken the dog for a walk through the cemetery and had found himself at the riverside park.

Boone scanned the shoreline for another stony victim. Selecting one, he pitched it after the first in a high arc, this time going for distance. The rock plunked into the river nearly to the halfway point. Over the past two years, the lanky teenager had undergone quite a growth spurt, and the phys ed coaches had been after him for both baseball and basketball. Boone didn't have much interest in either, despite dominating the basketball court when he played, his height and reach giving him an edge over the other boys.

He watched the ripples dissipate from his latest throw, then exhaled slowly and reached into his pocket. Withdrawing his hand, he held the object tightly in his fist for a moment before opening his fingers. The painted rock he'd earned from his first swimming lessons—the lessons his father had taken him to—lay in his palm, its painted eye staring up at him.

Boone swallowed as his mind drifted back to the last time he'd seen his dad. Unsurprisingly, his last memory of his father was dominated by one of his mother, red-faced and weeping, screaming at Dirk Fischer that she hated him.

The problem was, Boone knew that wasn't the truth. Even after all of the lies had blown up in his father's face... after the truth had finally come out that he was also married to a woman in the Netherlands and had fathered two children with her, Boone knew that his mother still loved the man.

And oddly enough, the woman in the Netherlands wasn't what had led to that final memory of his father, standing outside their resort room door, staring at his feet as his mother unleashed a torrent of fury and pain. At first, Boone had kept the late-night phone call from his mother, terrified of what it might mean if he told her. He still felt he had been a coward for not coming to her sooner with what he had learned. But no, it hadn't been that call that ended the marriage... it had been Dirk's dalliance with Chrissy.

The evening after that fateful phone call, Boone had sat at dinner with his parents. Both had wondered why he was so quiet, but Boone had deflected their concerns, making an effort to engage in conversation, all the while stealing glances at his father, wondering just who this man was. How had he fooled them for so long? After the dinner was over and they were waiting on the check, Dirk had announced he'd forgotten something over at the dive shop's storage shack. He excused himself, telling them he'd meet them back at the room.

Boone had quickly offered to go fetch whatever it was, but his father insisted the boy stay with his mother and keep her company. As the tall Dutchman strode away, his mother watched him for a moment, then turned to Boone with a searching look. Clearly, she had seen something in the boy's face, because she rose from the table, told the approaching waiter to bill it to the room, and asked Boone where the storage shack was. Boone hemmed and hawed, then offered to show her.

Mother and son had then gone to the gear storage room, a small wooden structure dimly illuminated by a security light. The door was locked for the evening but the sounds from within drew them to a side window that had been propped open for ventilation. A shaft of moonlight illuminated the interior, revealing two figures inside. Dirk and Chrissy were up against a wall, and what they were doing had nothing to do with gear maintenance.

A strangled noise halfway between a gasp and a sob had erupted from Boone's mother, and she'd fled from the hut. That sound had haunted Boone... far more than the sight of his father doing... well... pretty much what Boone had feared he might be doing.

A distant rumble of summer thunder rolled across the sky and Boone gave his head a violent shake, forcing the memories from his mind. Under the darkening clouds, the Clinch River lay before him. Clutching the painted rock in his fist, Boone cocked his arm... and then lowered it, just as he'd done the last four times. He dropped the stone into his pocket, retrieved Shingles's leash, and headed back toward the cemetery. Rain was coming and his mother would be home soon.

Boone's remaining time at Cherokee Middle School seemed to fly by as he kept himself busy with schoolwork and helped his mother around the house. He'd ultimately bowed out of basketball, opting instead to spend his limited extra-curricular hours on the cross-country team. Boone found long-distance running meditative, giving him precious time to himself, if only in his mind. What he really would have liked to do was join a swim team, but the middle school didn't have one. That would have to wait until he started at Roane County High.

The events in Aruba and the subsequent divorce had put a damper on any expectations of scuba diving in the near future, but nevertheless, Boone couldn't get his underwater experiences out of his head. Then, during the last summer before his freshman year in high school, the subject of diving resurfaced in an unexpected way.

Eugene Shelton's family had invited Boone to join them for a picnic and swim at Melton Hill Dam, not far from where Eugene's father worked in one of the Oak Ridge National Laboratory complexes. Now a hub for scientific research, Oak Ridge —the Secret City—had been built in World War II to provide enriched uranium for the Manhattan Project, and the reactor that provided plutonium to Los Alamos for Oppenheimer and his scientist buddies was located just three and a half miles from Melton Hill Dam. The world's first reactor designed for continuous operation, the X-10 Graphite Reactor had been decommissioned long ago, but that didn't stop Boone and

Eugene from spending the car ride from Kingston joking that they'd glow in the dark after their swim.

As they pulled into the parking lot near the swimming area, Boone noticed a patrol SUV for the Loudon County Sheriff's Department in the far corner near the boat ramp, next to a pickup truck with a boat trailer. The boat that belonged to it was probably the one Boone could see about fifty yards from shore, upstream of the dam. The Sheriff's patrol vehicle had tinted windows, but he thought he could make out two people inside.

"What do you think the police are doing here?" Eugene asked.

"Probably part of their patrol," Dr. Shelton suggested. He pointed across the reservoir at the forested ridge beyond. "Oak Ridge and Roane County are over there... but on this side it's Loudon."

As they got out and began gathering their picnic and swimming supplies, Boone looked out at the boat. It was a small bass boat, similar to many that could be found in the Clinch near his home, and there was a single man aboard.

"I don't know if I'd want to fish that close to the dam," Boone mused aloud.

"They have a loud siren that goes off when they're about to send water through," Dr. Shelton explained.

Boone nodded, watching the man in the boat. The occupant didn't have any fishing rod that Boone could see, and seemed to be scribbling something in a notebook. *Odd.*

Boone hurried after Eugene and his family, passing through the basketball court and pavilion to reach the grassy slope near the swimming area. After spreading out a picnic blanket and setting up a few towels and camp chairs, the two teens charged across the miniscule beach and into the cool water.

The swimming area was cordoned off from the rest of the dam reservoir by a floating barrier, and Boone swam out to the northwestern corner of it to look back at the fishing boat. His eyes were immediately drawn to a yellow ball floating just beyond it. Farther downstream, Boone saw another ball, and he guessed they were buoys of some sort. After a moment, the float nearest him seemed to move. *And are those... bubbles?*

"Hey, Boone!" Eugene called out. "Get your butt over here! We've been challenged to a chicken fight."

Boone turned to find his friend in waist-deep water, standing alongside a pair of swimsuit-clad girls, one a blonde, the other a brunette. Boone smiled and swam back to join them. His friend might be a Class A nerd, but he was quick with a joke and surprisingly popular with the girls at school. It didn't surprise him that he'd snared some so quickly.

"They're from Lenoir City." Eugene gestured to the pair. "This is Tiffany, and this is...?"

"Renee," the blonde said, nervously wringing out her sodden ponytail. She looked up at Boone. "I think you two have an unfair advantage, tall as you are."

"I'll bend my knees."

She grinned at his response, then turned to Tiffany. "Top or bottom?"

Eugene turned away from the girls and shot Boone a wide-eyed look while blowing out a breath. Then he shook his head violently and pointed at Boone. "Okay, Bigfoot. Assume the position!"

Eugene got onto Boone's shoulders, Tiffany climbed atop Renee, and aquatic shenanigans ensued. Round one went to the boys from Kingston, but Lenoir City came out on top in the second when Renee pressed up against Boone and blew in his ear. Startled, Boone stumbled and Eugene tumbled.

They were in the middle of round three with their giggling foes when Boone heard a commotion over by the boat. When he turned to watch, the momentary distraction allowed their opponents to topple Eugene again, plunging the smaller boy into spluttering defeat.

"Boone!" Eugene coughed. "We were winning!"

"Divers."

"What?"

Boone pointed toward the waters outside of the swim area. Two divers in full wetsuits and hoods were at the surface, talking to the man in the bass boat. The occupant of the boat nodded, then spoke into a walkie-talkie, looking toward shore. Boone followed the man's line of sight and saw another diver in a wetsuit on the shore beside the parking lot, standing next to a geared-up scuba tank. The diver was speaking into a walkie-talkie of his own.

"What do you think they're doing?" Eugene wondered.

"I dunno... but I bet it has something to do with the police car."

SIX

Boone watched the divers by the boat for a few more seconds, then started to make his way toward shore.

"Don't go!" Renee called out.

"He'll be back for a rematch!" Eugene shouted to her as he waded after Boone. "Hey, where are you going?" he hissed. "That blonde was into you!"

"I wanna talk to those divers," Boone said over his shoulder as he reached the beach.

"Well, I'm staying here," Eugene called after him. "I don't want our new friends to find another pair of opponents." With that, Eugene returned to the water.

Boone jogged to the Sheltons' picnic zone and quickly toweled off before donning a Handee Burger T-shirt and shoving his feet into flip-flops. He made his way to the adjacent parking lot as fast as his ungainly footwear would allow. The diver on shore was retrieving two tanks from the pickup truck with the trailer. He set them on the dock that ran alongside the boat ramp, then sat down beside his gear and lifted the radio.

Boone couldn't hear what the man said, but it was brief. He set the walkie down and picked up a bottle of water. He now seemed to be waiting.

Boone flip-flopped his way over to the diver. He could see fins, mask, and a hood alongside him on the pier. As he drew closer, he could see the man was older, maybe in his fifties.

"Hey, uh... sorry to bother you. I'm a diver... well, a newish diver, um..."

"It's okay, son. You looking for lessons, or...?"

"No. I... well, maybe. But I was wondering... what are they doing out there?"

"Um..." The man hesitated, glancing back at the Sheriff's Department vehicle.

Boone had a feeling he knew the answer, and he leaned in and said in a low voice, "You're looking for a body, aren't you?"

The man sighed. "Yeah. Fella went missing near here a few days ago, and yesterday they found some of his belongings at a popular cliff jump spot, upstream a bit."

"So, you're, like... search and rescue divers?"

"Well... search and recovery would be more accurate. When we're called in, it's almost always recovery."

"Are you with the police?"

"No. Volunteer. We work *with* the police, of course. A few police and fire departments in Tennessee have trained divers, but more often than not, they look to us. Honestly, most volunteer S&R divers have a lot more hours at depth than the paid folks. In this case, I wish we could've gotten a team from Knoxville over here. They have a side-scan sonar. We're hoping we can use it tomorrow."

Boone looked out at the boat. This time he could clearly see one of the yellow buoys moving along the surface, a diver's bubbles coming up beside it.

The man noted where Boone was looking. "Two of my buddies are down there right now, doing what we call a jack-stay search," he explained. "They've got a line pulled taut along the bottom—as taut as it *can* be, if there's debris. The line's got a mushroom anchor at either end to keep it in position, and one diver aligns on the right of the line, the other on the left. They stretch their free hands out to the side and feel along the bottom as they swim down the line. Then, when they get to the end..."

"They move the anchor!"

"Bingo. Two feet to the side. Then they go back along it to the other anchor, and move *it* two feet to the side. Rinse and repeat."

"A zig-zag pattern," Boone said, picturing it in his mind. "But... how far away was the place where they found the person's stuff? Why are you searching right there?"

"Well, we wouldn't normally dive on speculation, but since the evidence was found last night, we wanted to give it a try. The potential jump spot is up there." He pointed upstream to a ridge across the reservoir. "We searched at the base of that this morning. Didn't find anything. But we had some old side-scan sonar data for the area they're searching right now. There's a pair of fallen trees at that spot, so a body might get snagged on its way downstream toward the dam."

"What do you do if you find it? The body."

"Depends. The police call the shots at that point. But first thing we do is mark the spot. We have this dog cage, and—"

"Wait... what?"

The man sighed. "My old chihuahua passed away last year and I still had his collapsible carrying cage. Figured I could put it to good use. We send it down, put some rocks in it, then tie a line with a marker buoy to the top of the cage."

Boone looked over at the dam, a short distance down-stream. "Isn't it dangerous to be diving near a dam?"

"Definitely. But we've got a liaison with TVA. They've given us a three-hour window where they'll pause power genera-tion." He checked his watch. "We'll call it a day about a quarter hour before that window closes. And you'd get an extra kick-in-the-pants warning if the sirens go off." He laughed. "Man, one time, at the Norris Dam... I was still down when I heard the siren. Someone musta messed up with the timetable, but our safety diver up top called over and stopped 'em."

"You're the safety diver for today, then?" Boone asked.

"Safety and standby." Fred nodded toward the boat. "Lar-ry's got a rig with him, too. We always have at least one on standby. They'll take a break in a bit, and we may switch up if one of them needs more rest time, but it's not too deep. Almost seventy feet in the approach to the lock, but where they are right now, more like forty. But it's cold and the viz is next to nothing."

Boone nodded. "I snorkel in the Clinch sometimes. Pretty cold and murky. But I got certified to dive in Aruba a couple years ago. You could see a hundred feet!"

The safety diver looked over toward the swimming area. "You here with your folks?"

"I, uh... no. A friend's family brought me."

The man appraised Boone. "You from Kingston?"

Boone cocked his head. "Yeah. How'd you know that?"

The diver pointed at Boone's T-shirt. "I love those Handee Burger sliders!" He patted his stomach. "Maybe a little too much. I have a fix-it shop in Kingston, out on Gallaher."

"Fred's Fix-it?"

"Pleased to meetcha," the man said with a grin. "What's your name, son?"

"Boone. Boone Fischer."

"Well, Boone-Boone, when and where you thinking of diving next?"

"Um... not sure." Boone looked down at his flip-flops. "Not any time soon."

"Yeah, it's an expensive hobby. I tell ya what... Philadelphia Quarry's about twenty miles southwest of here. Our group trains there from time to time. They do classes, reasonable rates, so maybe you could brush up on your skills. It ain't Aruba, but they got some sunken boats down there. Some catfish, bass, bluegill. Saw a snapping turtle once. Almost put my hand on it."

Boone looked up. "That sounds cool, but... I'm not old enough to drive, yet."

Fred waved that off. "There're always divers looking for a dive buddy. Come by the shop sometime. I'll give you a list."

"Cool! Thanks!"

"You got a wetsuit?"

"No."

"Well, you'll definitely need one. And a hood. Once you get below the thermocline, it gets *very* cold." The walkie crackled and Fred's posture changed as he came alert.

"Fred, we're coming up on forty-five minutes."

Fred mashed the Talk button. "Roger. Bring 'em up."

Across the water, a trio of metallic bongs sounded as the man in the boat struck the aluminum hull. He repeated the signal a moment later.

"Time for their surface interval. Listen, I gotta get my head in the game," Fred said, extending a hand. "Good to meet you, Boone. Swing by the shop sometime. I mean it."

Boone shook his hand. "Thanks, Fred. I definitely will!"

Returning to the swimming area, Boone discovered the

Sheltons sitting around the picnic blanket. And they had company.

"There you are!" Eugene called out. "We invited Tiffany and Renee to join us."

Dr. Shelton looked up as he doled out potato salad. "Saw you talking to a diver over there. Everything okay?"

"Yeah, they, um... they're just..."

Mrs. Shelton saved him. "Probably just a training exercise. Right, Boone?" She handed him a plate. "Now eat up. You need to put some meat on those bones."

Boone gratefully took the plate and started to sit down beside Eugene, but a meaningful head tilt from his friend stopped him. Boone followed the direction of Eugene's lean, and found Renee flashing a smile as she scooted over on the edge of the blanket. Boone took the hint and sat beside her.

"Boone..." Renee said, a contemplative look on her face. "Cool name. Like... Daniel Boone?"

"Kinda. My mom says we're related to him. Great-great-great-grandfather... probably a few more greats."

"Well, I think it's great. Your name."

"Thanks." Boone lifted a forkful of coleslaw from the plate, then put it back. "Renee's a beautiful name," he added awkwardly.

Renee blushed, then shot him a sly smile. "After we eat... Tiff and I owe you a rematch."

SEVEN

Being young and carless, Boone didn't get to see Renee more than once before the end of summer, when the two of them joined a group going to The Lost Sea. Located down the interstate in Sweetwater, it was the largest underground lake in America. Cave divers had been mapping it for some time and still hadn't found an end to it. The otherworldly cavern lake was lit from above and below the water, and Boone had sat beside Renee on the glass-bottom boat as it trundled along, passing some of the largest rainbow trout Boone had ever seen. After the guided tour was over, the group returned to their cars, and Renee had suggested they try to get together again sometime.

But then, summer came to an end and Boone began his freshman year at Roane County High School. Unfortunately, it wasn't the most auspicious start. Two weeks into the school year, a trio of upperclassmen was hassling Eugene as Boone came around the corner. When one of them slammed Eugene into a locker, Boone hauled off and decked the kid with a punch to the face. Boone had never been in a fight before, but he held his own when the other two laid into him to avenge their bully buddy.

At the end of the day, Boone had earned himself a black eye, a split lip, and a stern lecture from his mother—along with a packet of frozen peas for his eye. On top of that, he was sentenced to two days in-school suspension. While Boone had felt justified dropping the kid who had shoved Eugene into the locker—stopping the bully before he had a chance to do any more than that—the principal considered the punch to be an escalation. That being said, Boone wasn't alone in the room; the three teens he'd tangled with joined him. By the end of it, they left on reasonably good terms, and Boone learned that Eugene had been hitting on two of their girl-friends.

During his freshman year, Boone focused on his studies and running with the cross-country team, but several days a week he found time to ride his bicycle over to Fred's Fix-it. Fred specialized in small engine repair, and much of his business involved marine engines for the multitude of boats in the area. Boone took an interest as he watched Fred work, and the man let him tinker with a few items he'd salvaged. Boone found he had a knack for it; he restored a busted lawn mower and an old outboard almost by himself.

Boone was still very interested in diving down at the quarry, but money was tight for his mother. And even if she had been rolling in dough, he wasn't exactly eager to bring up the subject of diving with her. Boone made a few bucks collecting fireflies for a cancer research project based in nearby Oak Ridge, but what little he made from that and from mowing lawns wasn't enough to get the wetsuit and other gear he'd like to have. But Fred had a thought.

"You definitely want your own gear if you're planning to dive more often. Tell you what... when's your birthday?"

"In February," Boone said. "But I can't accept a gift like that, sir."

Fred laughed. "Well, that's good, 'cause you ain't getting one. No, I'm asking 'cause I'm thinking of hiring you when you turn fifteen."

Boone's eyes lit up. "Hiring me?"

"Sure. I've watched you work. You're good. The state says I *could* hire you on now for a few hours a day, but I need to crunch the numbers first and *you* need to learn the trade. I'd be happy to teach you more between now and February. Call it an apprenticeship. And in the meantime, maybe you can fix up some more busted things I've salvaged. I'll sell them and give you a cut."

"Cool!"

"But school comes first."

"I know. Mom never lets me forget that."

"Hey, did you fix that underwater metal detector you've been puttering around with? Bet we could find a buyer for it."

"Actually, I kinda want to keep that for myself and try it out around some boat recreation spots. Besides, it's still dead. I'm waiting on a replacement coil."

The next year, Boone started working for Fred for a few hours here and there during the week. By the time his freshman year ended, Boone had made enough to purchase a wetsuit and a better mask and fins. Fred let him borrow his regulator and BCD and Boone was able to join a few local divers who were driving down to the Philly Quarry, where he took a refresher course. The quarry was down a dirt road shrouded in trees. A makeshift snack bar doubled as a sign-in desk, with a cooler of drinks and packets of chips set on an old picnic table under a pop-up University of Tennessee Volunteers canopy.

Fred hadn't been kidding about the temperature. Even in early summer, the water was cold... and became even colder when you descended below the thermocline—a layer of water where the temperature drops rapidly when you dip beneath it. On the other hand, Boone was surprised that the visibility wasn't that bad... almost fifty feet, if he had to guess. The quarry went down to eighty feet, but Boone spent much of his dives much shallower than that, on one of the training platforms.

That August, while sitting at the kitchen table reading over a dog-eared book that Fred had given him about automobile maintenance and repair, his mother called him into the living room to join her and Shingles on the couch.

"What's up, Mom?"

"Come watch the Olympics with me. They're covering swimming right now."

Boone had nearly forgotten that the Athens Summer Olympics were going on. Just as he sat down, a tall, lean swimmer filled the screen. At the bottom of the screen, the name "Michael Phelps" appeared beside the American flag.

"You look a lot like him!" his mother exclaimed. "Or you will in a couple more years, at the rate you're growing."

Boone wasn't sure he saw the resemblance, but he had to admit he'd grown even more over the past year and was easily the tallest boy at school. And while Phelps was certainly more athletic in build, Boone was in excellent shape from his frequent cycling and running. He still heard the moniker "Beanpole" from time to time, but his skinny frame was developing a fair amount of lean muscle.

The swimmers took their positions on the platforms and a

short buzz signaled the start of the men's 200-meter butterfly. As the participants dived into the water, the commentators noted that Phelps had won this same event in the Sydney Olympics when he was only fifteen. And in this contest, Phelps won handily, beating the second-place competitor by nearly a second.

"I know you were thinking of doing cross-country your sophomore year, but maybe you should join the swim team," his mother suggested.

The following semester, Boone joined the high school swim team, the Roane County Yellowjackets, and broke several regional records in freestyle and butterfly. Shortly after his sixteenth birthday, his swim coach suggested he take a life-guard certification class in nearby Oak Ridge during the upcoming spring break. Then he could work as a lifeguard, either at the small community pool in Kingston, or at any number of other pools in the area. Boone hadn't yet gotten his license—and didn't have a car, for that matter—so he couldn't drive himself to Oak Ridge for the classes. But as luck would have it, the swim coach had made the same suggestion to a few others on the team, including a junior who had both license and car.

The class was held in an indoor swimming pool in the Oak Ridge Civic Center, a complex built in the seventies in the middle of town beside the public library. Boone was familiar with the facility; a pungent tang of chlorine stung the nose as you walked down the hall toward the locker rooms. Kingston didn't have an indoor pool, so their swim team occasionally traveled there to train during colder months.

The lifeguard course spanned five days, and by the end of it, Boone had acquired Red Cross certifications in Lifeguarding, First Aid, CPR, and the use of an AED, or automatic external defibrillator. During his final day, while he waited for the other swimmers to finish up their paperwork, Boone found himself wandering the halls of the civic center, proudly carrying a manila envelope with his certificates. The main gymnasium had a vigorous basketball game going on, but Boone was drawn to the sound of slaps and thuds coming from one of the smaller gyms. Curious, he sidled up to a glass wall beside the door and discovered the source of the noise was a martial arts class; the slaps and thuds were from bodies striking the large gym mats laid out across the room, as gi-clad occupants practiced throws, takedowns, and tumbles.

Not wanting to disturb the class, Boone snaked a long arm into the room and snagged a brochure off a chair just inside the door. Retreating to the hall, he headed back toward the swimming pool wing, examining the brochure. *Brazilian Jiu-jitsu.* Skimming the first page, he saw that this was a martial art that focused on grappling, takedowns, and joint locks rather than punches or kicks. *If I'd known something like this, maybe I'd've avoided that suspension,* Boone mused, thinking back to his freshman-year scuffle when he'd clocked that kid in the face.

"Hey, Boone! We've been waiting on you, man!"

Boone looked up and saw his classmates in the lobby area. "Oh, sorry!" He stuffed the brochure into the manila envelope and hurried to catch up with his ride back to Kingston.

Arriving home, he found his mother had picked up some Buddy's Bar-B-Q for dinner, and when they sat down to dig in, Boone proudly presented his certificates.

"Wait, before we get barbecue sauce on our fingers ... look,

Mom!" He slid the papers out of the envelope. "If I want, I can be a lifeguard this summer!"

"I'm so proud of you, Boone." She looked at each certification, then paused. "What's this?" She held up the brochure.

"Oh, that... they were having a martial arts class in the same building the swimming pool was in. I watched them for a while."

"Is this something you'd want to do?"

"I... well... maybe." He went on to explain his thinking about the fight he'd gotten into.

"I don't think you're supposed to learn martial arts to get into fights, Boone."

"No, 'course not! But... with this... I was just thinking... that bully who was hurting Eugene... maybe I coulda stopped the guy without hitting him, is all."

His mother looked thoughtful. "Well... maybe. When would you take the class, though? You've got so much on your plate already. School comes first!"

"I know. I was thinking this summer. I was hoping to work at that huge outdoor pool in Oak Ridge; my swim coach said they're always looking for lifeguards. And then I could pop over and take the jiu-jitsu class."

"Pop over..." His mother sighed. "If you're planning on a job in Oak Ridge, you'll need a car. And money is tight, Boone..."

"Hey, don't worry. I think I might have that covered."

"It's older than *you* are, you know that, right?" Fred said, as the two of them walked around the old Toyota Tercel. "They don't even make these anymore, so parts might be an issue."

Boone shrugged. "But it's cheap. The guy's practically

giving it away." He had spotted the little gray car on his bike rides over to Fred's Fix-it. The For Sale sign in the window was faded from sunlight, so he figured it had been sitting there for a while.

"Wouldn't you prefer a pickup truck or something?"

Boone smiled. "Sure, but that would cost a lot more. This is plenty for me. And having a hatchback is great... I can haul dive gear in it. What do you think? Can you help me fix her up?"

"Yeah, of course," Fred said. "I mean... you'd have to buy any parts we need, and you'll do most of the work, but I can steer you in the right direction."

"Thanks, Fred."

"Is your mom gonna help with the insurance?"

"Uh... no. I've saved enough to handle it. Barely."

"Well, with you having a car... I can send you to some of the nearby marinas to work on boats. That is, if you can find the time with your busy lifeguarding schedule this summer."

Boone laughed. "I'm just doing that a few days a week. Along with some classes I'm taking."

Fred raised an eyebrow. "Classes during summer? What kind of kid *are* you?"

"These'll be fun classes, I hope. Oh! One more favor. Um... after I buy the car... can you drive it? Take me over to Rockwood? I need to get my driver's license."

EIGHT

That summer, Boone started working at the enormous public swimming pool in Oak Ridge. The Army Corps of Engineers had built it in 1944 to provide recreation for the community that had sprung up to service the Manhattan Project. Constructed on the site of a preexisting spring-fed pond, it was one of the largest swimming pools in the world and the fifth-largest in the US.

Nine lifeguard towers ringed the acre-and-a-quarter pool, with a snack bar at one end, changing rooms at the other, and a vast grassy area between them that ran along the gentle slope on the north side. There was a day of orientation for the lifeguards as the recreation department put them through their paces, and then the facility was opened to the public. Swimmers descended on the pool from all over the surrounding towns, and Boone was kept busy, bleating his whistle at children running on the concrete, and occasionally tending to skinned knees for some who didn't obey the whistle fast enough. His first summer, there was only one water rescue:

during his second week of lifeguarding, a not-so-strong swimmer ventured into the thirteen-foot-deep part of the pool and had begun to thrash. Three lifeguards knifed into the water, but Boone reached the swimmer-in-distress first, bringing him to the side of the pool with no harm done, other than to the man's ego.

While Boone sat on the edge of the pool to catch his breath, one of the other lifeguards who had dived in—a tall girl with dyed-pink hair named Liza—kicked him playfully in the thigh with her foot, her toes sporting fluorescent pink nail polish.

"Hey. You lost something."

Boone squinted up at her and Liza held out his sunglasses.

"You saved the guy... I saved your shades. Guess we're both heroes."

Boone grinned at her as he plucked the sunglasses from her pink-nailed fingers. "Thanks, Liza."

She put her foot on his shoulder and gave him a gentle shove. "You. You are *fast*."

"Oh... yeah, I guess. I'm on my school's swim team."

"I know. And I'm on mine." She pointed east toward Oak Ridge High School, visible from the pool. "I watched you compete this spring. And then the girls' teams were up and you watched *me* compete."

"I did?" His eyes flicked up at her hair.

She laughed and ran a hand through the wet, pink locks. "This was under a swim cap. Also... I think it was blue that month."

Boone stood. "Did you win?"

Liza just smiled and tapped a fingertip against his chest. *Tap, tap, tap.* "So... Boone..." *Tap, tap.* "Some of us are going to Big Ed's Pizza after the pool closes. You should come."

"I would, but I've got class."

She blinked. "Really? In summer? What for?"

"Brazilian jiu-jitsu."

"I have no idea what that is, but it sounds hot." She gave him one final, gratuitous shove. "Rain check, then."

Two evenings a week, Boone would drive to the nearby civic center to take classes in Brazilian jiu-jitsu. He quickly learned that his great height, long limbs, and flexible joints gave him a significant advantage in BJJ, keeping an attacker at bay and allowing him to lock up an opponent in difficult-to-break submission holds. His teacher encouraged him to enter competitions once he attained a blue belt, but between swim team, lifeguarding, working for Fred, and helping out his mother—on top of the homework he'd have to complete once back at school —Boone didn't see how he could take that on. And then, of course, there was the diving.

Before the summer was out, he found time to join some local divers on two trips: one to nearby Loch Low-Minn in Athens, and another to Gray Quarry, all the way out in Johnson City. The latter was notable for having a small school of paddlefish. The prehistoric-looking fish were nearly five feet long, with long snouts that looked a lot like an oversized shoehorn. By now, Boone had acquired a secondhand Aeris dive computer, and he spent some time getting acquainted with it.

In addition, the magnetic search coil he'd been waiting on arrived and he repaired the old metal detector he'd been hanging on to, using it in the Clinch River to hunt for coins and jewelry. He also continued to practice his freediving skills; by the end of the summer his breath-hold was up to three and a quarter minutes.

During the last weekend in August, he finally joined some of the lifeguards at Big Ed's, but by then Liza was dating a lifeguard named Chad. The phrase "You snooze, you lose," was whispered in Boone's ear on her way back from selecting a song on the old jukebox.

His junior year was jam-packed, and Boone didn't find much time for socializing. He continued to break records with the swim team, work for Fred, train in BJJ, and somehow managed to eke out a B+ average in his schoolwork. On Sundays, Boone would grab his mask and fins and travel to a pair of small golf courses in Oak Ridge and Farragut, where he collected golf balls from the water hazards, selling them to the managers of the course pro shops. The following summer, Boone once again commuted to Oak Ridge to work at the pool.

In addition to regular swimming hours, the pool would occasionally allow groups to book the facility for parties, starting thirty minutes after closing and running for two hours. Lifeguards had the opportunity to make some extra money, and on an evening when he didn't have a martial arts class, Boone worked one of those pool parties. He was assigned to the tower nearest the wooden swim platform.

Boone had heard they were planning on replacing it with a solid island of some sort, but at that moment, the swim-up raft was still the same one he remembered from his youth. In addition to providing a spot to climb onto and dive off of, the platform had another feature that kids and teens quickly discovered: you could swim up under it. Once you broke the surface beneath the raft, you found yourself in a shadowy little grotto surrounded by the echoing sounds of lapping water... and the distant whistles of lifeguards if they figured out you were under there.

Boone was sitting atop his lifeguard tower with a watchful

eye on a group of teens in the shallow end near the snack bar when a voice came from below.

"Well, well, well... look who it is! The great-great-great-great-great-grandson of Daniel Boone. Fancy meeting you here."

Boone glanced down at the base of the tower and found a beautiful blonde in a light blue swimsuit smiling up at him, a towel draped over her shoulders. She had grown since he'd last seen her, but he recognized her immediately.

"Renee! You... you're with the party?"

"No, I snuck over the fence to steal bathing suits." She laughed. "Yeah, I'm with the party. It's for Tiffany's birthday. You remember Tiff? She was on my shoulders when we beat your ass in chicken."

"I remember. It's good to see you, Renee. You... you look great." In the waning sunlight, Boone thought he detected a blush.

"You, too. You been working out?" Renee came around the front of the tower and started up the ladder.

"Uh... we're not allowed to let anyone up here with us."

"Okay." She halted on the second rung. "Then I'll just hang out right here." She leaned her forearms on the fifth rung and looked up at him. "So, what've you been up to, Boone? Haven't heard from you since the Lost Sea."

"Yeah, sorry about that... high school kinda took over my brain."

Renee shrugged. "Same here." Then she laughed. "And now college is looming over me."

"You're already looking at schools?"

Renee wrinkled her brows at him. "I'm going to UT in the fall. I'm a grade above you."

"Oh! Sorry, I guess I didn't realize..."

"I don't think I ever mentioned it," she said. "We only went out that one time. Didn't seem like it mattered."

The pair chatted for a while, each filling the other in on what they'd been doing over the past three years. Every so often Boone's eyes scanned his area of responsibility, but as the sun slipped below the horizon, the party was coming to a close and there weren't that many people left in the pool.

"So... what's it like being a lifeguard?"

"Well..." Boone gestured to the tower he sat atop. "Mostly, I sit here all day and blow my whistle at kids running at top speed on the wet concrete." He pointed over at the wooden platform. "And I keep an eye out for swimmers going under that. We leave them alone if they're there for just a little bit, but then..." He lifted the whistle, then let it fall against his chest.

Renee's gaze followed the whistle, then she looked up at him with a mischievous sparkle in her eyes.

"What happens if they ignore your whistle?"

Boone shrugged. "I gotta go get 'em."

Renee looked out at the platform, then descended the ladder and curled her toes over the edge of the pool. She shrugged the towel from her shoulders and looked back at Boone. "Then I guess you better come get me."

With that, she dove into the water and swam for the platform. Boone looked around and spotted Liza on her nearby tower, watching them with a grin on her face. Renee reached the platform, stuck her tongue out at Boone, and ducked under.

Liza laughed, then called out, "Go on! It's almost closing time. I'll cover for you."

Boone dived in and swam underwater to the platform, angling up when he reached Renee's kicking legs. He popped up inside the raft and found her hanging from the underside of the platform, the fingers of one hand gripping a gap between the boards overhead.

"It's freezing!" she gasped.

"Spring-fed water. And the sun's going down." Boone reached up and snagged a board as well, hanging beside her in the gloom. For a moment, there was no sound but the lapping of water against the sides of the platform. Strips of shadow danced across their faces as the waning light reached the surface of the water.

"So... Mr. Lifeguard... you ever rescue anyone?"

"A few. One last year... a couple this year."

"You ever give anyone mouth to mouth?"

Boone blushed, but fired up a crooked smile. "No. But I know how, if I have to."

Renee shifted her grip on the board-gaps overhead and swung closer. "Prove it."

NINE

Senior year began and Boone's schedule felt even more jam-packed than before, which scarcely seemed possible. On top of school, swimming, quarry diving, and his increased hours working for Fred, Boone had started back up with cross-country. And then Eugene dropped yet another chore in his lap.

"You've got to start applying for college, Boone. Like... now."

Boone looked up from his sandwich and stared out at the Clinch. The two of them were taking their lunch break out at the river park near the high school. "I... I'm not sure what I want to do..."

"That's step one. Figure that out." Eugene took a swig of soda. "I know you, Boone. I bet you have a few ideas bubbling in that head of yours."

"Well... I could stay here. Keep working. Decent money in engine repair."

"True. But is that what you want to do? What about all your diving and swimming? And you used to talk about the islands all the time." He held up a hand. "I realize whatever happened with your dad might've put a damper on that, but... I bet that spark is still in there."

Boone nodded, then asked, "Where are *you* going to college?"

"Nice deflection. I've got a short list of my top picks and some backups." He rattled off a few.

Boone put his half-eaten sandwich down on its wrapper and stood to pace a bit. "Actually, I *have* thought about it. A lot. I was looking at options for marine science. You know... oceanography, ecology, conservation. Marine biology."

"Where would you go for that?" Eugene asked.

"There are a few colleges that are highly rated for it, but there's one I keep coming back to. University of Miami. But it isn't cheap."

"Boone, if anyone can get an athletic scholarship, it's you," Eugene declared. "You're one of the best swimmers in the region."

Boone cracked a rueful smile. "They don't have a men's swim team there. Just a women's."

"Oh..."

"They have diving, though."

"Scuba diving? Well, there you go!"

Boone laughed. "Nope. Diving board diving. And I've never done that. But they *do* have scholarships for cross-country."

"That's why you started running again!"

"Yeah. And they have track and field scholarships, too, so... maybe. But I gotta get my grades up. And keep socking away money."

Eugene looked at his watch. "Oh, shoot, we gotta get back!"

They tossed their trash in the bin beside the pavilion and headed across the road to the school, arriving just before the bell. Eugene split off to head toward his next class but turned back.

"Hey... are you still seeing that Lenoir City girl?" Eugene asked.

"Not really," Boone said with a sigh. "She's staying on campus in Knoxville. I drove out to see her a few times, but... we're in different worlds now."

"Oh. Darn. Sorry to hear that."

"S'okay."

"No, I meant, 'sorry to hear that' because I wanted you to get her friend Tiffany's number for me." Eugene threw him a wink and rushed off to class.

Shortly after his eighteenth birthday, Boone received a belated gift: an acceptance letter from the University of Miami, along with an athletic scholarship for cross country. Beaming with pride, his mother took him out for a celebratory dinner in Knoxville before returning home and sitting him down at the kitchen table, where she had laid out all of her research on various student loans.

"I know you've been working and saving, Boone... but you'll need a loan."

Boone took her hand across the table. "Thanks, Mom."

"When does the semester start?"

"Late August. I'll go straight there from my summer job."

"Lifeguarding again? Or working for Fred?"

"Probably a little of both. Although Fred said he might have something else for me."

After high school graduation, Boone worked for Fred for two solid weeks, banking as much cash as he could.

"I gotta admit, I was kinda hoping you'd stick around," Fred announced one day, as the two of them finished up work on an old Evinrude outboard. "You really have a knack for this."

"Well, I've got even more of a knack, thanks to you, Fred. And I suspect this is a skill that'll come in handy no matter where I end up."

"So... marine science, huh? At least you'll be able to use your scuba diving skills!"

"Yeah... and thanks for your help with that, too."

Fred flashed a crafty grin. "I ain't done helping just yet. You don't need to come in tomorrow."

"Why not? I was planning on finishing up the Yamaha."

"I'll handle that. You've got somewhere to be." He went over to his makeshift desk and grabbed a large envelope, then tossed it onto Boone's workbench with a slap.

Boone opened the envelope and pulled out the contents. His eyes widened at the coversheet. "Ripley's Aquarium of the Smokies?" He lifted the cover and looked at the next sheet. "A job application?"

"They want you there at eight in the morning, so you'd better get an early start. Traffic into Gatlinburg is insane in summer."

"I've always wanted to work at an aquarium...."

"I know. Your little buddy came by here one day, looking for you... Eugene? Anyway, we got to talking about your diving. He said you told him one time you wanted to dive at an aquarium. I know Chattanooga's is closer, but one of my Search and Rescue buddies knows the dive safety officer in Gatlinburg. Last month, I called him up. Rattled off some of your swim team records, your lifeguarding certs, your PADI cert... that was already enough to spark their interest, but then I mentioned your freediving. Told him you could hold your breath for three minutes. That impressed him."

"I'm up to three and a half now."

Fred whistled appreciatively. "Well... correct the record when you get there," he added with a laugh. "Anyway, the job's not a done deal. They'll give you a swim test, and they require a chest X-ray and medical clearance... but since I know you're gonna ace all that, I had them go ahead and send over tax documents and the application. Have all that filled out when you show up. And bring your gear."

The resort town of Gatlinburg lay just within the borders of the Great Smoky Mountains National Park. A "gateway" of sorts between the bustle of Pigeon Forge to the north and the natural beauty of the Smokies, Gatlinburg drew about twelve million visitors each year, as vacationers from all over the country descended on the mountain town for entertainment, food, and shopping. If you were planning on visiting the National Park— and didn't know about the winding Gatlinburg Bypass—there was a good chance you'd have to run the "Gatlinburg Gaunt-let," navigating its traffic-packed streets.

Boone had taken Fred's suggestion to heart, gotten an early start to arrive before the crowds, and made his way to the massive Ripley's Aquarium of the Smokies, easily one of the largest structures in town. Gathering his scuba gear in a mesh bag, Boone made his way to the front of the aquarium and approached the glass doors. The aquarium wasn't yet open and there was no sign of anyone in the ticket booth, so Boone pulled his recently acquired flip phone from a shorts pocket and called the number he'd been provided.

"This is Ray," a voice answered, speaking loudly, as if competing with background noise.

"Hey, Ray, this is Boone Fischer. From Kingston? I'm out front."

"Oh, yeah! Hang tight, I'll send someone to come get you."

Boone waited for several minutes, then spotted a young man in a polo shirt fast-walking through the lobby. He opened the door and waved Boone inside.

"Good morning," the man said, speaking with a Carolina drawl. "Ray's got his hands full, so I'll bring you back to him. Boone, right?" He held out a hand. "Alex. I'm an aquarist... on loan from the original Ripley's Aquarium in Myrtle Beach."

"What's an aquarist do?" Boone asked.

Alex chuckled. "Everything, it sometimes feels like. We take care of the animals, making sure they're eating properly and keeping them safe and healthy. And we monitor the tank and water cleanliness. That alone could be a fulltime job."

Alex steered Boone out of the lobby to the left, then led the way up some stairs to a walkway that overlooked the massive main tank on the right. At the end of the walkway, a small, boxy boat was tied up alongside.

"The glass-bottom boat is new. Well, not so much a 'boat' as a raft... we use that line there to pull it across and back. They might have you man the boat from time to time." He pointed at a treasure chest full of gold doubloons. "Hang a left there. I'll buzz us in."

Alex used a keycard to open a metal door at the end of a corridor and led Boone into a large space with brightly colored walls. A pair of doors painted like dive flags stood out along a yellow wall to the right.

"Men's and women's locker rooms are there." He opened the men's and pointed inside. "Just set your gear bag there and we'll go find Ray."

Boone stepped in and felt his heartbeat kick up a notch. Cubbyholes ran along one side, but the other side was filled with wetsuits, booties, BCDs, regulators, masks, and fins. He set his bag down in a corner and rejoined Alex. "Wow. How many divers work here?"

"A lot. I'm just visiting for this month, so I don't know the full count here, but just among the aquarists, there are eighteen. But you need a degree for that. You'll be part of the dive staff that helps with tank maintenance and assists husbandry with feeding." He pointed toward a kitchen in the back corner, where Boone could see the door to a large walk-in freezer. "There's a lot of food prep. Different animals like to eat different things."

"Like what?"

Just then, a burly man stepped out of the freezer and proceeded to toss large bags of frozen fish onto the floor, calling out in a measured cadence, "Herring!" *Thud.* "Squid!" *Thud.* "Mackerel!" *Thud.* His hands empty, the man returned to the freezer.

Alex laughed. "That answer your question? We also use a lot of shrimp, clam, krill... we even cultivate our own brine shrimp."

Boone could hear voices around the corner, echoing off walls and water, a sound reminiscent of the atmosphere at the indoor pool in Oak Ridge. One voice rose above the others.

"That's it... easy does it!"

Alex led Boone around a corner, and he found the behind-the-scenes area opening up into an even larger space. Hoses, different-colored pipes, and holding tanks ringed the walls, and one section looked like something out of a mad scientist movie, with clear rubber tubes and blue plastic tubs lined up near shelves of glass jars, many containing liquids of differing shades of green. But the sight that dominated the cavernous room was a large, open tank with a gate at one end. Above it, a crane on a rail was just retracting; a sling-like stretcher hung from it, dripping water. Boone could guess what had occupied it moments earlier: a large, brown shark was slowly moving along the side of the tank, two men in wetsuits gently encouraging it.

"That's the acclimation tank," Alex explained. "One of the sand tigers was in quarantine, but our marine veterinarian gave her a clean bill of health, so she'll be in acclimation for a while before they open up that gate there and let her rejoin the others in Shark Lagoon."

A man with close-cropped hair and wearing a purple polo shirt stood at the edge of the pool talking on a radio. Spotting Boone and Alex, he signed off, clipped the radio to his belt, and came around the pool.

"Hi, Boone. I'm Ray. Fred told me all about you. Sounds like you'd be a good fit. I'll go over your paperwork and certifications, then we'll give you your swim tests and arrange for the medical."

"Yes, sir."

"None of that 'sir' stuff—we're all one big happy family. C'mon, let's step into the offices."

The rest of the morning was spent going over Boone's paperwork, undergoing some basic physical tests, and demonstrating his diving and swimming skills, after which he sat down with Ray for some lunch in the alley between the main building and the Marine Science Building behind it.

"What's in there?"

"The MSB? Well, at the moment, we're getting ready to try and breed sawfish. They're critically endangered, and we've had great success with our eagle ray breeding program, so we're branching out. But you won't be spending much time in there. You'll be doing a lot of cleaning dives... and maybe some show dives, if you're any good at performing."

Once—and one time only—Boone had been in a school play, and Eugene had proclaimed him "the worst actor he'd ever seen." But Boone simply smiled at Ray and said, "Sounds great to me."

"All right, then. You passed everything with flying colors. You're done for today, apart from heading over to this address for a chest X-ray and medical exam. Assuming everything checks out, you'll start this Thursday."

Thursday morning, bright and early, Boone arrived at the aquarium to begin his first day. As part of orientation, he watched a group of six divers enter the acclimation pool, largely ignoring the docile sand tiger shark. When they were suited up, Ray held a large pole in the water, guiding the shark away from the main gate, which another aquarist lifted partway up, like a castle portcullis. The divers ducked under the gate and descended into the tunnel beyond, trailing long vacuum hoses behind them. Ray then beckoned to Boone to follow him out a door that opened into a dimly lit area in the public part of the aquarium.

Boone joined Ray on the moving walkway that ran under the acrylic tunnels of Shark Lagoon. At nearly 750,000 gallons, this was the main attraction of the aquarium. The conveyor-belt tunnel was quite dark, and strains of Vivaldi's "The Four

Seasons" filled the air with string music. Overhead, a massive sawfish swam by, its bottom-set mouth and flattened underbelly making it look like a cross between a shark and a stingray. Beyond the "glass," Boone lost count of how many sharks he saw, surrounded by a wide variety of tropical fish.

Ray pointed ahead as the divers swam down from the entry tunnel. "This is a lot of what you'll be doing. We're almost always cleaning one tank or another on a daily basis. For the main tank, you'll have a team of four scrubbers and two guards."

"Guards?" Boone watched the two divers with white PVC pipes wrapped in spirals of black tape as they occasionally intercepted an approaching shark, presenting the poles as a barrier. "Are they there to keep the sharks from biting you?"

"More to just gently guide sharks away from the divers and hoses. We've never had an unprovoked bite. The sharks are quite chill. No, it's Sally you have to watch out for."

"Who's Sally?"

"That's our four-hundred-pound green sea turtle. She's adorable, but she's got quite a beak. Sally loves to sneak up on you and nip your hair or go after your mask or fins. In fact..." He pointed.

Sure enough, Sally was calmly swimming up behind one of the scrubbers, who was fixated on a patch of imitation coral, scrub brush in one hand and vacuum hose in the other. This diver, whose name Boone remembered was Tessa, had her brown hair in a long braid. No doubt a tempting target.

Ray stepped over to the acrylic wall and rapped on it. The diver looked around, then turned and spotted Ray, who pointed at the stealthy turtle's approach. Tessa flashed an "OK" sign and oriented face-on to the turtle. Her potential victim alerted, Sally seemed to lose interest and swam away toward the center of the tank, where she settled on the bottom. Immediately, a school of fish with yellow-and-white horizontal stripes and two thick, black vertical stripes descended on the turtle, nibbling at the surface of her hide.

"Guess Sally decided to get groomed herself, instead of grooming Tessa," Ray said. "That's Sally's grooming station; when she goes there, the porkfish know to come give her a cleaning."

"How long has Sally been here?" Boone asked.

"Since the beginning. She's a rescue. We got her from Miami Seaquarium."

Boone blinked. "On Virginia Key in Biscayne Bay?"

"Yeah. You been there?"

"No, but... that's right next to the University of Miami's marine science campus. I'm going there this fall."

"Congratulations! Well, once you get a degree from there, you could come back here as an aquarist." Ray gestured ahead. "C'mon, I'll show you the other tanks. The aquarium opens to the public in fifteen minutes, and it's about to get crowded."

Ray wasn't kidding. The summer crowds soon poured into the aquarium, and Boone and Ray retreated to the employee areas to complete the orientation.

"So... what do I do first?" Boone asked.

"For now... go help Barry with the food prep. You'll dive tomorrow."

TEN

Boone had been on "scrub-n-suck" duty in Shark Lagoon for several hours, and had just finished with a corner he'd been assigned to when something odd passed through his peripheral vision. Backpedaling from the corner, he turned to make sure he hadn't imagined it.

After a moment, the bizarre sight proved itself real. A triggerfish—Boone wasn't sure what kind—rounded an outcrop of polyurethane "coral" and swam into the open. Triggerfish mouths possessed some impressive teeth, but this one's mouth was tipped with something else: a pacifier. An honest-to-gosh rubber Binky, like you might find plugged into the mouth of a human baby.

Boone released the scrub brush and stretched out a long arm, trying to snag the pacifier as the triggerfish passed, but it turned on a dime and instantly changed direction. Fortunately, it chose that moment to decide the chunk of rubber wasn't edible and released it. As the pacifier slowly sank toward the bottom of the tank, a small blacktip shark spotted the object and angled toward it. Boone shot forward with a flutter kick and grabbed the pacifier while holding out a loop of the vacuum hose as a barrier to redirect the shark from his outstretched hand. Tucking the pacifier into a pocket on his BCD, Boone retrieved his scrub brush and swam over to his next cleaning assignment.

After their time was up, the six divers returned to the exit tunnel and swam toward the acclimation tank. The sand tiger from before had rejoined her pals in the main tank, so the pool was empty of any marine occupants when the divers emerged from under the gate. Boone was second to last in the tunnel, with a guard bringing up the rear, in case Sally decided to try and pay the gate a visit.

"What was that you grabbed?" Tessa asked Boone as she removed her gear.

Boone dug in his BCD pocket and held up the pacifier. "Triggerfish had it."

Ray was nearby and barked a short laugh. "You know, when I started here... the first time we opened up the skimmer to clean out the filters... we found twenty-eight pacifiers in the skimmer guard."

Tessa laughed. "Why so many?"

"It was one of the attendants in the lobby area who figured it out. Apparently, one thing that parents love to do is hold their kids up over the main tank and let them see all the pretty fish down below. And a lot of those kids are babies... with pacifiers. So now we clean out the skimmer guard frequently. In fact, Boone, you'll handle that today. Any pennies you find—and you *will* find some—go in the jar over by the breakroom microwave."

After cleaning out the skimmer guard, Boone detoured to the concession area to buy a bottle of water. While he waited in line, he watched the live demonstration in Ray Bay. The second-largest exhibit at 87,000 gallons, it was filled with spotted eagle rays, southern stingrays, and cownose rays, as well as a few sharks—primarily bonnetheads—along with a few hard-to-spot epaulette and bamboo sharks.

Lane, a white-bearded veteran of the aquarium, was the current show diver in the tank. While one of the exhibit educators narrated over a loudspeaker, describing the various animals inside the tank, the show diver came down to the glass —or, acrylic, more accurately—to interact with the children, who quickly filled the front of the viewing area.

Boone reached the cashier and paid for his water. Turning to leave, he spotted a child gesturing with hand signals toward the show diver. Lane waved, sank to the bottom beside the child, and began signing back. In moments, the two appeared to be having a conversation. Boone recognized the back-and-forth gestures as American Sign Language. Eugene had once tried to teach him ASL, but Boone had never gotten further than alphabetical fingerspelling, and had no idea what these two were saying to each other.

Returning to the employee area, Boone added the pennies he'd gotten from the skimmer into the jar by the microwave, then set down another pacifier and a pair of scrunchies beside it.

"Pretty good haul," Ray said as he passed by.

"Lane was using sign language to have a conversation with a kid," Boone recounted. "How cool is that?"

"Was it a little girl, black hair, about yea big?" Ray held a hand a few feet off the floor. When Boone nodded, Ray explained, "That's Tricia. Her mother brings her here every other week, if Lane's working. She also loves the mermaid show."

Boone blinked. "You mentioned mermaids during orientation, but I thought you were joking."

Ray laughed and glanced at his watch. "Swing by the Coral Reef tank in forty-five minutes and you'll see that I wasn't. But in the meantime, I'll need to give you something to do."

"He can take my place and clean Race Track," Tessa said from the breakroom table as she poked at a cup of yogurt with a spoon.

Boone knew she was referring to the tank that was a continuous loop filled with schooling fish that had learned to swim in a particular direction.

"Tall as Boone is, that's probably not a good idea." Ray nodded to Boone. "It's claustrophobic enough as it is. Divers have to use a hookah. Not enough room for a tank on your back."

"I feel like I'm being penalized for being small," Tessa complained.

"Aw, now, Tessa... you're not small. You're the perfect size. To clean Race Track." Ray's radio squawked and he pulled it free of his belt.

"Go for Ray."

"Hey, Ray, it's Lisa... can you bring me some vinegar and Adolph's?"

"You get stung?"

"Yeah, just a brush with a sea nettle. I'd grab the stuff, but I'm kind of in the middle of something."

"On the way." He pointed the radio antenna at Boone. "You know where the first aid locker above the Coral Reef tank is?"

"I do." One of the first things he'd learned during orientation was the location of each and every one of the first aid stations.

"Go grab some vinegar and a shaker of Adolph's and bring

it down to Lisa in the lab where they've got the poison arrow frogs. The back walls of the jellyfish exhibits are down there."

"Okay!" Boone started away, then came up short. "Wait. What's Adolph's?"

"Meat tenderizer."

Boone hurried to the first aid locker he'd been directed to, clonking up the metal steps to the room above the Coral Reef exhibit. Passing the tiled shower stall at the top of the stairs, he crossed the small room and opened the tall locker. There, on the top shelf, beside the defibrillator and in front of the green hardcase for emergency oxygen, were two store-bought shakers of Adolph's Tenderizer and a plastic bottle of vinegar. He grabbed one of each, scrambled back down the steps, then rushed into the lab where Lisa was waiting. She was in her late thirties and wore a stylish pair of horn-rimmed glasses on her face, the lenses of which were currently focused on a stainless-steel tray. She held a long pair of tweezers and was examining an amorphous blob of goo. Her eyes flicked up at Boone, then back to her work.

"Well, hello New Guy! Ray sent you, I take it. You find everything?"

"Yeah."

"Just shake some out in a little pile next to the sink... add some vinegar to it... then grab that little spatula and mix it into a paste, please."

"Um... okay." Boone did as she asked. "You got stung?"

"Comes with the territory. We've got an emergency envenomation kit up on the shelf there for stings from some of the nastier beasties, but for a nettle, good ol' vinegar and meat tenderizer is plenty."

She set down the tweezers and joined Boone at the sink.

Lisa held up her wrist, and Boone could see several red stripes across the skin.

"Does it hurt?"

"Sure. But pain is just a signal." Taking the spatula from him, she gathered some of the paste and slathered it on the injury.

"That really works?"

"I wouldn't be doing it if it didn't. There are lots of folk remedies out there that don't do diddly-squat, but this isn't one of them. The tenderizer contains an enzyme that breaks down proteins. Venom... is mostly protein." She set down the spatula. "Back to work. You can return the vinegar and tenderizer to first aid, but leave that paste there, in case I need some more."

With that, she returned to her examination of what Boone assumed was a jellyfish. He grabbed the Adolph's and vinegar and went back to return them to their shelf. Climbing up the stairs, he passed the tiny shower stall just as a topless young woman started to step out. Startled, Boone dropped the vinegar and tenderizer and abruptly turned away as the woman squeaked in surprise and slid the shower curtain closed.

"Oh, jeez, I'm so sorry!" Boone blurted.

The woman laughed, not sounding offended in the slightest. "No, *I'm* sorry! I didn't think anyone was up here. I was just using the shower as a changing room."

Boone heard the curtain slide on the railing. Out of the corner of his eye, he saw her poke her head out. A cascade of auburn hair framed blushing cheeks and hazel eyes. She burst into laughter.

"Oh, the look on your face! C'mon, no harm done." She

snaked an arm out from behind the curtain and held her hand out. "I'm Faye. Or you can call me Finny."

Boone reached back and tentatively took her hand. "Boone Fischer. I'm new."

"Ooh, fresh meat!" She squeezed his hand, then laughed again and released him. "I'm kidding. Hey, sorry to trouble you, but could you hand me my top? You scared the bejeezus out of me and I dropped it." She pointed at the floor just outside the shower stall.

Boone reached down and picked up the bikini top from the floor. It was composed of two scallop seashells, rimmed with iridescence. He held it out to her. "Here you go, Faye. Or...?"

"Finny. It's my mermaid name."

After returning the vinegar and tenderizer to the locker, Boone started back to the employee area, but paused beside the huge fractionators. The sound of machinery echoed off the walls and high ceilings as the system filtered out particulates and organics. *Ray did say to swing by Coral Reef and watch the mermaid show,* he thought. Smiling, he turned around and headed to one of the exit doors that led into the public part of the aquarium, emerging near the Coral Reef tank, the third largest of the exhibits.

The darkened viewing area was already packed with kids inside a ring of parents, so Boone took advantage of his height and found a spot against the wall in the back. The tank was full of tropical fish—primarily Pacific species—and tall pillars of imitation coral rose out of sight. The children were excitedly pointing, and Boone spotted a large, turquoise-blue mermaid tail hanging down from above. He'd been at the top of that tank, and knew there was a platform along one side with some stairs leading down into the water. After a moment, another tail joined the first, this one bright orange.

Kid-friendly calypso music started up and the two mermaids dove in, drawing oohs and ahs from the audience. The turquoise fin belonged to Faye—or Finny—and her long, auburn locks streamed out behind her as she descended toward the glass, smiling broadly and waving at the children. The other mermaid with the orange tail, her hair platinum and shoulder-length, swam in a curving spiral as she descended to a spot a few feet to Faye's left. She waved as well, as the same narrator from the show diver performance at Ray Bay keyed the intercom mic and began to spin tales about the mermaids and their performance.

The pair were clearly freediving, and Boone was impressed by how they took turns using their underwater acrobatics to end a particular move at the surface for a breath, always keeping one mermaid below to maintain the focus of the children.

Boone watched closely, observing several things: he could see wetsuit-clad legs at the top of the glass, back where Faye had been sitting, so he knew they had a safety diver on standby. Next, he noticed that the mermaids would occasionally glance down at the bottom and adjust ever so slightly before performing a tumble or roll. There was a rock at that spot, so Boone assumed they were using it to orient themselves. Without masks, everything was likely a blur, especially the audience of children, and yet you would never know it from the wide-eyed, smiling faces the mermaids directed at the kids on the other side of the acrylic.

After about ten minutes, the music crescendoed and "Orange Tail" moved off to the side as Faye/Finny came down with a fresh lungful of air. She centered herself over the rock, then arched her slender body and back-rolled three times, spiraling through the water in a graceful arc. The material on her tail and seashell bikini-top sparkled with each rotation. Completing the third backward somersault, she turned to face the audience, placed her fingertips to her smiling lips, and blasted a gust of bubbles through them as she rapidly moved her hands in a pair of sweeping curves. The maneuver created a heart composed of streams of tiny bubbles, eliciting piercing squeals from the kids. With a wave of her hands she shot to the surface, no doubt to fill her depleted lungs after that impressive trick.

The music stopped, and Orange Tail moved in to give final waves to the children, pressing her hands to the glass. Faye soon joined her as the announcer thanked everyone for coming. After a moment, the two young women returned to the surface, lifting themselves out of the water, where Boone knew the shallow steps were.

He pushed off from the wall he'd been leaning against and made his way back toward the nearest employee door. He was impressed. And maybe... if he was honest with himself... a bit smitten.

ELEVEN

Boone continued to work in Gatlinburg several days a week, filling the remaining days at either the fix-it shop or at nearby marinas that Fred sent him to.

Although Boone spent much of his time at the aquarium on cleaning duty in the various exhibits—including the ever-popular Penguin Playhouse—Ray let him do several show dives a week. Boone was a graceful swimmer and he proved to be quite popular. He soon learned how to blow bubble rings and became fairly skilled at it. One trick was to send one ring floating to the surface, then ascend through it headfirst, giving himself a bubble halo. Or he'd launch a big ring upward, then expel another after it. Launched with greater force, the second ring would shoot up through the first.

On one particular morning, Boone was in the middle of a presentation when a flash of auburn hair caught his eye. A woman was watching from off to the side of the small crowd, and he thought it was Faye, but when he next looked her way, she was gone. Faye hadn't been back to do the mermaid show for several weeks; Boone had learned that there were quite a few different mermaids—and at least one merman—who took turns.

After performing a few more tricks, the show dive came to an end. He turned to wave to the children and found Faye right beside the glass, off to one side near where the exhibit explainer had her microphone. Faye was watching him intently with a lopsided grin on her face. Catching his eye, she waggled her fingers at him, then turned and spoke with the announcer who had just finished up her part of the presentation. Boone saw Faye borrow a hand-held radio from the woman, but then a tow-headed little boy plastered himself up against the side of the tank, waving at Boone and pressing a palm on the glass-like acrylic.

Boone sank to the sand and mirrored the hand move, placing his own palm-to-palm with the boy's. He waved with his other hand, then removed his mouthpiece, tilted his head back, and fired off three quick bubble rings. The boy backed away, clapping, and turned toward his parents. A second hand slapped into place on the glass, a few feet above where the boy's had been, its fingers long and slender. Boone looked up to find a pair of hazel eyes looking at him. Faye's small smile grew into a grin when Boone reached out to place his palm over hers, but she withdrew her hand before he could. She pressed a piece of paper to the glass.

It read: *You are my safety diver today. See you at noon.*

"Faye?" Boone called from the base of the metal stairs. "You up there?"

"That you, Boone? Right on time."

"Are you... are you decent?"

Faye laughed. "Well... that's a loaded question."

Another voice snickered and Boone heard whispering. Then Faye appeared at the top of the stairs. "I have my clothes on, if that's what you're asking. So does Yvonne. C'mon up, you're early."

Boone shouldered his gear and climbed the steps toward Faye. She was wearing a loose-fitting T-shirt and blue spandex swim shorts. Boone could see the straps from her mermaid top beneath the shirt, so he imagined she was ready to go, except for the tail. When he reached the top, he set his tank down to the side and turned to greet Faye and a brunette woman in her twenties.

"Hi Boone, I'm Yvonne," the brunette said with a smile. "Faye's been telling me all about you."

"She has?"

Faye rewarded Yvonne's statement with a punch to the arm. Yvonne yelped, then punched her right back before offering her hand to Boone.

Boone shook it. "Is Yvonne your, uh... your name-name? Or your mermaid name?"

"When I've got the tail on, I'm Nixie."

Boone looked at the clock on the wall. "We've still got a half hour before the show, right? Ray walked me through my responsibilities, but if there's anything you want me to know...?"

"You'll be fine," Faye reassured him. "So... there are three shows today... 12:30, 2:00, and 4:30. You'll be our standby for all of them."

"Yeah, Ray told me. I was supposed to be on penguin duty this afternoon, but he reassigned me." Boone looked Faye in the eyes. "When I was doing the show dive, I saw you borrow a radio. Did you...?"

"Call Ray and ask him to put you on the mermaid dives?" she asked with a playful smirk. "Gee, I can't recall."

"That's what she did," Yvonne said. "She told me she liked the way you moved."

Faye rounded on her. "I'm going to murder you when you least expect it." She turned back to Boone. "But yeah... you're a natural. The way you move underwater is very... well, I'll just say 'effortless.' The kids loved you." She snorted a laugh. "And so did the moms."

Boone blushed. "Uh... cool. So, I'll just get geared up." He assembled his equipment on a bench nearby, then stripped down to his red swim trunks and started to pull his wetsuit over his legs.

"Were you a lifeguard?"

Boone looked up to find Faye drinking a bottle of water, watching him. She pointed at the top of his swimsuit.

"Yeah. Last couple years."

"Of course you were." She gestured at him with the water bottle. "You'd make a great merman."

Boone chuckled nervously. "Nobody wants to see that." He quickly pulled the wetsuit up and slid his arms into the sleeves.

"Oh, you're wrong about that. And Ray told me you could breath-hold a crazy long time. You'd be perfect."

"He told you that on the radio?"

"No. It was another time." Faye watched him as he zipped up the wetsuit. "We lost our merman... he's going off to grad school."

"I'm leaving for college in late August," Boone quickly said. "Florida."

"I'm from Florida!" Yvonne declared. "Where are you going?"

"University of Miami."

"Very cool. I'm a Gulf Coast girl, myself. Hey, Faye... quit flirting and get suited up."

"I'm not...!" Faye protested, then gave Yvonne a light shove. "You do realize you're about to be underwater with me."

While everyone got ready, Boone went over his gear one last time, then brought his rig over to the bench closer to the pool. Faye stripped off her shirt and tossed it at Boone as she made her way to the platform above the tank.

"Hey Boone, grab my tail."

That elicited a snicker from Yvonne, who was carrying her own pink tail over to join her. Boone picked up the turquoise-blue tail from beside the shower and was surprised by how heavy it was. He said so, as he set it beside Faye.

"Yeah, it's silicone, with a monofin built into the tail, and I've got a couple soft weights added to help me stay down. It's got a lot of surface area, so it needs the extra weight. The whole thing's about thirty pounds." She grabbed the waist of it and slid it closer. "Hey, Boone..." She put on a husky voice. "Gimme some lube."

"I... what?"

"Quit teasing him," Yvonne scolded. "She means that tube of lubricating jelly over there, next to the alcohol." She pointed. "Getting these tails on and off can be a pain."

Boone grabbed it and handed it to Faye, who winked at him. "Thanks." She squirted some on her hands and spread it around the waistband of her spandex swim shorts. "Do I make you nervous?"

"Yes," Boone replied without hesitation. "But I'll live."

The first show went off without a hitch, and Boone joined

the women for some lunch in the alley at the back of the aquarium. He learned that Faye had dropped out of college to travel
the southeast, performing at several aquariums and occasional
pool parties. Yvonne had just gotten engaged, and showed off
her ring.

"You don't dive with that, do you?" Boone asked.

"Of course not. I put it with my stuff when I suit up."

The remaining two dives went well, with the trio hanging
out between the shows. The two girls shared some absolutely
outrageous "mermaid tales" that ranged from scandalous to
side-splittingly funny. Boone had never been much of a
laugher, but he found himself thoroughly enjoying the stories,
with the two mermaids dissolving into giggling hysteria on
several occasions.

After the final show, Boone was pulling off his wetsuit and
Finny and Nixie were transitioning back to Faye and Yvonne,
when Yvonne suddenly moaned in distress. Boone was on his
feet in an instant.

"What is it?"

Yvonne didn't answer as she tore through a little pocket on
her backpack. "Oh no... no, no, no, no, no!" She started opening
other parts of the backpack, then turned to Boone with tears in
her eyes. "My ring! I... it's not here!"

"Did someone steal it?" Faye asked.

"I was up here the whole time," Boone reassured them. "No
one came up during the shows."

"I... I don't remember putting it away," Yvonne said, wide-
eyed. "We were having so much fun... I just..." She turned and
took two steps to the side of the tank, looking down at the
surface of the water. "I must've had it on. I've lost a little
weight since I got it, and..." She started to cry.

"Do you know which dive you lost it on?" Faye asked.

"You had it at lunch, but I don't think you had it on between the second and third shows," Boone said, visualizing their interval.

"Oh, no! So, I might've lost it hours ago?"

"Hey, look, we'll find it," he assured her. "Let's go down to the public area and see if we can spot it through the glass."

Boone grabbed the radio Ray had given him for the afternoon and called to explain the problem. Ray quickly joined them in the viewing area beside Coral Reef, bringing two other employees to assist. After a thorough search from outside the glass, they hadn't spotted it. Yvonne got more and more upset as the minutes ticked by.

"Wait... I've got an idea," Boone said. "Ray, we close at nine tonight, right?"

"Yeah. After they lock up, some of us can suit up and—"

"Let me have first crack at it," Boone interrupted. "I'm an idiot for not thinking of this sooner." He placed a hand on Yvonne's shoulder. "We're going to find it. I promise."

TWELVE

Ten minutes before closing, Boone ran out to the parking deck behind the aquarium and raised his car's hatchback. Wrapped in a towel, beside some spare gear and a small toolbox, he found what he was looking for. Grabbing hold of it, he returned to the employee area where Ray and the mermaids were waiting. He was pleased to see that Ray was distracting Yvonne from her situation with the wonders of the "feeding tube massage chair." Along one wall was a series of tubes that sent various foods to various tanks. The tubes hummed with vibration, and if you leaned against one you could enjoy a sensation not unlike a massage chair at the mall.

Boone held up the underwater metal detector he'd fetched. "I fixed it up not long ago and used it in a few places where recreational boaters anchor. I've gotten pretty good at finding jewelry. People jumping in and out of the water tend to lose watches, earrings, necklaces... and a few rings. May I ask what your ring is made of?"

"White gold."

"Great, I can find that." He raised the detector above his head. "Shall we?"

"We shall," Ray answered with a grin.

Yvonne rose from the chair. "Let's go!"

With Ray's permission, Boone left the scuba gear behind and freedived with just a wetsuit and weights. Ray joined him in full gear as a safety backup.

"I can be a second set of eyes, if you need me," Ray said at the surface.

"Hang up top," Boone said. "I want to minimize disturbing the sand with our fins." With that, he performed a brief freediver "breathe-up," then drew in a deep breath and ducked under.

As he descended, he located the rock the mermaids used to center themselves for many of their stunts. Although it was quite possible the ring had come off during the entry or exit, Boone had a hunch the backward somersaults were the likely culprit, and those were performed over that rock. As the mermaid show continued, the sweeping motions of the two monofins might have covered the ring with enough sand that they hadn't been able to see it when they'd looked through the glass a few hours ago. Dropping down to the rock, he adjusted his waterproof headphones and activated the metal detector. Swimming in concentric circles around the rock, he began sweeping it over the sand.

When he'd first searched for jewelry in Watts Bar Lake, Boone had noticed that different metals made different sounds. Gold, for instance, sounded a lot like aluminum. A few hours on the internet had taught him that gold in jewelry was often a combination of metals. White gold usually had zinc or nickel added to the gold, and all of those metals were non-ferrous, and therefore non-magnetic. They were harder to detect, but since they were conductive, they would still register on the detector.

After a couple of minutes, Boone went back for a breath. When he popped up, Ray was waiting with an eye on his dive watch.

"Thought you said you could breath-hold for three and a half minutes."

Boone laughed. "If I focus on nothing else, sure. But there's no reason to show off."

"Fair enough. Anything yet?"

"No... I did two circles in the sand around the rock they perform over, and..." He trailed off, then ducked his mask under, looking at the rock. He popped his head back up. "Back in a jiff."

Boone prepped his breathing, filled his chest, and dropped straight down to the rock. When he glanced up at the acrylic wall, he could see Yvonne and Faye watching him expectantly. He looked down at the rock, focusing on a little bump on the back, almost like a tiny outcrop. Putting the head of the detector under that spot, right up against the base of the artificial stone, he triggered the device and got an immediate tone. If this was a typical lake search, he'd expect to come up with a pull-tab from a soda can, but he knew in his gut he'd found the ring.

He swept the detector a little to either side, then set it down and dropped closer to the rock. Boone reached out and gently slid his long fingers into the sand, careful not to push the object any deeper. Because Yvonne had lost it just hours ago, he doubted it'd had time to migrate too far from the surface of the sand. He scooped his hand underneath where he thought it would be, then slowly lifted it, letting the sand sift through his fingers. There, atop his palm, was the white gold diamond engagement ring.

Closing his fingers around it, he flutter-kicked over to the onlookers, grinning broadly. Boone pinched the ring between two fingers and held it next to the glass. The look on Yvonne's face made the entire summer worthwhile. And as he ascended to the surface, he glanced down and saw Faye looking up at him, her face close to the glass.

While Yvonne's expression had been filled with gratitude and relief, Faye's face held other emotions.

The following day, Boone was back on cleaning and show-diver duty, but he kept an eye out for Faye; he knew the mermaids were performing again, but he hadn't seen her. During the lunch break he spotted Yvonne and another girl under one of the umbrellaed tables in the alley.

"Hey, Boone! Thank you so-so-so-so-so... *so* much for finding my ring!"

"Think nothing of it."

"This is Lindsey. She stepped in—or *swam* in—for Faye today."

"Oh. I thought Faye was here for the whole weekend. Is she okay?"

"Yeah... she's fine. She..." Yvonne looked like she was going to say something else, then shook her head. "She had to take care of something. She'll be back tomorrow morning for Breakfast with a Mermaid."

"Oh, right... that's tomorrow." Boone had been around for one of those, even helping set up the catering tables. The event was popular with families looking to get an early start at the aquarium. The kids got to meet—and take photos with—a mermaid, while mom and dad scarfed down scrambled eggs and coffee.

At 10:00 p.m., Boone was in the Ray Bay exhibit, performing his last show dive of the day, when a familiar face appeared in the dwindling crowd. Faye approached the tank and beckoned to him with a finger. She was wearing a light summer dress with a tiny purse dangling from one bare shoulder, her auburn hair cascading over the other. He descended, and when he was face-to-face with her, she pressed a note against the glass.

Meet me in the gift shop after work.

Boone raised his eyes from the note and looked at her. She raised an eyebrow and one corner of her mouth lifted in a half-smile, dimpling her cheek. Boone raised his hand in an "OK" sign. Her smile broadened and she turned abruptly away, vanishing into the shadows of the viewing area.

Twenty minutes later, Boone entered the gift shop near the entrance lobby and found Faye standing by a carousel of stuffed marine animals. She waggled an octopus at him as a greeting, then tossed it back with its plush friends.

"Good. You left your gear."

"Yeah, I'm working tomorrow—"

"I know. C'mon." She took his hand and dragged him to the exit.

Outside, the night air was humid with a whiff of ozone. From the puddles, it was clear a summer rainstorm had passed through while Boone had been at work. Faye latched on to his upper arm with both hands, guiding him down the steps toward the pedestrian bridge that crossed the Little Pigeon River in the direction of the main drag.

"Where are we going?"

"Depends. Did you eat dinner?"

"Yeah."

"Then you and I are going to have a drink."

"Um... I'm eighteen," Boone said. "And a half," he added.

She laughed as she pulled him along. "Then *you* are going to watch *me* have a drink, while you sip a Shirley Temple."

"Can I get an iced tea instead?"

"We'll see."

They crossed through a parking lot and reached the main thoroughfare, lined with shops of all varieties. Since it was almost eleven, most storefronts were dark, but Faye led him across the street and into a brick-paved shopping area: a cul-de-sac of candy stores, boutiques, and eateries.

"There's a pub back here that stays open pretty late in the summer," she explained.

"Where were you today?" Boone asked. "Everything okay?"

She squeezed his arm, and replied, "Let's wait until I've got a drink in front of me, okay?"

They walked the rest of the way in silence. Ten minutes later they were in a corner booth of the cozy pub, Boone with an iced tea and Faye with a margarita.

"What you did for Yvonne was very sweet," she said, after taking a sip.

"Ray would've found it if I hadn't," Boone replied with a shrug. "I just happened to have something to speed things up a bit."

Faye looked at him over her salted rim. "You've got an 'aw shucks' way about you... and it isn't an act, is it?"

"Uh... I don't think so." He picked up his iced tea.

"I like you, Boone."

Boone was caught mid-sip but managed to swallow without incident. "I... I like you too, Faye."

"Thought you might." Faye stirred her margarita with the straw, round and round... then pushed her drink away and sighed. "You wanted to know why I wasn't here today..."

"I was just worried about you, is all. You don't have to—"

"I wasn't here because I drove to North Carolina," she interrupted. "I've been living there for almost a year, while I travel to various gigs. Been calling it 'home base.'" She dragged the drink back to her, took a long pull on the straw, shoved it away again. "I broke up with my boyfriend."

Boone opened his mouth... closed it. "I didn't..."

"Didn't know I was seeing someone? Why *would* you, the way I was flirting with you? Anyway... it's over."

"Oh... jeez... I'm sorry to hear that, Faye."

"Don't be. I've been meaning to do it for a while now. And I wanted to do it in person." She laughed at herself. "Also, I needed to get my stuff." She smiled, looking down at the table. "I'll need a new home base... and it just so happens Yvonne is moving in with her fella, so I've got an option for a few weeks."

"Why did you...?" Boone began. "Never mind. None of my business."

"I broke up with him because it was time. And because I didn't want to cheat on him. Because I met someone."

Boone said nothing, waiting for more.

Faye abruptly smiled. "Where did you say you live? Kingston?"

"Yeah."

"How far away is that?"

"About an hour and a half."

"Long drive. And you have to be back here crack of dawn, right?"

"Yeah. Six in the morning."

"Seems pretty silly to have to drive all the way home, sleep for a few hours, then drive all the way back."

Boone took a deep breath, let it out, then locked his gaze on her hazel eyes. "I suppose I could sleep in the back of my car. Unless you have an alternative suggestion...?"

A wicked grin crept onto Faye's face and her eyes sparkled. "As a matter of fact, I do." She took a final sip of her margarita and retrieved her little sling bag. Faye took out a twenty-dollar bill and set it on the table. Boone scrambled to get his wallet out to pay, but she snatched it from his hand and bounced it off his forehead with a leathery smack. The two of them burst into laughter at that.

"You're about to go off to college," Faye said when her laughter subsided. "You'll need the money more than me. Now, finish your tea. Whenever I work a full weekend with a mermaid breakfast gig, I get a hotel room. Good news for you, is... you won't have to sleep in your car."

Hours later, as Boone drifted off to sleep, his drowsing mind declared that he may in fact have found something he enjoyed more than diving.

PART THREE

THIRTEEN

MIAMI, FLORIDA

For a rural East Tennessean, Miami was quite a culture shock... but in a good way. In Boone's freshman year, he spent most of his time on the university's Coral Gables campus, tackling all of his core curriculum classes and running for the college cross country team, but he found time to venture out, discovering a vibrant city with a melting pot of cultures.

The food scene in particular was an eye-opener. While Boone would never turn down a heaping plate of good ole southern cooking, in Miami he experienced all sorts of food he'd never tried before. Sure, Knoxville had a wide variety of eateries, but he hadn't been to many of them. He quickly gravitated toward cuisine of the Caribbean variety, seeking out good Cuban and Jamaican food.

Faye had been "mermaiding" on the other side of the state at Weeki Wachee Springs north of Tampa, and came to visit Boone during spring break. The two of them took a road trip down to Key West, and Boone managed to fit in some diving on the way back up, stopping in at Islamorada for an afternoon dive.

"You sure you don't wanna join me?" Boone asked. "I know you didn't bring any gear, but we could rent some."

"No, that's okay," Faye said. "I'm actually not that into scuba diving." When Boone looked surprised, she laughed. "I'm sorry, I've been hiding that from you. I know, I know... I'm a mermaid... we met at an aquarium full of divers. But it's my ears... I've never been good at equalizing. Anything deep is just agony. We mermaids like to keep it under fifteen feet."

"Hey, it's cool. We can just head back. I don't need to—"

"Boone Fischer, if you don't get on that dive boat, I will kick your ass six ways from Sunday. I don't care how good you are at that jiu-jitsu stuff... I can take you."

"I bet you could."

"Besides, it'll give us something cool to talk about the rest of the drive back. Given what Miami traffic's like, make sure you see a lot of cool things down there to tell me about."

Boone smiled and pulled her to him for a brief kiss. "If you're sure..."

"Damn sure. I'll go shopping while you Jacques Cousteau it out there."

It had been a long time since he'd dived in anything other than a rock quarry or aquarium tank, and the sloping walls and massive spurs of Victory Reef teemed with fish, including a massive goliath grouper that dwarfed anything he'd seen in Aruba. Boone couldn't wait to apply for a semester abroad at one of the university's Caribbean conservation programs.

After the dive, Boone joined Faye at her SUV and piled his rinsed gear into a bin she kept in the back for storing her mermaid tail after a gig.

"You see everything there was to see under the sea?" she asked.

"I did. And then some. You keep yourself amused?"

Faye rubbed her hands together with an evil laugh. "Oh yes. More than you know. My shopping spree bore fruit. Close your eyes and hold out your hands."

Boone heard the car door open, then close, then something was dropped into his hands. He opened his eyes. Staring up at him were multiple yellow Sponge Bobs and pink Patrick Starfishes populating a light blue pair of swim trunks.

"The swimsuit you had on in Key West was about to fall apart. Not that I would have minded, come to think of it... but I figured you could use an upgrade."

Boone stared at the gaudy shorts. "Not really my thing..."

"Oh, who are you kidding? They're awesome! You can wear them ironically."

"I feel like anyone that stares at these for too long might have a seizure."

Faye laughed. "Well, tell you what. When we get back to the dorm, you can model them for me. And if you don't like them... I can take them off for you."

At the end of the spring break, Faye went back to her mermaid gig and Boone returned to his studies. Over the summer, he returned to Tennessee to work for Fred, spending just two days a week at the aquarium, usually Saturdays and Sundays. One Friday night, as he sat down for dinner with his mother at the kitchen table, he worked up the courage to ask if she'd like to come along to the aquarium.

"I could give you a behind-the-scenes tour. And I'm on show diver duty tomorrow, so you could watch me perform."

His mother gave him a sad smile. "I... I know you love

diving, Boone... but it brings back some memories that I'd rather not think about. Is it okay if I say no?"

Boone looked across the table at her. Her eyes gleamed with a hint of tears, but the smile remained on her lips. "Sure, Mom." He swallowed, then took a breath before asking, "Mom... you ever wonder what...?" He trailed off, stopping himself from using the term "Dad."

But his mother knew what he was going to ask. Boone was surprised to see that the smile remained on her face, although a tear broke free and ran down her cheek. "Do I ever wonder what your father is doing? Where he is? Who he's with?" She sighed. "Of course I do, Boone. But I know in my heart that it's something I don't *need* to know. And I think I'll be happier *not* knowing." She dabbed her eyes with her sleeve, then continued. "He's never reached out, and I'm strangely grateful for that. And I haven't tried to contact him either. But, listen... Boone... he is your father. If you ever want to try and contact him—"

"No," Boone interrupted her in a soft voice. "No... I don't want to talk to him. I hate him."

His mother reached across and patted his hand. "Maybe a part of you does... but I'm sure there's still a little love in there, too. Don't dwell on the hate, Boone. It never does anyone a lick of good."

During his sophomore year, Boone began taking several classes a week at the marine science campus over on Virginia Key. When he felt he had a handle on his studies, he added lessons in Brazilian jiu-jitsu at a martial arts gym not far from the Rickenbacker Causeway. As his skills improved, a chance meeting at a nearby beach introduced him to another martial art, one that was as different from BJJ as night and day.

Boone would often visit Hobie Island Beach Park, as it was very close to the Rosenstiel campus and not too crowded. On top of that, it was a dog-friendly beach, and owners would often bring their four-legged friends. Boone missed Shingles, who had passed away last year, and there he could relax beside the lapping waves of Biscayne Bay, punctuated by occasional visits from friendly pups.

Early one Sunday morning, as Boone was strolling along the beach an hour after sunrise, he spotted a small cluster of people beside a copse of palm trees. They were gathered in a half circle with coolers and camp chairs spread about. If Boone had to guess, it was three or four families, complete with kids of all ages and a pair of dogs. Pulsing island rhythms emanated from a small boombox, and as Boone drew closer, he could hear distinctive Caribbean accents emanating from the group. A picnic party on the beach was nothing unusual, but what grabbed Boone's attention was what two of the men were up to.

As the families looked on, clapping to the beat of the current song, the two men whirled with flashy, acrobatic movements, appearing to be dancing one moment and fighting the next. Both looked to be in their late thirties; one had dark skin and dreadlocks, while the other had a shaved head and a lighter complexion than his opponent. Both were shirtless and barefoot and wore long, white pants.

Baldy spun a high kick and Dreadlocks backflipped away from it, turning the flip into a cartwheel at the last second and tumbling to the side. He dropped low on his haunches and snapped a kick straight out, but Baldy executed a cartwheel of his own to remove himself from the targeted area. This sequence done, the two faced off, mirroring each other with odd, shuffling, side-step movements. Then one would launch another attack, the other would evade, and the contest would continue. After each kick or evasion, the crowd would cheer and clap.

Boone observed the sparring match for several minutes, and decided that each attack was somewhat telegraphed, offering the opponent an opportunity to mount an impressive defensive move. But then, as one song ended and another began, the two gave each other a knowing look, and Boone could literally see their focus and body language change.

Now we'll see something, Boone thought, leaning against a palm trunk. This time, there was a lot more jockeying for position, and even the onlookers quieted down as the men circled each other. Then, Dreadlocks attempted to flank Baldy with a tumble to the side, but was hit with a quick snap-kick as he passed. He rolled with the impact but was still sent sprawling. Not to be discouraged, he shot out a kick from a prone position, one that Baldy barely batted away. Rising, Dreadlocks began spinning, sending one, two, three sweeping kicks arcing through the air, advancing with each rotation and driving his opponent back. Then, Baldy abruptly ducked under the last kick, spinning on one knee in the sand as he swung a kick to sweep the grounded leg out from under Dreadlocks and dropped the man on his back.

Tumbling away, Baldy hopped to his feet amidst wild cheers and applause, a broad grin on his face. Dreadlocks rose and brushed himself off, laughing breathlessly while he waggled a finger at the winner of the bout. Then the two did something Boone was very familiar with: they faced each other and dipped their upper bodies in bows of respect.

Boone was about to turn away and walk back up the beach

when a young boy from one of the families suddenly appeared him.

"You're very tall," the boy declared, looking up at him.

"I suppose I am," Boone admitted. "But I can make myself shorter."

"Really?"

"Sure." Boone gathered in a deep breath and held it, puffing out his cheeks. He locked eyes with the kid, then abruptly faked a sneeze. As he snapped his head forward for the "a-choo," he tumbled into a shoulder roll often used in jiu-jitsu, but instead of continuing the roll to come up standing, he let himself land on his back with a sandy flop. "There," he squeaked, pretending to have had the air knocked out of him. "Now you're taller than me."

The boy laughed uproariously at that. Boone turned his head and saw the fighter with the shaved head smiling and watching him, a balled-up T-shirt in one hand. The man approached, standing over Boone and looking down at him.

"You know... when you roll like dat, you supposed to land on your feet."

"Unless you're entertaining a kid," Boone replied from the sand. "That was impressive, that fighting you were doing."

"It's called *capoeira*!" the boy said, then launched into some kicks and tumbling of his own, soon ending up flat on his back himself. Laughing, he dashed off to rejoin the party.

"Ka-poo-air-uh..." Boone sounded the word out. "Is that Spanish?"

"Portuguese. Well... Brazilian Portuguese. But de word 'capoeira' may come from de Tupi language in de Amazon. Dere's some debate on dat."

Boone listened carefully to the man's accent. "You're not Brazilian, though... are you?"

"No, mon. Bajan." He pulled on the T-shirt he was holding and spread his arms out, showing it off. A flag was in the center, blue vertical stripes on either side of a yellow stripe, with the head of a trident in the middle. The T-shirt declared: *I'm not yelling. I'm Bajan.* "From Barbados," the man clarified. "But I've got some Brazilian on me muddah's side. My ancestors went to Brazil from Barbados to work in de rubber plantations for a few decades." He held out a hand to Boone, who was still on his back in the sand.

Boone took it, rising to his feet and giving the helping hand a shake. "I'm Boone."

"Keith."

"That fighting you were doing, the, uh... capoeira... it looked a lot like dancing."

Keith shrugged. "Dat's because it is. But it's also fightin'. It was developed by slaves in Brazil; dey disguised martial arts as dance, so dey could practice it in de open without de authorities realizin' what it was. Well... until dey did. Capoeira was banned for a time, under pain of death... or having your Achilles tendon cut."

"Yeesh."

"But now, it's quite popular. Me bruddah-in-law—dat's de man I knock *katspraddle* in de bout—he and I teach it to some of de Bajan kids in de community." He stretched out his T-shirt, showing off the flag. "Most Bajan-Americans live in de outer boroughs of New York City, but dere are a lot of us here in Miami." He gestured over to the group. "We get togeddah here most Sunday mornin's for breakfast and lessons, den we head back to de mainland for church."

"Do you only teach Bajan kids?"

"Why... you looking to learn?"

"I... maybe. I go to school just over there, past the Seaquarium." He pointed toward the east. "I come to this beach fairly often."

"Tell you what... you come over here and meet my family. You have breakfast?"

"Not yet."

"Myra! Plate up some fish cakes and bakes for me new friend, 'ere." He led Boone over and introduced him to several of the adults in the gathering. "Eat up, den sit you down and watch de trainin' wid de little ones. If de spirit move you, you can take a jump-up and try some moves."

An hour later, Boone had been introduced to some of the basics, especially the *ginga*, which was a shuffling step that kept the body in motion, ready to transition in an instant to attack or evasion. Boone even took to the "mat"—a flattish area of sand the men were using—to perform some of the techniques. At one point, Keith sent Boone to the ground with a flashy move, and when Boone rose to his feet, instinct took over and he squared off with Keith and gave a bow of respect.

"I knew it," Keith said with a grin. "You already a fighter."

"I've never done this before today," Boone said.

"No, not capoeira... somet'ing else. De way you move. And de way you picked t'ings up so quickly. And dat bow was right out of a dojo. What you do?"

"Brazilian jiu-jitsu."

Keith grinned. "In close and down on de ground." He looked around for his brother-in-law, the fighter in the dreadlocks. "Hey, Willis!" When Willis came over, Keith pointed at Boone. "BJJ."

"Very cool. How far you gone?"

"How far...? Oh... I'm a purple belt, but my instructor says I can progress to brown belt next year."

"*Kawblema!*" Keith exclaimed, and Boone guessed that

meant something like "wow." Keith nodded, thinking. "Okay, dis is what we do. We teach you some capoeira, you teach us some BJJ."

"Yeah, dat *irie*," Willis agreed. "Capoeira is great for certain t'ings, but you got to keep you distance for most moves. And if you facin' someone who gets in close... like in a real *bassa-bassa*... a real fight... t'ings can get messy."

"Would be great to have somet'in' unexpected to surprise dem wit'," Keith added.

"Like a shift to jiu-jitsu," Boone finished. "Okay! Deal."

FOURTEEN

I n the fall semester of Boone's junior year, his class load was almost entirely at the campus on Virginia Key, though he often traveled to the mainland campus to train with the cross-country team. Boone often finished among the top three runners and his team won numerous regional meets, even advancing to the Division I championship. They were demolished by Oklahoma State, but just reaching that competition was quite a feat.

Boone had continued his PADI training on the side, and had become a certified divemaster the previous summer, with plans to take the instructor course the following year. Over Columbus Day weekend, he joined a group of classmates on a dive trip over to nearby Bimini, taking the two-hour high-speed ferry from Fort Lauderdale. Boone was amazed that a tropical foreign country, the Bahamas, was little more than fifty miles from American shores; he drove farther than that to get to Gatlinburg from home. They traveled over in the morning, dove three dives, then returned on the 8:00 p.m. ferry. Before they'd reached American waters, Boone had already signed up for an upcoming weekend trip to Key Largo to dive with Rainbow Reef.

Boone returned to Tennessee for the holidays and took his mother to Dollywood to enjoy the Christmas lights. They had wanted to do this the previous winter break, but the universe had decided to treat the little town of Kingston to the opposite of a Christmas miracle that year, when the local fossil fuel plant's coal ash pond was breached. A retaining pond's dike had broken just after midnight, three days before Christmas, inundating a massive area around the breach in six feet of sludge and slurry. Fortunately for most Kingstonians, the spill had largely flowed north, sparing the town and most of the infrastructure and homes—but not everyone had been so lucky. Boone and his mother had spent much of Boone's winter break helping displaced families at a local shelter.

Arriving at Dollywood, they parked as close to the entrance as they could. For their sanity, his mother had taken off work, and they went over on a Tuesday to avoid the holiday weekend crush. After the Parade of Lights, Boone and his mother retreated to a back corner of Granny Ogle's Ham 'n' Beans for dinner. Once their food arrived, his mother cleared her throat.

"So... you're going to study abroad next semester."

"Yeah. It's all set. I'll be working on a study of coral bleaching in the reefs. Coral propagation techniques. A few other disciplines."

"You told me it was in the Caribbean, but where exactly?"

Boone poked at his collard greens. "Bonaire."

His mother nodded. Took a sip of sweet tea. "That's the Dutch island near Aruba, isn't it?"

"Yeah. Other side of Curaçao from Aruba."

"And that's why you just said 'Caribbean' the first time I asked where you were going."

Boone nodded.

"Boone... while I appreciate you trying to spare my feelings... you're my son. And I want to know everything there is to know about what you're up to."

"Okay, Mom."

"And on that subject... where's that mermaid girl of yours? Why isn't she here right now, enjoying the Christmas lights with you?"

"Uh... Faye and I have kinda fallen out of touch, Mom. You know how it is. I'm working on my degree and trying to make money here and there. I just didn't have time to do all of the things she wanted to do."

"Did you break up?"

"Sort of. I guess. She was pissed I wouldn't join her last summer on a trip to Vegas, and just said to look her up again after I graduated." He shrugged. "Seemed fair."

"I'm sorry, honey."

"S'okay. Hey, how about you, Mom? You mentioned you might consider dating again. Now that you've successfully kicked me outta the nest, why not?"

His mother smiled, eyes on her plate. "Boone... I'm still thinking about it. Let's just say I have trust issues. I suppose my faith in men hasn't fully recovered." She raised her eyes to his. "Present company excluded, of course."

"Oh, yeah, I'm a knight in shining armor," Boone said with a laugh.

"You know... in a way... I suspect you are. Then again, I'm biased! So... you lost the mermaid. Are you seeing anyone else?"

"Nope. Been too busy. But hey, maybe I'll meet someone in Bonaire."

Arriving on Bonaire in January, Boone and three of his fellow University of Miami classmates joined a small cadre of students from other schools for an orientation. The group gathered in a shaded outdoor area beside the green-and-yellow headquarters of STINAPA Bonaire. The *Stichting Nationale Parken Nederlandse Antillean*—the national park foundation for the Netherlands Antilles—was responsible for the care and maintenance of the Bonaire National Marine Park, and the visiting students would be participating in several studies.

During the next four months, the group would be researching and monitoring the health of the reef, studying instances of coral bleaching, and keeping an eye out for various coral diseases. In addition, they would be performing multiple marine life surveys in various patches of reef, providing a census of sea life in each area. Finally, they would learn about the coral reproduction techniques being employed in several nurseries around the island, focusing on restoring populations of endangered staghorn and elkhorn corals.

The lodging for the quartet of Miami students was a small house on a dusty lane in the neighborhood of Hato, a half mile inland from the ocean. After unpacking their things and stocking up on groceries at the nearby Zhung Kong supermarket, they piled into the communal rental Jeep and traveled to the Cliff shore dive site to assess everyone's skills. All of the students passed muster and the very next day, Boone went to work under the sea.

Under the supervision of a marine park diver, Boone and three other students began with a survey of the Klein Bonaire dive site Munk's Haven. Due to its exposed location on the far side of the offshore island, the site had taken some damage from Hurricane Omar in 2008, and STINAPA was monitoring the reef's recovery.

Midway through the survey, Boone dipped below a coral ledge and came face-to-face with a creature he'd been warned about at orientation: a lionfish. In other parts of the Caribbean, these predators were becoming a problem. Back in 1985, a single fish had been spotted off Florida, followed by several more in the nineties, but only recently had the population of this voracious Pacific species exploded across the Caribbean. Given how far away Bonaire was from the initial outbreak, it had taken a while for the invasive species to reach her shores, but one had been spotted and officially confirmed just a few months ago, on October 26, 2009.

Boone had seen several in his dives in the Keys, and the Gatlinburg aquarium had them; it was an undeniably beautiful and impressive creature. Nevertheless, these remorseless eating machines needed to be stopped. There were only a few divers on the island who were officially sanctioned to cull them at this time, so Boone signaled the marine park diver with a tank bang and pointed out the interloper.

The man flashed an "OK" sign, then dug in his BCD vest pocket and extracted a small object wrapped in thin twine. He descended to the overhang and found a small chunk of coral on the bottom. Attaching one end of the twine to it, he unspooled the rest of the length, revealing a wine cork at the other end. Releasing it, the object floated up, making a little buoy above the lionfish's hiding place. This done, he took out a slate and began taking notes.

Later, as the dive boat returned to shore, Boone asked him about the cork.

"I'll pass along the sighting to the park rangers that handle lionfish culls, and they'll be by this afternoon to find the cork and kill the fish. They'll retrieve the marker at that time."

"Isn't there a danger something might eat the cork? Or get entangled in the twine?"

The man nodded. "It's a concern, but the twine and corks are biodegradable. And the cork itself will be digested if eaten. Still, there's already some debate about it. I wouldn't be surprised if they stop the method in the near future."

Boone's first week flew by, and he was stunned by the quality of the diving here. The visibility was astonishing, the current minimal, and the reefs were teeming with fish. There didn't seem to be many larger animals on most dives, but he did spot a huge pod of dolphins transiting the channel between Klein and the mainland. He hoped to see one underwater sometime, but was told it was an extraordinarily rare occurrence in Bonaire.

Late in the afternoon of the second Saturday of their stay, the students all gathered at Captain Don's Habitat, the very first dedicated dive resort on Bonaire. The resort was hosting STINAPA's conservation gala, featuring a seminar with a very special guest: Jacques Cousteau's grandson, Philippe Cousteau, Jr.

In addition, Captain Don Stewart himself was in attendance, sporting his trademark Greek fisherman's cap. The founder of Habitat and a legend of underwater exploration in his own right, Cap'n Don was widely credited with bringing recreational diving to Bonaire. When they arrived, he was holding court in one of the corners, entertaining guests with tales of his adventures. Though wheelchair-bound, he exhibited boundless, youthful energy while recounting his exploits.

STINAPA staff handed out name badges on lanyards and sat the students at a pair of tables at Rum Runners for a pre-seminar dinner. The meal wouldn't start for another twenty minutes, so Boone went up to the Deco Stop Bar to order a soda. But there didn't seem to be anyone manning the bar.

"What can I getcha?" a woman asked from out of sight below the bar, her voice blessed with a musical, lilting accent—Irish, if Boone had to guess. A moment later, a freckled face popped up. "Sorry, dropped me bar blade." She rose and tossed a long, flat bottle opener on the counter with a dull clink. The bartender was quite tall, her red hair tied back in a ponytail. Dark brown eyes flicked down to Boone's nametag lanyard and she lifted it in her fingers. "Well, hello... Boone. This badge entitles you to a complimentary rum punch, if you're interested." She jabbed a thumb at a large, glass beverage dispenser full of an orange liquid.

"Oh, uh... tempting, but I've still got a month to go before I'm twenty-one," Boone said.

"Well, lucky for you, the drinking age here is eighteen." She smiled, then her eyes strayed to something over Boone's shoulder. "Phwoar, that's a fine thing, that one."

Boone looked over his shoulder and spotted Phillippe Cousteau speaking to a pair of guests. When he turned back to the bartender, she was staring at Boone intently, then at Cousteau, then back to Boone.

She raised her eyebrows. "Like lookin' in a mirror, so it is."

Boone glanced back at the guest of honor, noting the man's brown hair, his build, his height. Admittedly, he could see what she was talking about. Boone was quite tall at six-four and Cousteau looked to be exactly the same height.

"Sorry for me wandering eye... ye came here for a drink. Punch or no?"

"Aw heck, why not? Punch me."

She laughed at that. "Some patrons, I wouldn't mind doin'

119

just that, but I'd hate to mar your pretty face." She filled a cup from a spigot on the jar. "Fair warning, you might want to switch to beer after this 'un. We don't stint on the rum, and two or t'ree of these'll leave you ossified."

"I'll keep that in mind, miss."

She grinned. "I'll take miss over ma'am any day, but you can call me Penny." She looked to the opposite side of the bar, where a group had just settled onto the stools. "Duty calls. How long you here for?"

"Until May."

"I'm here T'ursday to Sunday. Hope to see you again, Boone."

FIFTEEN

Boone did indeed see Penny again. Quite a lot of her, in fact. The conservation studies program kept him busy most days, but there were several times during the week when their schedules synced up. As it turned out, the two had quite a lot in common. Penny was Boone's age, having finished a semester early at a vocational college in Ireland. Her hometown was even smaller than Boone's, with a population of under 2,000: the little resort town of Dingle in County Kerry. And most surprising of all, she had also worked in an aquarium. Dingle Oceanworld was situated right on the harbor front, catering to visiting tourists. Penny had gotten certified to dive by one of the aquarium staff and had worked two summers there.

Boone had gotten into the ritual of practicing his capoeira on the beach at sunrise, and Penny would often join him, albeit as an observer. Bonaire wasn't blessed with as many beaches as Aruba, with most of her coastline consisting of jumbles of broken coral and rocks or jagged ironshore, but Penny would occasionally drive them down to Te Amo Beach by the airport.

While most of Boone's diving was classwork, he managed quite a few recreational dives of his own. Diving with several different shops, he noticed that the divemasters and dive instructors came from all over the world, with quite a few from the States and various Commonwealth countries, despite this being a Dutch island. By the end of April, as the semester abroad came to an end and he logged his two-hundredth Bonaire dive, it occurred to Boone that being a divemaster in a tropical paradise might be a career worth considering.

Back in the States, Boone spent the summer before his senior year working with Fred, with occasional weekends at the aquarium. On one particular occasion, while helping Fred repair the engine on a houseboat, a call came in for search and recovery divers. Since Boone had his equipment in the car, he joined Fred in a search for a drowning victim. It was a stark contrast between diving in warm waters with a hundred feet of visibility... and crawling along the muck in a cold river when you couldn't see your hand in front of your face. Boone was grateful that the divers found the victim's body, but equally grateful that he hadn't been the one to discover it.

Embarking on his final year at the University of Miami, Boone threw himself into his studies, applying what he'd learned in Bonaire whenever possible. He was taking all of his classes at the Rosenstiel campus now, since his double major in Marine Science and Biology had been locked in. He found time to attain a brown belt in Brazilian jiu-jitsu, and his informal Sunday morning capoeira lessons continued. Soon, he was able to beat Keith in sparring matches two times out of three, although Keith chalked that up to Boone's arms and legs being "freakish long and freakish strong."

Over spring break in his final semester, Boone joined a short research trip to Sint Eustatius, or "Statia," another Dutch island, for a two-week intensive course. The school had booked two weeks with Golden Rock Diving, and the students were put up in an old hotel in the lower town. Boone enjoyed the diving in Statia. The island was so rarely visited that the patch reefs were pristine, and he encountered large numbers of flying gurnards, a bottom-crawling fish with pectoral fins that fanned out like a pair of peacock tails. A dive on the *Charles L. Brown* was also notable, the former cable-layer ship being one of the largest wreck dives in the Caribbean.

Back in the States, Boone completed his studies. Finally, diploma in hand, he left Miami for Tennessee. While he didn't have a *summa* or *magna* in front of his *cum laude*, Boone now had a degree that would allow him to work as an aquarist at any aquarium in the States. But now that he had the choice... he wasn't so sure that was what he wanted to do.

Arriving back in Kingston, he slept in his old room until one in the afternoon, then called Eugene. He knew his old friend had graduated a year early from M.I.T. and was already working at an engineering firm in Boston, but he hoped he might be available to chat. No dice. Boone left a voicemail. Next, he drove over to Fred's Fix-it, but the place was closed. It turned out Fred had taken his family to Yosemite and wouldn't be back for two weeks.

Finally, Boone called Faye. She picked up right away.

"Well, well, well... Boone Fischer, if my Caller ID doesn't lie."

"Hi Faye. I'm afraid your phone is telling the truth."

"So... you graduated?"

"I did."

"And now you're calling me, just like I told you to."

Boone laughed. "Yeah, I guess I am. Just wondering if you'll be in Gatlinburg this summer."

"Um... no. Still in Vegas."

"Really?"

"Yeah, there's a casino here with a full-time mermaid display. And... even if I were in Gatlinburg..."

"Yeah?"

"Well... let's just say, if you had to go searching for a mermaid's engagement ring again... it might be mine."

"You mean, you're...?"

"Engaged to a magician. Because of course I am."

"Congratulations, Faye!"

"Thank you, Boone. And 'con-graduations' to you. You have a job lined up?"

"I thought I did... I mean, I probably could. If I wanted to. But, well..."

"Tell me."

And Boone did. He gave her a quick summary of what he'd been studying and his time in Bonaire. When he reached graduation, she interrupted him.

"Stop. You should go be a divemaster."

"Really? Probably not a lot of money in that..."

"So? People spend half their paychecks going diving... and you have a chance to get paid to do it? Come on... I could literally hear your voice change when you were talking about Bonaire... and that time we drove back from the Keys to Miami? I've never seen you so animated, talking about a single dive. Let's face it, Boone... you're not exactly a talker. But when you're talking diving, it's like someone shot you full of sunshine."

Boone laughed. "That'd probably sting."

"That degree you got... it doesn't have an expiration date on it, does it?"

"Well... no."

"So... hop on the internet and start looking for a divemaster job. The aquarium isn't going anywhere."

After his conversation with Faye, Boone set about unpacking his suitcases from college. Reaching the bottom of the last one, he came across the garish Sponge Bob swimsuit Faye had gotten him, wrapped around a small object. Opening it up, he came eye-to-eye with the painted rock he'd earned for learning to swim. Boone thought back to Aruba, wondering where his father might be. Then, he reminisced about Bonaire, and the spectacular diving there. Finally, he dug in his backpack and found his passport. Opening it, he looked at the pages and remembered his childhood determination to one day fill his passport with stamps from all over the world, although that childhood passport was back in Kingston with only Aruba in it. Flipping through his current passport, he saw stamps for Statia —and Saint Martin, where he'd flown into to get to Statia— The Bahamas, Bonaire... and one for Curaçao. Boone knew there were direct flights to Bonaire, but for whatever reason, for the research semester, the University had opted for the Curaçao flight with the puddle jumper to Bonaire.

Sitting at his laptop, Boone opened a browser and typed three words into Google: divemaster job Curaçao.

PART FOUR

SIXTEEN

CURAÇAO, DUTCH CARIBBEAN

"Fish on! Fish on!"

Boone Fischer scrambled over to the fighting chair to assist, but the tourist from Texas seemed to have things well in hand, battling whatever it was he had on the line. After a vigorous fight, the sunburned man landed an impressive wahoo.

Boone had been in Curaçao for over a year, working as a divemaster at two different dive shops and subbing for a third, but he supplemented his modest income with occasional stints crewing for deep sea fishing and catamaran cruises, both of which paid quite well. His aptitude for all things mechanical was an added bonus, and had come in handy on a number of occasions when a marine engine needed a tune-up or repair.

Boone assisted the Texan with the removal of the hook, transferred the fish to an icebox, then set the man up for another go. The irony of working for one recreational pastime that relied on taking marine life *out* of the ocean, only to go back to one that relied on seeing marine life *in* the ocean, was not lost on Boone. He was a bit conflicted, but the fishing was kept well outside of the protected areas. And it wasn't like he wasn't eating seafood himself nearly every other meal, although he had made a personal decision to no longer eat grouper. In his eyes, the big fish were like puppies... and local divers said the average size seemed to be getting smaller every year.

As the late afternoon sun sparkled across the water, Boone's cell phone vibrated in the pocket of his board shorts. Glancing at the screen, he saw it was Gustav Groen, the Dutch owner of the catamaran cruise company, Green Flash Cruises. Looking at the sun's current position, he figured Gus would be out of luck if he needed him for this evening. Ducking into the cockpit, he tapped the talk button.

"Hey Gus, what's up?"

"*Hallo* Boone. What's your availability tomorrow?"

"If you need me for a day trip to Klein Curaçao, you're out of luck. I'm supposed to do certification dives tomorrow morning and probably won't be off until two or three, depending on where we take the students."

"It's a sunset cruise. I need you at Mood Beach at four to help with prep."

Boone thought about the traffic through Willemstad in the late afternoon and sighed. "I dunno, Gus, that's cutting it close. Don't you have enough coverage? What about Linda? She loves doing the sunset cruises."

"Well, you see... it's a bachelorette outing, and they asked for an all-male crew. And you're, um... popular... in that regard."

Boone laughed. "Please tell me you're not asking me to rush down there just to be eye candy."

"No, of course not! Okay, yes. But I also like to have you

aboard in case we have engine trouble. I can offer double your normal rate. Wealthy client, last-minute booking."

"Should've led with that."

Just then, there was a commotion outside, and shouts of "Fish on!" Boone looked astern toward the fighting chair and saw the Texan's rod bending under the strain of what was likely a sizable catch.

"Hey, Gus, I gotta run! I'll see you tomorrow at four."

In short order, the fishing trip was at an end and the captain took them back to the protected bay of Spanish Waters and over to their slip in a marina in the neighborhood of Jan Thiel. Arriving back at the dock, Boone assisted the clients with the offloading of their gear and their catch, then walked to his car, a used Kia Picanto.

When Boone had first arrived, he had tried to get by with a bicycle he'd bought used, but what had worked in Bonaire didn't work in Curaçao. The island was substantially larger than Bonaire or Aruba, and surprisingly hilly in places, the topography being far less flat than on her sister islands. Having the car had allowed him to move farther out from Willemstad, the capital of Curaçao. His tiny apartment there had been centrally located but quite pricy, and what he was saving in rent easily made up for the cost of the car.

He now lived in a little green house in the small coastal town of Boka Sami, conveniently close to one of the dive ops he worked with—Snake Bay Divers beside the Sint Michiel Harbor —although "harbor" was a bit of a misnomer, as it was basically just a small, L-shaped jetty. His other primary divemaster gig, a shore-dive op called Scuba Dooby Do, operated out of a minibus, and took clients to shore diving spots all over the island. Given Curaçao's size, many dive boats tended to go to sites within twenty minutes of their docks, so the traveling shore-dive op proved popular.

Leaving the marina, Boone drove west, navigating the late afternoon traffic through Willemstad to the massive Queen Juliana Bridge, which rose 185 feet above St. Anne Bay. Boone risked a few glances out the windows toward the historic Willemstad waterfront to the south and the huge inner harbor to the north, lining a bay that sheltered one of the largest deep-water ports in the Caribbean.

Exiting the main road and going west toward Boka Sami, Boone stopped at the Centrum Supermarket to stock up on a few things. As was so often the case in island stores, prices were high compared to the States, since everything had to be shipped in. Once back in the car, he took a shortcut and slowed as he reached an odd feature this tree-lined stretch of street was known for: dolls and dolls' heads hung from branches along the left side of the road. Boone had asked around, but so far no one had any idea who had put them there.

Arriving home, Boone pulled into his dirt driveway, put away the groceries, popped open a bottle of Polar beer from Venezuela, then called up Scuba Dooby Do.

"*Bon tardi*, Boone," a Dutch voice answered, giving the Papiamentu greeting for "good evening."

"Heya Laura, how was today?"

"Very good. We took a group up to Playa Lagun. Saw a bunch of cornetfish. Ended up staying on the beach there for an extra-long surface interval."

"Love that beach. One of the best on the island."

"I know! Sorry you missed it. You could have shown off some of that spinning, kicking thing you do."

"Good beach for it. Hey, I've got a sunset cruise tomorrow and the money's too good to miss out on. Any chance I can bring my own car and just meet the minibus? I know we've got some open water certs, right?"

"Yes, that should be fine. This is dive number one and two for them. Easy day. A father-daughter duo from the Netherlands, and the father's already certified."

PADI certifications required four open water dives. Often, the classwork and swimming pool portions were done elsewhere, and then—rather than dive in a gravel quarry in their home country—the diver might come to Curaçao to take the open water portion of their certification.

"Sounds good. Can we do Tugboat and Double Reef? That'll put me close to where I need to be for the sunset cruise.

"I'm sure that will be fine. I'll see you tomorrow."

Boone rose before the sun, scarfed down a quick breakfast, then drove to Willemstad and crossed the bridge. He soon passed the Jan Thiel marina he'd been in yesterday, but this time he drove across to the opposite side of Caracas Bay, past the remains of Fort Beekenburg, and down the rutted road to the parking area beside Tugboat Beach and the rustic wooden structure known as Tugboat Bar.

As he exited the car, Boone was greeted by a quartet of dogs that had claimed the area as their territory.

"Hey, gang!" Boone fetched a container of dog biscuits he kept in the trunk. Grabbing four, he doled them out, then set about gathering his gear. It was still quite early, and the Tugboat Bar was closed, so Boone had the area to himself as the sun rose, out of sight behind the limestone ridges to the east.

Setting his gear down, he walked through the area by the beach, an eclectic hodge-podge of seating, from salt-encrusted wicker furniture to faded lounge chairs, with wooden cable spools here and there that served as makeshift tables. Overhead, brightly painted bits of driftwood decorated every surface, and a variety of homemade mobiles and wind chimes hung from wooden beams.

Finding a small patch of sand, he sat down in a lotus position and quieted his mind. He took stock of his thoughts, then let those go as well, aware only of his breathing and the sounds of the ocean breeze and the lapping water a few yards in front of him.

Shortly after arriving in Curaçao, Boone had gone in search of a Brazilian jiu-jitsu dojo. He couldn't find one, but did come across a yoga studio during his search. On a whim, he joined it and had attended it for a few months before letting his membership lapse. He found the meditation skills useful, and now combined a few minutes of that with his morning capoeira exercises.

Rising from the sand, he ditched his shirt on top of his gear and went around to the backside of the bar, where there was a small, pebble-strewn patch of ground that lay between the back wall of the building and the edge of a limestone drop-off into the water. Curaçao had many soft, sandy beaches with lots of room for tumbling acrobatics, and those were certainly more fun for his capoeira exercises, but Boone liked to practice on this spot whenever he came here. The confined space and uncertain footing provided a challenge, restricting him to controlled and less flashy moves, more suited to combat in many real-world situations.

Boone was thirty minutes into his workout when the sound of barking dogs heralded the arrival of a vehicle. Coming around the back of the bar, Boone saw the Scuba Dooby Do van trundling up the road. The eighteen-passenger minibus was decorated to resemble the Mystery Machine from the *Scooby-Doo* show, painted aqua and lime green with "Marine Machine" in orange lettering. In addition, there were red-and-white dive flags on the driver's and front passenger's doors, and another on the hood. The owners had told Boone that he'd originally wanted the whole thing to look like a dive flag, but there was already a "Scuba Bus" on the island with that paint job. Boone had seen it a few times: an old school bus, the entire thing painted red with a white roof and diagonal white stripes running down the sides.

Laura gave a wave from the open window as she pulled the minibus up beside Boone's car. In her late twenties, she, along with her husband, owned the dive op. Boone jogged over and slid open the panel door at the rear. He was greeted by a burly passenger with a handlebar mustache, the tips waxed up in little curls.

"What on earth have you been doing?" the man asked. Boone could tell he was Dutch, but his English was excellent, with little accent. "You're drenched in sweat and it's not hot yet."

"Boone's been practicing his martial arts, I imagine," Laura said, calling out from the driver's seat as she gathered up some paperwork. "Hope you saved enough energy for the dive."

The big man stepped down and offered an oven mitt of a hand. "I'm Noah, and your student for today is my daughter, Anika." After shaking hands with Boone, he turned back to assist a willowy teenager down from the van. She seemed quite young and practically exuded shyness.

"Pleased to meet you, Anika. I'm Boone and I'll be your dive instructor, along with Laura."

"He'll be doing most of the work," Laura said. "I'll be looking around for seahorses and frogfish to show you after you finish with the Dive One certification drills."

Boone joined her at the back of the Marine Machine and began removing tanks. Noah grabbed two of them, ignoring Boone's protestations that they could take care of it.

"No, no, I've got them. Where do you want us to set up?"

"You'll see my gear on a bench in there," Boone said, pointing. He grabbed another pair of tanks and followed.

Boone watched Anika as she set up her own gear and was pleased to see her father remained off to the side, offering no assistance. The young girl had no problem at all, assembling everything like a veteran. Once finished, Boone went over the dive plan.

"'Tugboat' is a very shallow dive with zero current. Everyone's swimming skills and comfort level are different, so I like to use this site for the first certification dive. You can take all the time in the world to work out your buoyancy, which is something you don't want to be struggling with in a current or on a deeper dive."

"I like the sound of that!" Anika said.

"You won't have as much of an opportunity to practice equalizing here, since the max depth is under thirty feet. We'll tackle that on the second dive."

Many beginner divers were so focused on the novelty of breathing underwater that they neglected two other necessary skills: buoyancy control and equalization. If you didn't master the former, you'd be bobbing up and down, popping to the surface, dropping down onto fragile coral, and constantly adding to or purging air from your BCD.

And divers needed to "equalize" as they descended; the surrounding pressure increased the deeper you went but the pressure in the middle ear remained the same. This skill was quite easy for some but a challenge for others, and if you weren't able to equalize, a deep dive could be excruciating or even impossible. In most cases, a diver could simply pinch their nose shut and gently blow to relieve the pressure. Boone didn't even need to do that; he simply worked his jaw as he descended.

Boone went over the dive plan, then they crossed the "beach" of crumbled coral and pebbles and began the dive. While Laura and Noah swam over to the nearby pier to search for critters under the massive pilings, Boone led Anika to a sandy area that was clear of any coral and put her through her paces. She practiced clearing her regulator mouthpiece, retrieving a lost regulator by sweeping an arm back and along the hose, and then cleared her mask from a partial flood. Finally, he had her inform him of how much air she had—almost a full tank at this shallow depth, of course, but he was more interested in her proper use of signals for the amount of pressure in the tank. She accomplished everything with ease, so it was now time to simply enjoy the rest of the dive.

Boone chopped a hand toward the pier and the pair swam to the nearby staghorn coral nursery, passing carefully through a gap between the tree-like structures, their "branches" festooned with chunks of coral. Nearing the pilings, Boone spotted Laura, who excitedly beckoned for them to join her, then she crooked her wrists and made a gesture like she was holding the reins of a horse. *Seahorse.*

Sure enough, there was a good-sized yellow seahorse at the base of one of the columns. This one was often here, and he usually had company, though of another species. A few minutes later they found the yellow frogfish, wonderfully camouflaged to blend with a patch of sponge.

Finally, the group swam back across the area Boone had been training Anika in and visited the wreck that gave the site its name. At a depth of less than twenty feet, the little tugboat was encrusted in corals from bow to stern, and the entire site teemed with schools of tropical fish.

Once they'd reached an hour of bottom time, Boone had Anika demonstrate an air check for him again, then led the group back to the shore.

The moment her regulator left her mouth, Anika shouted, "That was amazing!" All vestiges of shyness completely gone, she gushed about everything she'd seen.

Boone grinned. "Well, if you liked that... wait'll you see Double Reef."

SEVENTEEN

Boone followed the Marine Machine back to Willemstad to the southwest corner of the Otrabonda neighborhood, where they parked by the Tula Monument, a site commemorating the ill-fated Curaçaoan slave revolt of 1795. At the nearby concrete jetty, a large naval vessel was docked. Boone recognized it as a Dutch warship that was often in the area. Not for the first time, the sight reminded him of his father.

An enthusiastic Anika quickly took his focus, and he went over the dive profile while everyone geared up.

"The conditions look good, but I may need to adjust our plans, depending on the current. We'll enter along the seawall, then swim to the edge of the breakwater and descend to the shallow reef there. Then I'll take us down to the sandy valley between the two reefs to run the certification tests. If you have any trouble equalizing, let me know. Once in the sand, we'll do a complete mask flood and clearing, then we'll perfect your buoyancy."

"And then, we'll visit the junkyard," Laura added.

When Noah gave them a quizzical look, Boone explained, "We use it as a navigation aid. It's a stop sign stuck in the sand beside some old pipes... and there's a shopping cart down there. Divers will sometimes put trash they find into the cart. Last time I was here, it had a bunch of bottles and shoes in it. The Marine Park cleans it out periodically."

"Be sure to check in the pipes," Laura suggested. "There's a big green moray that is often in one of them."

"Once we finish there, if the current is playing nice, we'll swim to the deeper reef and follow it to the west, then cross back to the shallow reef and return to the east. Once we see the junk pile on the return leg, we'll angle back toward the shore. Then we'll do the last certification test: offering your spare air to a diver in an out-of-air situation. Noah, do you mind playing the victim?"

The big man laughed. "I'm an air hog, so it wouldn't be the first time."

"Good. Anika, you'll get the signal from your dad that he's out of air... then..." Boone trailed off.

"Boone?" Laura asked.

"Sorry, my mind wandered there. Anika, you'll give your dad your yellow octopus reg, then the two of you will do a controlled ascent, nice and slow. We'll come up right where we started the dive and surface swim to shore. Any questions?"

There were none, and the group proceeded to the seawall to start their swim. Boone looked up at the looming Dutch warship just to the east and sighed. For his own certification dives in Aruba, he had done the out-of-air ascent with his father.

The dive proceeded according to plan and the current had allowed for a leisurely looping exploration of Double Reef, treating Anika to several morays, a big school of southern sennets—which looked like mini-barracudas—and so many sea turtles, Boone lost count. Once back on shore, Anika again bubbled with excitement, listing all of the sights she'd seen.

The group gave their gear a quick rinse at the back of the Marine Machine. In Tennessee, Boone's mother had used a simple pump-sprayer for homemade weedkiller, and Boone found one at a Curaçao home improvement store. Filled with tap water, it made for a quick and easy way to get the salt and sand off of gear before loading it into the minibus. Once the Mystery Machine got back to home base, the equipment could be given a proper dunking. Boone began slotting empty tanks back into the carrying racks and noted where the sun was in the sky.

"Where will we go tomorrow for the last two open water dives?" Anika asked.

"Well, it'll be Laura's turn to choose," Boone said. "After that, the pool's open and you can dive for fun!"

"Hey, are there any large wrecks?" Noah asked. "I'd love to dive one before we leave."

"Yes, Curaçao has a fantastic one, the *Superior Producer*. But that one's advanced, and it's best dived from a boat."

"You should go, *Vader*," Anika suggested encouragingly.

"I can set that up for you, if you're interested," Boone offered. "It's a great wreck, 165 feet long. She sank in the seventies. Apparently, she was overloaded, and her cargo was improperly stored, and much of it was liquor and clothing. She started listing near the entrance to Willemstad's harbor and the crew began tossing cargo overboard, but she took on water and finally sank off to the side, upright in a hundred feet of water less than five hundred feet from shore. Many islands will sink a ship deliberately for a reef, but this one was an accident that ended up perfectly situated."

"Well, not exactly," Laura said. "It's close to the harbor mouth, so you have to watch out for boat traffic. And they're talking about adding a cruise ship pier over there."

"The rest of the story of the *Superior Producer* is a hoot," Boone continued. "In the days after the sinking, lots of local residents helped "rescue" the cargo and were soon seen staggering around town enjoying salvaged whiskey in their new clothing."

Noah laughed, then asked, "Where is the wreck?"

Boone pointed to the east. "It's just past that frigate that's docked over there."

"Ah, you mean the *Holland*? She's actually a patrol boat."

"Oh, you know it?"

"I was in the Royal Netherlands Navy and served on a frigate, quite a bit larger than that. They use those patrol boats for drug interdiction mostly."

"When did you serve?"

"In the late nineties until about ten years ago."

"Really? Did you know a Dirk Fischer? Or Diederik Fischer? He'd be about your age, maybe a few years older."

Noah frowned, thinking. "The name sounds familiar, but I'm pretty sure I didn't serve with him. I could ask around."

"I... no, that's okay." Boone looked at his dive watch. "I should probably get a move on. Laura, are you good?"

"Yes, I can handle it from here," she said, then walked Boone to his car. "Fischer is your last name... the man you asked about, are you related?"

Boone worked his jaw. "You could say that. Hey, I gotta get to the catamaran. See you tomorrow."

Before pulling out of the parking lot, Boone saw he'd missed a call from the owner of the cruise company. He rolled down the car windows to let the hot air out, then rang Gus back.

"Boone! Hey, have you left yet?"

"I'm in Otrobanda, leaving now."

"Oh! Good! Don't come straight here! Swing by the Floating Market. We need twenty each of avocados, mangos, and limes... and a few papayas."

"Okay, on my way."

Once again, Boone crossed the Queen Juliana Bridge. High above the harbor, he could see his destination far below out the passenger side window: the canal on the north side of the trendy Punda district was lined with boats docked alongside an entire street of stalls and tents. Boone took the next exit and wound his way through the historic downtown until he reached the bayside. He paused at the intersection, waiting for a large group of tourists to cross the street to the famous Queen Emma Bridge.

A pedestrian pontoon bridge dating back well over a century, the "Swinging Old Lady" could be opened to allow ships in and out of the inner harbor. The Queen Emma had hinges on the Otrobanda side of the channel, and a shelter with an operator who controlled two diesel engines on the Punda side. When Boone heard a siren through his open windows and saw people on the bridge start to scramble for one side or the other, he looked to sea and spotted the Dutch patrol ship *Holland* on approach, on its way to the inner harbor. In moments, the security gates would close and the pontoon bridge would swing to one side.

He turned right up the famous *Handelskade*. Lined with

brightly painted buildings, the historic trading district was a UNESCO World Heritage Site, and one of the most recognizable waterfronts in the Caribbean. But Boone wasn't looking at the sights; his eyes were focused on the sparse parking spots along the water. Many had "NP" painted on them—prohibiting parking—and some individual spots had actual chains across them. Fortunately, the parking gods saw fit to smile upon him; an SUV left a spot just as he approached, and he slipped in.

Exiting the car, he jogged around the corner to the market. A fixture in the historic city center, the Floating Market was a great place to get the freshest fish and produce on the island. Every morning at sunrise, Venezuelans would make the fifty-mile journey from the mainland and dock there to sell their wares. With no time for browsing, Boone went straight to the largest collection of produce he could see and quickly gathered what Gus had requested. On his way back, he spotted a boat with a basket of strange, spiky fruit that the vendor called guanábana. On a whim, Boone bought several, then hustled back to his car.

Threading his way through the old city, he was soon on the coastal road and arrived at the Mood Beach pier fifteen minutes later. After leaving his keys with the Green Flash Cruises valet, he grabbed the fruit and a backpack with a change of clothes and hurried to the dock.

"You get everything?" Gustav called out from the pier as Boone approached.

"Yep, right here. I need to hit the head and shower and change. Unless there's anything sweat-inducing you need me to do first."

"No, you go ahead. Give the produce to Zimmy on your way in."

Boone stepped aboard the *Green Flash*, a 75-foot catamaran

decked out with a large, shaded seating area, a top-notch sound system, a bar, and a small kitchen with a grill behind the bar.

Hubert "Zimmy" Zimmerman, a local Curaçaoan chef, was currently fileting yellowfin snapper for fresh ceviche. Balding and in his thirties, he was wearing one of the light green polo shirts the crew wore, decorated with a setting sun embroidered on the breast.

"You got de limes?"

"And everything else," Boone reassured him as he set down the bags of produce. "Oh, and I grabbed these just for the heck of it." He set down one of the spiky fruits.

"Ah! Sorsaka!"

"The Venezuelan who sold it to me called it guanábana."

"Dat fruit's got more names den I got hairs left on me head," Zimmy said with a laugh. "Dey call it soursop in most other islands. Haven't had any in a while." He set aside his fileting knife and selected a chef's knife to slice through the spiky skin. The blade slid through with ease, halving the fruit and revealing a white interior with black seeds. "Grab a spoon and scrape a bit off. Don't eat de seeds."

Boone dragged a spoon across the white flesh, then popped the morsel in his mouth. "Wow!"

"It's good, right?" Zimmy ate some as well. "*Hopi bon!* Smells like pineapple, feels like banana, tastes like strawberries, mango, and citrus. I'll cut some up for de guests."

Boone left the kitchen, nodding to Mark on the way, a handsome young man from Australia. Boone figured Mark was another "eye candy" choice for this evening's crew.

As a cruising catamaran designed for large groups and day trips over to Klein Curaçao, *Green Flash* was blessed with two marine heads, including one with a shower. Boone rinsed off his two-dive day and pulled his crew polo and white shorts from his backpack before shoving his dirty clothes into a plastic bag he kept inside. Once dressed, he left the head, stowed the backpack, and went looking for Gus. He found the Dutchman beside the catwalk and retractable stairs that ran down the middle of the two trampolines. The two nets, stretched taut between the dual bows, provided lounging areas over the water below. Gustav was toeing one of the tramps as Boone approached.

"This one is getting a little loose, but it will do for tonight," he grumbled. "One more thing for the to-do list."

"At least the engines are shipshape," Boone reassured him. On a recent trip, one of the two engines had cut out at the end of the cruise. Unable to maneuver the large ship back into the protected pier, the crew had had to ferry the passengers ashore in the rubber dinghy. Boone hadn't been on that cruise, but he'd spent two days fixing the issue with a few ten-dollar parts.

"Yes, thank you for that."

"And the wind is cooperating today," Boone noted, eyeing the Curaçaoan flag fluttering gently from the gaff overhead. "Should be a nice night for sailing."

"We're being paid handsomely, so I want everything to go well tonight. I'll be aboard to make sure it does."

Boone was surprised but didn't show it; as long as Boone had worked for him, Gus had been more of the owner-in-the-office than the owner-on-the-boat, ever since a skin cancer scare. But a sunset cruise wouldn't be a problem for the man's sun-weathered skin.

Mark was standing on the port side when he gave a low whistle of appreciation at something he was looking at on the grounds of the Mood Beach restaurant.

"Crikey. If that's our charter, I'd've worked for free! Every one of 'em a stunner."

Boone stepped across to join the Aussie and watched a group of young women making their way to the pier, all of them dressed in what Boone assumed were expensive leisure clothes. Some were wearing gossamer-thin shawls or wraps that had a better-than-even chance of winding up in the drink once the *Green Flash* was under full sail. Boone made a mental note to keep an eye on that.

The women were all smiling and laughing, and Boone guessed this evening of entertainment had begun with drinks somewhere else. As they walked, they were engaged in multiple conversations, and Boone picked up a lot of Spanish being spoken. Most of them appeared to be of Latin American heritage, not unusual this close to Venezuela and Colombia. Once his eyes took in the entire group, he turned back to Gustav.

"Hey, Gus... I thought this was a bachelorette party."

"It is." Gustav joined them as Boone pointed at the approaching group.

"So, what's with the suits?"

Two men were with the group of women. Deeply tanned and dark-haired, they were dressed in light, tropical suits. One was talking with one of the women, but the larger of the two was at the rear, his head on a swivel, occasionally looking back the way they came.

"Oh, yes... they said they were going to bring their own deejay for the music," Gustav said. "The other one is probably their limo driver or something."

"Or something..." Boone replied.

"Welcome to the *Green Flash*!" Gustav called out. "It's going to be a beautiful cruise tonight!"

The group increased its pace as they came up the pier.

"Boone, ya long-armed gibbon, why don't you help the ladies step across," Mark suggested. "I'll take bags and coats."

Boone joined Mark at the entrance step, and they assisted the charter guests as they boarded. One of the last women on the pier took his hand, stepped across, then laid her other hand atop his forearm.

"*Gracias*," she purred, treating Boone to a quick but intense moment of eye contact with her brown eyes, their hue so dark as to be almost black. Then she was stepping past him, and Boone was helping the larger suit to board.

When the man reached out his arm, his suit coat billowed open slightly. Boone helped the man across, then found Gustav and took him aside.

"The 'limo driver' in the suit? I think he's more likely a bodyguard."

"Why do you think that?"

"Because he's got a gun."

EIGHTEEN

When everyone was aboard and Gustav had given the safety briefing, the captain started the engines. Boone and Mark cast off the lines and stepped aboard as the *Green Flash* motored out of the little marina and turned to the east. The first stop of the cruise would be the Spanish Waters area, then on to Fuik Bay as sunset neared. The prevailing winds were easterly, so the captain kept them under engine power for the first part of the trip, to make sure they were in position for the sunset.

Boone circulated amongst the guests, taking food and drink orders and offering to stow the occasional hat or shawl. The deejay who had come with the group had ditched his suit coat and was currently serving up some tunes that pulsed through the speakers and subwoofer. Boone was happy to see the man didn't have a shoulder holster like his buddy.

He kept an eye on Mr. Suit, who largely kept to himself. From time to time, the man took a small pair of binoculars from a side pocket and scanned the waters around the catamaran, often focusing on nearby boats. At one point, Boone decided he'd see if the man wanted a drink. He knew what the answer would be, but he did it anyway.

"No, *gracias*."

"See anything interesting?"

"*Qué?*"

"The binoculars."

When the man frowned, thinking, Boone made circles with his fingers and held them up to his eyes. That triggered the lightbulb for Mr. Suit and he took them out of his pocket. "Oh! These. I... like the... *aves*." Another lightbulb sparked. "Birds."

Boone had found that most Spanish speakers on the island had an excellent command of English, so he assumed this one wasn't a local.

"Excuse me..." A light touch on Boone's arm accompanied the voice. He turned to find the dark-eyed woman he'd helped aboard standing close beside him. She was breathtakingly beautiful, her tanned skin standing out in stark contrast to a delicate white blouse. Her thick, raven hair shone in the late-afternoon sun. "If you're not too busy, I would like a drink."

"I... yes, of course. What can I get you?"

"An aguardiente sour."

"I have no idea what that is, but I'll ask the bartender."

She smiled. "He's so busy, why don't I show you how to make it?"

"I... uh... sure. Always happy to learn new skills."

"That is an admirable sentiment. May I know your name?"

"Can we trade? My name for yours?"

The near-black eyes sparkled and her mouth quirked up with amusement. "How very transactional. My name is María."

"Boone."

"Boone..." she repeated, stepping back and looking him over. "Unusual name. It suits you."

"Hope so. It's the one I'm stuck with. So... how do you make this... something-or-other sour?"

"Aguardiente. It is the most popular liquor where I am from."

Now it was Boone's turn to smile. "How about another trade? I'm from Tennessee. In the United States."

"And I am from Medellín. In the mountains of Colombia."

"Your English is perfect," Boone observed. "You don't have much of an accent."

"I will, once I drink the cocktail you're going to make for me," she replied. "I went to school in Europe, and I have lived in Curaçao for over a year now."

"Same here." Boone replied. "The Curaçao part. Not the Europe part."

"Hey, Boone, we need some more tucker over here!" Mark called out from the trampolines at the bow. "Quit flirting with the guests and grab some skewers of shrimp from the barbie."

Boone chuckled. Mark liked to dial up the Aussie lingo when among guests. "María, can I get you that drink in a moment?"

"Of course. But don't keep me waiting long. This is *my* party, after all."

"Oh! You're the...? I... congratulations."

She laughed. "No, no... my sister Maricela is the one getting married. I'm the one who put this all together for her, and for my other sisters and their friends." She swept her hand around at the party. "I will see you at the bar."

After Boone made several trips with food, he returned to the bar-and-grill area to find María eating some of the unusual fruit he'd bought, spooning the white flesh from a cup.

"I hear you are the one who brought the guanábana! What a lovely surprise. I have not had this in a while. Now, let me show you how to make an aguardiente sour."

After Boone's bartending lesson, María returned to her friends as the captain maneuvered the boat into a sandy area and anchored well clear of any reef structure. With the sunset nearing the horizon, the deejay turned off the music so everyone could enjoy the sounds of the ocean and breeze. As the sun dipped below the horizon, there was no green flash, but the sunset was spectacular, nonetheless. Once the lightshow began to fade, the catamaran's sound system sprang to life and the evening lighting switched on as strings of soft, white lights provided gentle illumination for the second part of the cruise.

Under Gustav's supervision, Boone, Mark, and one other local crewman deployed the sails, and the catamaran coasted back to the west. Drinks continued to flow as the *Green Flash* sailed toward the bustle of the Willemstad waterfront.

After radioing the harbormaster and ensuring there was no inbound or outbound traffic, the captain brought the catamaran into the mouth of the inner harbor, so the guests could get a view of the Queen Emma pontoon bridge, which was lit up with multi-colored arches along its length. To either side of the entrance bay were repurposed forts: Fort Amsterdam and Water Fort on the right and the Rif Fort on the left. Fort Amsterdam contained government offices and a museum, while Rif and Water had been converted into shopping malls with restaurants and shops; both were aglow with lights.

The sails were lowered, and the *Green Flash* lingered near the bridge for a while, then the captain took her back out to sea under engine power. Boone spotted a small fishing boat approaching and figured that might have been the reason for their departure. Mr. Suit stepped up to the starboard side nearest the fishing boat, one foot on the lifeline railing, his eyes locked on the vessel. Boone was pretty confident it was a run-of-the-mill fisherman on that boat, but he watched one of Mr. Suit's hands moving to the interior of his jacket.

It was at this moment that one of the bachelorettes—no doubt well into her third or fourth complimentary rum drink—stumbled as the catamaran began its turn. She pitched sideways into Mr. Suit, who lost his balance and promptly fell overboard, arms flailing. She nearly followed him in, but Boone was close enough to grab hold of her arm and pull her back even as he shouted "Man overboard! Starboard side!"

Without hesitation, Boone raced to the small, stern steps built into the ends of the twin hulls. There was enough illumination from the moon and the nearby shore lights to enable him to spot the man, spluttering in their wake; he didn't appear to be the best of swimmers and he was still wearing his suit coat. Boone quickly assessed their speed—only a few knots, and slowing—then grabbed a life preserver ring that was mounted on the side of the steps, unhooked the coil of line, and hurled the ring with all his strength. It landed in the water with a satisfying smack, just beyond his target. Kicking off his shoes, Boone propelled himself into the sea with a picture-perfect dive. He surfaced less than five yards from the man and closed the distance with several powerful freestyle strokes. Spotting the life ring's line, he snagged it in one hand as he reached the man.

"I've got you!" he shouted, coming around behind. He looped an arm under the man's armpit and dragged the life ring toward them on its line.

"*No sé nadar,*" the man gasped.

Boone knew enough Spanish to know the man was saying he couldn't swim. "Just stay calm... uh... *tranquilo.*"

Boone could feel the man's handgun under his arm, but decided not to request he ditch the weapon; he could already see the *Green Flash* coming about. Instead, he brought the float around and pressed it to the man's chest. "*Aquí toma!*"

As the catamaran drew nearer, he could see Gustav at the bow. "Do you need help?" he shouted.

"No, we're all right..."

"Should I drop the bow stairs?" Mark called out.

"No, the waves are coming from behind... it'll be much easier for us to use one of the stern platforms. Have the captain idle the engines and keep her steady. See you around back!"

With that, Boone swam with Mr. Suit along the port hull. The man was much calmer, now that he had an armful of life preserver.

"*Gracias, mi amigo,*" he said.

"Just doing my job. And I'm guessing your job was to guard one of the guests?"

"*Sí...* yes. I was hired to guard the Cabrera sisters. I am Tomás. Again, thank you."

Boone had a feeling the man's English was better than he'd let on earlier.

"Your gun... you're gonna want to clean that thoroughly. Salt water is incredibly corrosive."

As they reached the stern, Boone helped Tomás get his footing on the molded stairs, then followed him up. Boone was greeted by cheers from the bachelorettes as Gustav led Tomás toward the main cabin area.

"Good on ya, mate!" Mark slapped Boone on the back of his soaked polo shirt. "Hope you didn't have your phone on ya."

"No… I leave all that with my street clothes, just in case something like *this* happens. I'm gonna go towel off."

As the *Green Flash* made her way back to Mood Beach, Boone ducked into the nearest head with his backpack. He decided the dirty street clothes inside were a better option than his soaking-wet crew outfit, so he quickly changed and went back outside. María was waiting for him, holding his shoes.

"You left these."

"Oh, right. Thanks." He took them. "These are dry, at least."

"That was very impressive. You must have been a lifeguard in a previous life."

"I was a lifeguard in this *current* life."

She laughed. "And what else are you, in this current life?"

"Well… I guess I added 'bartender' to the list a little while ago. How was that drink, by the way?"

"Adequate. But the fault was not yours. You need egg whites to do an aguardiente sour properly. You really should try one. In fact… I know a little place on the waterfront. What are you doing after this cruise?"

Boone had planned on getting himself home and in bed ASAP, given that he had two training dives in the morning, but he found his mouth saying, "Nothing. I have to help clean up, though."

"Actually… you do not. I have already spoken to your employer. Given that you saved our… our assistant, treating you to a drink is the least I can do."

"Is he *your* bodyguard?" Boone asked.

"Tomás? He's a friend of my overprotective brother. He was on the cruise to look after all of us. That being said…" She leaned in close and whispered in Boone's ear. "You and I will have to 'give him the slip,' as they say."

The following morning, an hour before dawn, Boone's alarm went off and he snatched up his phone to silence it as quickly as he could. María rolled over and mumbled in her sleep as Boone stealthily slipped from the bed and padded barefoot across her bedroom to the door. Stepping through, he was greeted with a view of the expansive open-plan living room and kitchen on the first floor below, dimly lit by track lighting.

He texted Laura: *Where are we diving first?*

Laura tended to rise later than Boone, so she might not respond for a while. When he went down to the kitchen area, seeking caffeine, he found a single-cup brewer, grabbed a mug and made himself a cup of coffee. Sipping it, he went over to the floor-to-ceiling windows and looked out at the manicured grounds in the back. The trunks of palm trees were lit with small spotlights, the spillover illuminating flowering bushes along the walls. A swimming pool glowed with blue light beside a small gazebo.

The previous night, after securing the catamaran, Boone had taken María to a waterfront bar in Willemstad where the two of them hit it off. Since her transportation was tied to Tomás the Bodyguard, they'd gone in Boone's car, and he was a bit embarrassed to take such a sophisticated woman in his tiny used Kia, stuffed with gear. She'd surprised him when she informed Boone that she actually drove the same model. After drinks, she'd asked him to take her home. The Jan Thiel neighborhood she lived in was filled with elegant homes, their plots walled and gated. It was clear María Cabrera wasn't hurting for money, but she didn't behave like it. He had parked right beside her car, and sure enough—apart from being a different color—it was nearly identical.

Boone was just brewing a second cup of joe when Laura called.

"Morning, Laura."

"I'm thinking Kokomo Beach," she said without preamble. "We can have lunch there for a surface interval, then see what Noah and Anika want to do for the last open water dive. Could either stay there and dive Car Wrecks... or drive up the coast to Playa Lagun."

"Sounds good."

"Kokomo's right up the road from you, so I'll swing by and—"

"Actually, I'm not home. I'll just meet you at the beach."

"Where are you?"

"Somewhere in Jan Thiel."

Laura laughed. "Wait a minute. You're waking up in another town after you played cabin boy for a bachelorette cruise? Oh, I can't wait to hear this."

Boone shook his head with a grin. "See you at Kokomo," he said as he disconnected the call.

"*Madre de Dios*, do you get up this early all the time?"

Boone looked up at the second-floor balcony that ran along the back of the living area. María was standing at the railing, dressed in a robe that looked more comfortable than expensive. She yawned and pointed.

"Make me a cup, please. Black."

"Coming right up."

She descended the stairs and joined him in the kitchen, running a hand up his back.

"You have to go, yes?"

"Yes."

"Will I see you again?"

"Also yes." Boone handed her the fresh cup of coffee. "I'm

free most evenings, but... well, I'm not much of a night owl, I'm afraid."

"Because you rise at an ungodly hour." She leaned against the counter and sipped from the mug.

"Well, I don't *have* to get up this early, it's just habit." He went on to describe his morning routine. "The first dive doesn't actually happen until about nine. But I've got students this morning so I should get there early. And I really ought to grab some fresh clothes, so I need to swing by my place, first."

"Then I will let you go. But... I want you to teach me to dive."

"I'd love to."

"Good. I am embarrassed that I have lived here for so long and not gotten certified. And some of my friends back in Medellín go diving all the time in San Andrés and Providencia, and it makes me jealous."

"I don't know those places."

"They are Colombian islands near Nicaragua. Very beautiful. My uncle has a house there. I have visited twice, but only snorkeled."

"Well, I'll have you diving in no time. Next time I see you, I'll bring you the PADI manual."

"Manual?"

Boone smiled. "You can't just put on a tank and jump in the ocean. And we'll need access to a swimming pool... but I see you've got that covered."

"Yes." She smiled. "Would you like to try it out?"

Boone leaned in and gave her a lingering kiss. "Next time."

NINETEEN

Boone did indeed teach María to dive, and by the end of their first six months together, she was a PADI Advanced Open Water Diver. To celebrate, Boone arranged a spot on a dive boat he occasionally worked for and took her to Watamula and Mushroom Forest, his two favorite dives. Afterward, on the drive back to Willemstad, María announced that she had a thank-you gift for him.

"You and I are going out for a proper dinner," she declared.

"You mean to tell me all those fancy places we've been eating at didn't qualify as 'proper'?"

María was quite the foodie, and had taken him to a wide variety of restaurants. At first, she tried to pick up the checks, but that didn't sit well with Boone, so they took turns. He wasn't exactly sure what she did for a living—she was "between jobs," she said—but he knew her family was quite well-off.

"Tonight, we are going to the restaurant in Fort Nassau."

"The one way up on the hill over the harbor?"

"The same. But first... you and I are going shopping. You're going to wear long sleeves and pants if it kills you."

"It might."

"And shoes. You need new shoes."

"So, you're going to dress me?"

María turned in the passenger seat with a lascivious smile. Boone glanced over at her, then back to the road.

"You're thinking about making a crack about *un*dressing me, aren't you?"

"Yes... but it seemed too obvious. But seriously... the few times I've stayed at your house, I've gone through your closet while you were in the shower."

"Of course you did."

"So I know you have nothing suitable. Come on, it'll be fun!"

As it turned out, the experience wasn't entirely miserable, since María took them to only one men's clothing store and Boone had new shoes, shirt, and a pair of slacks in record time. They returned to María's home, where she changed into a stunning red dress—one that skirted the edge between classy and scandalous. Once Boone had his new clothes on, she dragged him beside her to a full-length mirror.

"Very presentable, don't you think?"

"I think *you* look like a princess, and I look like... well, don't be surprised if diners ask me to recite the daily specials."

María smacked him on the shirt sleeve, then straightened his collar. "You look perfect."

As they were getting into Boone's car, María told him to wait a moment while she fetched something, then returned with the PADI manual that he had loaned her. "I figured I should return this. Your father wrote on the first page, so I imagine this holds sentimental value."

"Oh... yeah. Thank you." Boone tossed it in the back, and they got on the road.

"Your father... did he teach you to dive?"

"No." Boone didn't say anything else for a few blocks, then added, "He encouraged me, though. Signed me up for classes. In Aruba."

"You have mentioned your mother before. In Tennessee. But never your father."

"He left when I was young." Boone quickly changed the subject. "What about *your* family? You haven't told me much about them."

"Well... it is complicated. You met my sisters on the cruise. We are very close. Especially Maricela... she was the bride-to-be."

They chatted about Maricela and her new husband, then María directed Boone to turn off the main highway onto Fort Nassau Way. In minutes, they were climbing a steep road lined with cacti and low brush. Reaching the top, they pulled into a parking space beneath the high stone walls of Fort Nassau.

Much like the forts near the entrance of Willemstad's harbor, Nassau was part of a network of forts built to defend Curaçao from the English, French, Spaniards, pirates, or whoever else might want to invade or raid the island. Many were now in ruins, but eight forts still stood. This one was perched 223 feet above sea level, with a commanding view of every nook and cranny of the inner harbor. In addition to providing a scenic lookout for tourists, the fort served two other purposes.

At the highest point, a square tower with all-around, sloping glass windows had been erected. Lined with radio antennae and looking very much like a 1960s air traffic control tower, the building served as a vessel traffic control center, monitoring and directing the comings and goings of ships into and out of the harbor, including coordinating the opening of the Queen Emma Bridge.

The other occupant of the fort was the venerable restaurant María had brought them to. Boone followed her up the stone steps and through an arch in the outer defensive wall. They entered a courtyard lined with yellow-painted buildings, and María led him to the left. Following a stone wall, they suddenly came upon a restaurant tucked into a corner of the old fort.

"This restaurant has been here since the fifties," she said. "And you can't beat the view!"

"I am seeing plenty of shorts and T-shirts in here..." Boone said, with a tinge of accusation in his voice.

"I didn't say there was a dress code," María responded with a laugh. "I just said *you* had to wear something nice. For me."

They had drinks at the bar, then were seated at their table in the far corner of the fort, beside a small cannon poking through a gap in the ramparts that lined the restaurant. Boone gave María the seat facing the impending sunset, while he sat with a view across the dining area. They were still perusing the menus when Boone spotted a familiar face.

"Hey, it's Tomás!"

María's smile abruptly faltered. She turned in her seat and looked toward the entrance as Tomás and several other men entered the restaurant. Several wore suits, but a few were in stylish linen shirts and slacks.

María turned back to Boone and ducked her head. "*Mierda*," she muttered.

"What's wrong?"

"It's my brother, Santiago."

"Oh? Which one?"

"The one in the white guayabera shirt."

The man she indicated looked to be in his early thirties and exuded confidence. Another man, similarly dressed in a blue guayabera with elaborate embroidery, seemed more nervous than confident. Boone didn't like the vibe he felt from the man.

"Who's the guy in the blue shirt?"

"That is Maximiliano Mesa. He is a... business associate of my family."

After a moment, the men went to a table in a distant corner, each sitting opposite the other. Two of the suits sat at an adjacent table. Tomás began making the rounds through the restaurant, giving the patrons a quick once-over. When he reached their corner, Boone rose with a smile.

"Tomás!" He reached out to offer a handshake.

The big man appeared surprised, but then he spotted María and the surprise turned to unease. He shot a glance back at his group, then turned to Boone. "You should not be here."

"Uh... happy to see you, too, Tomás."

"I thank you for what you did, but... I do not know you. Do you understand?" He turned away, as if scouting out the rest of that side of the restaurant. "*Señorita* Cabrera," he said without looking at María, "I have kept my side of the bargain." With that, he went back toward the group of men, continuing his reconnaissance.

Boone sat back down. "Okay, what was that?"

María sighed, holding her menu like a shield. "You may remember... that I said my brother is very... protective."

"Overly protective, I believe you said. On several occasions. But to be honest, I don't know much more than that about him."

"I do not know how he would react to my dating a... well..."

"A gringo?" Boone asked.

"Oh, no, no. It's not that. Let's just say, I want to live my own life. And how I live it, and who I spend it with, is none of his business."

"What did Tomás mean about a bargain?"

She sighed. "My brother put him on the sunset cruise. For protection, yes, mostly... but also to keep an eye on me and my sisters. And when you and I snuck off in search of a proper aguardiente sour, Tomás threatened to tell Santiago."

"But he didn't."

"No. Because I suggested to him that if he kept that to himself, then I would also remain silent on his falling overboard. And not being able to swim. And letting me get out of his sight. We came to an understanding. He is the only one who knows I have been seeing you."

"Well... that's probably about to end. Since he did a sweep of the restaurant, there's no way he'd be able to say he didn't see you." Boone watched as Tomás leaned over and spoke to Santiago. The man frowned and looked their way. "Yep. Incoming."

María swallowed. "Well... so be it. Listen. You are my dive instructor. Yes? I just finished my certification dive, and this is a celebration."

"Well, how lucky for us that those things are actually true," Boone said with an easy smile, as his peripheral vision tracked the approach of María's brother. "Don't worry. Just chill and roll with it." He turned his menu to face her, ramping up his Tennessee twang a bit. "Hey, what's this 'velouté' sauce on this here red snapper dish?"

María looked at where Boone was tapping his finger and played along. "Oh, that is a French sauce... probably herbs, butter, and stock."

Santiago appeared at the side of their table. "María. *Que sorpresa... encontrarte aquí.*"

"Santi! I am surprised to see you, as well!" she replied, shifting the conversation into English. "How good to see you!" She turned around, searching the restaurant. "Are you here with family? Or a date?"

"Neither. Business dinner. But what about you?" He turned to look at Boone, then back to her. "Is this a date?"

Boone knew that a denial would need to come from María. As a young man sitting across from a stunningly beautiful woman, any protestation on his part would ring false, so he remained silent, appearing confused.

María took over. "No, Santi, this is a celebration! This is Boone... um...?"

"Fischer," Boone supplied.

"Yes, Boone Fischer. From America. He was my dive instructor." She sat up with an air of pride. "I am now, officially, an advanced scuba diver!"

"Oh? Impressive."

"Boone, this is my brother, Santiago."

"Pleased to meet you, sir! You have a very talented sister. She learned everything in record time."

"Well, that's good to know," Santiago said. He reached behind to grab a chair from an empty table and set it beside theirs, then took a seat and looked at María. "What a lovely red dress. I haven't seen you wearing that before."

"As I said, this is a special occasion! Now I can go diving here! And the next time we stay at Uncle's place in Providencia, I can dive there, as well."

"Do you scuba dive, sir?" Boone asked. "I'd be happy to offer you a friends-and-family rate."

Santiago smiled at that, then leaned back in his chair. "Thank you, no. I'm far too busy, I'm afraid."

"Oh, that's a shame," Boone said. "This island is just made for diving."

"So I hear."

María leaned toward her brother and asked quietly, "Santi, the... business dinner. Is all well?"

Her brother looked at her, then inclined his head toward Boone, as if implying this wasn't the best company to have a discussion in front of. "I believe we have reached a satisfactory outcome," he said.

Boone knew he should keep his mouth shut, but he just couldn't help himself. "What line of work are you in, sir?"

Santiago shrugged. "Nothing as interesting as teaching scuba diving, I fear." He lifted one of the menus, examining it. "I am in the import/export business. Mostly agricultural products."

"Oh. Cool." Boone left it at that. He could tell that Santiago was still suspicious, and it didn't help that María had worn a dress that would've tempted the most celibate of monks to break every possible vow. Boone hated to lie, but he decided he could skirt the truth.

"This place is amazing," he said, playing up the easily impressed yokel. "Bit fancier than I'm used to. I can't wait to bring my girlfriend here."

"Oh? She is in Curaçao?" Santiago asked.

"Yeah, she's here," Boone said, flicking a glance at María.

"And you have not yet brought her here?" Santiago asked.

"No, but I will now!" He picked up the other menu. "Hey, what would you order? I admit, I'm a bit out of my depth, here."

"Anything you choose will be excellent," Santiago said, rising. "María, I congratulate you on your new skill."

Just then, Tomás approached, and Boone overheard a burst

of Spanish that he managed to understand as, "Maximiliano wants you back at the table."

"Maxi *puede esperar*!" Santiago hissed back. Then, turning to Boone and María, he asked, "How did the two of you get here?"

Boone didn't see an easy way out of this, but María took over. "Boone drove us. I wanted him to know how to get here, so he could bring his girlfriend. I was going to take a taxi home..."

"Don't be silly," Santiago said. "Tomás... after our meeting is concluded, you will escort María home." He turned back to the table. "Mr. Fischer, upon reflection... I recommend the rack of lamb. Thank you for teaching my sister to dive, and I wish you a safe journey back to your own home."

Santiago returned the borrowed chair to the nearby table and returned to his group. Tomás gave María a look, then shook his head and followed his boss.

Boone and María both lifted their menus, staring through them.

"Your brother is... intense," Boone said.

"All things considered, I think that went very well," María replied. She looked at him over the top of her menu. "So... you have a girlfriend, I hear. Who you'd like to take to this restaurant?"

"Sure. She's sitting across from me right now. And since she took *me* here today, I can't wait to return the favor and bring *her* here." Boone tossed his menu down. "But for this visit, I think I will go with that lamb."

TWENTY

Another six months passed, and Boone and María continued to see each other, although Boone found himself looking over his shoulder from time to time. María told him not to worry, that the odds of running into Santiago again were slim, as he was rarely in Curaçao.

In addition to dining and shopping, they spent time at María's place—quite a lot, in fact. Boone would be the first to admit that the sex was fantastic, but he wasn't one to stay in one place for too long, so he pressed her to get out and explore the island with him. He took her cliff diving at Playa Forti, bicycling at the blowholes on the rough coast of Shete Boka National Park, and hiking up the 1,200-foot Mount Christoffel.

And, of course, they gave her new diving certification a proper workout, hitting most of the major dive sites, watching the coral spawning at Snake Bay, and enjoying a long night dive at Tugboat Beach. That last trip ended with a visit to the abandoned Quarantine House, up a rough road on the hill overlooking the dive site. Using their dive lights, they explored the creepy old hospital, with occasional peeks out the windows; they were less worried about being visited by ghosts than about Boone's Kia being visited by car thieves.

Boone had stopped crewing for the deep-sea fishing charter, but he continued working for several dive ops as well as Green Flash Cruises. On one of their outings—a day trip to Klein Curaçao—María and her sisters came along, accompanied by a few of their friends. Once again, Tomás accompanied them. Boone was pleased to see that one of the first things the bodyguard did after coming aboard was to put on a life vest—although he left the front unsecured. Likely so as not to hinder access to his gun, Boone figured.

Mark was aboard—the Australian loved Klein Curaçao and rarely missed a voyage there. Zimmy was there as well, manning the kitchen and bar with another local. And once again, Gustav had left his reservation desk to make sure the trip went well.

The day trip began at half past eight, when the *Green Flash* made its way from Jan Thiel Beach to Klein. The wind was coming out of the east at twenty knots—not unusual for Curaçao—so they decided against a zigzagging, sail-assisted crossing, opting to save the sailing experience for the afternoon return. They cruised across at a leisurely nine knots, arriving at just after ten in the morning. From time to time, they passed—or were passed by—other day-trip vessels, from catamarans to motor yachts.

Even though the nearest point of Curaçao was only seven miles away, Klein's desolate appearance made it seem remote. Boone thought back to his dive trips to the offshore island of Klein Bonaire, just twenty-five miles away to the northeast. While both of the Klein islands were extremely flat, rising no more than a few feet above sea level, that was where the similarities ended. The interior of Bonaire's "Klein" was quite green, with a variety of bushes and low trees, including a few of the iconic divi-divi trees. Klein Curaçao, on the other hand, was almost completely devoid of large vegetation, a true desert island, sun-blasted and barren.

As the *Green Flash* neared Klein, the first thing that came into sight was the white tower of a lighthouse. As they drew closer, a weathered pink building at its base came into view. Boone was taking a pause from his duties, sitting beside María on one of the bow trampolines. María was decked out in a lightweight beach cover-up with a blue bikini underneath. She had been sunning herself for the first part of the voyage, but there wasn't a cloud in the sky, so she'd donned the cover-up a while ago as the sun rose higher. Boone had been allowed to skip the crew outfit and was currently wearing his Sponge Bob swim trunks and an Amstel Bright T-shirt.

"Where on earth did you get this ridiculous thing?" María asked, giving the hem of Boone's garish swimsuit a tug.

"It was a gift."

"Did the gift-giver have a grudge against you?"

Gustav suddenly appeared by the trampolines, his leathery face lit up with excitement. "One of the other captains radioed that there's a mola mola near the reef! We'll drop by there, if anyone wants to snorkel with it."

"Great!" Boone exclaimed. "María, you'll want to jump in for this. They're one of the largest bony fish in the ocean. I studied them in college, but I've never seen one."

"That sounds delightful," she said to Boone, and then turned to Gustav. "Excuse me, that lighthouse... is it operational?"

Gustav nodded. "Yes. It was abandoned a long time ago, but it's now automated with a solar-powered beacon. With the prevailing direction of the trade winds and with Klein Curaçao being so hard to see until you're right on top of it, a lot of boats and ships end up running aground on the windward side. There's a rusty old section of an oil tanker up against the coast, and the last time I was here, two small yachts had been washed ashore."

As they drew closer to Klein, a thatch-roofed observation tower came into view, and soon they could see several boats anchored in the shallows, the largest of which was a two-decker trawler. Ashore were groups of day-trippers, sunbathing amidst the beach palapas in front of a small pavilion. Just to the north of this area, a single dock stood by some small fishing shacks.

"That big pleasure boat, that's the *Mermaid*," Gustav said.

When Boone chuckled, María cocked her head. "Why are you laughing?"

"I dated a mermaid for a while."

"Oh, really?"

"You think I'm joking, but I'm not." He snapped the waistband of his Sponge Bobs. "These were from her."

"But mermaids are half fish," María said with a mischievous smile. "How did you...?" She tipped her sunglasses down and raised her eyebrows at him.

"Well... the tail was removeable." Boone got up from the tramp. "Gus, I'll get the snorkeling gear out, then do a head count of who wants to take a dip with the mola mola."

Boone went aft and opened up one of the bench lockers, taking out bins of masks and snorkels, fins, and lightweight snorkel vests. Satisfied, he went to make the rounds of the guests. Spotting Tomás near the stern, he went to him first.

"Tomás, can I assume you won't be joining us for snorkeling?"

The man had his binoculars up, one hand gripping the lifeline to steady himself. When he didn't reply, Boone called his name again.

"That boat has been following us," Tomás said, lowering the binos.

Boone looked out to sea and spotted the boat on the horizon. He came closer and held a hand out. "May I?" Taking the binoculars, he focused them on the distant vessel. It was a small boat, perhaps twenty feet long, with a partially enclosed cockpit.

"Looks like a local fishing boat. Fishing is allowed in most of the area around Klein. They're probably on their way to those fishing huts to take a break or clean their catch. Although... huh."

"What?"

"Trip outboards." When Tomás furrowed his brow, Boone elaborated. "Three engines."

"This is unusual?" Tomás asked.

"For a smallish boat like that, yeah. Local fishermen, if their boat uses outboards, they have just one or two. If you were coming out to Klein to fish, you would want two, in case you lose one. But three...?"

Tomás took the binoculars back and looked again at the boat. "Three men aboard. If they are local fishermen, they are not Curaçaoan."

"Might be Venezuelan. They come across to fish. That might explain the third outboard." Boone spared a glance toward Klein, watching as they approached the spot where the other captain had said he'd spotted the mola mola. He had another minute or two. "Hey, Tomás... the few times I've seen you, you seemed on edge."

"Edge?"

"Uh... tense. Alert. So, I gotta ask... what's up with María's brother?"

Tomás lowered the binos and looked at Boone. "Has she told you... anything?"

"No. I mean... I haven't exactly pressed her for details, but... well, I have an idea his line of business might not be entirely... legal."

Tomás returned the binoculars to his eyes. "This is not something I can speak of. You should go do your job, and let me do mine."

***

The mola mola turned out to be a large one. A bizarre-looking fish, it had a tiny mouth on its enormous, flat body. Extremely long dorsal and anal fins made the fish as tall as it was long, and when they came upon it, the mola mola was floating on its side, sunning itself near the surface. This behavior was what gave the fish its other common name, the ocean sunfish.

The snorkelers dropped in around it, keeping a respectful distance; Boone had made it clear no one was to approach closer than ten feet and to keep their splashing to a minimum. After a few minutes, the leviathan wobbled its ungainly fins and dropped down, turning upright. As it slowly moved away, Boone led the snorkelers back to the catamaran, where they climbed aboard at the stern, with some assistance from Mark.

Once everyone was accounted for, the *Green Flash* got underway. Boone spotted the fishing vessel again, a quarter-mile away. He couldn't see any wake and could just make out a fishing rod extending over the boat's side. There was a brief flash as something glinted in the sun from the fishing boat's cockpit. He was about to find Tomás when María suddenly clutched his arm, her eyes wide with excitement.

"Boone, that creature was magnificent! I have never seen such a thing!"

"My first time, too."

María grabbed a nearby towel and dried herself off before tying it at her waist. "When we go ashore... shall we visit the lighthouse?"

"If Gus can spare me, sure."

The catamaran motored into the turquoise shallows near the beach, then anchored and lowered its bow stairs. The metal steps dropped down between the two hulls and the trampolines, allowing bathers to descend right into the warm water.

"All ashore who's going ashore!" Mark called out, as the Aussie manned the tiller of a dinghy that was available to bring anyone ashore who didn't want to get wet. Many opted to swim, but the dinghy made several trips. Boone and María stayed behind until it returned for the third time. Then, after Boone gathered up a bag with some bottles of water and one of the sets of binoculars they kept aboard for whale-spotting, María donned a straw sunhat and stylish sunglasses, and the two of them took the dinghy with Mark, who nosed into the sandy beach near Tomás and the Cabrera sisters.

Boone helped María out of the dinghy, then turned to its skipper. "Hey, Mark, can you let Gus know María and I are going to the lighthouse?"

"Sure thing, mate."

Within earshot, Tomás whirled around and approached. "Wait... no," he protested. "*Señorita* Cabrera, your sisters are staying on the beach."

"Good for them," María said.

"But *Señorita* Cabrera... María... *por favor...*"

"We'll be fine, Tomás."

Boone thought the bodyguard seemed more than merely protective, and he grew agitated.

"Your brother said I must watch all of you!" he pleaded, then switched to Spanish, lowering his voice to an urgent hiss. "María... *hay problemas con la familia Mesa. Santiago tiene miedo de que nos ataquen.*"

The Spanish was rapid-fire, and Boone wasn't able to understand the last part, but he picked up most of the first sentence: there were problems with the Mesa family. And he recognized that name from the business dinner at the fort— that squirrely man in the blue guayabera had been named Mesa. Maximiliano Mesa.

"Tomás... my brother worries too much," María assured her bodyguard. "We will be fine." She swept her arm toward the lighthouse and the vast emptiness around it. "There is no one around. Stay here with Maricela and the others. I insist." Her last words had a bit of steel behind them.

Tomás sighed. "Very well. But please be quick."

"Come along, Boone." María started down a rough, lime-stone walkway that ran from the beach to the distant lighthouse.

Boone looked at the bodyguard, then stepped closer. "Hey, I don't know exactly what you said to María, but it didn't sound good."

"No. There has been peace, but..." He bit his lip. "I cannot say." He turned away, then reconsidered. Turning back, he leaned close. "Listen... Mr. Cabrera is in Colombia right now. If something happens, it will probably happen there. But... he considers his sisters in Curaçao a..." He waved his hand, searching for the word.

"A vulnerability?"

Tomás thought for a moment, perhaps translating the word Boone had supplied, then he nodded. "Yes."

Boone breathed out a long, slow breath. "Tomás... I think I understand. But listen to me... there's almost no vegetation on Klein; if anyone comes toward the lighthouse, I'll see 'em." Boone pointed at the thatch-roofed observation tower beside the beach. "And that's a perfect lookout spot. If you go up there, you'll be able to see the whole island."

Tomás nodded. "Is good."

"And keep an eye out for that boat from before," Boone said. "They had a fishing line out when we were snorkeling, but... better safe than sorry."

Tomás grunted, then pointed after María. "Go. Watch her for me."

Boone turned and jogged after María. Reaching her, he handed her one of the water bottles he carried. "Here. There's zero shade out here, so you'll probably want this. Just gimme the empty when you finish."

"What were you saying to Tomás?"

"He's worried about you, is all. Although..." Boone sighed. "Maybe this is a conversation that can wait until we get back, but... I think I need to know what line of business your family is in."

María stopped on the sandy walkway and looked at him. "What if you don't like what you hear?"

"Won't know 'til I hear it." When she looked down at her feet and was silent, he added. "But like I said... it can wait 'til we get back."

She looked up at him, her eyes hidden behind her sunglasses, but from the tremor in her voice, he wondered if there might be tears in her eyes. "I will tell you everything. But can we enjoy today?"

Boone nodded. "Yeah. We can do that."

TWENTY-ONE

Boone and María completed the sun-scorched quarter-mile walk to the lighthouse. The central tower's base was flanked by two pink buildings that once housed the two lighthouse keepers, who took turns manning the lighthouse until it was abandoned. The plaster on the outer walls was weathered and crumbling in places, and most of the windows were mere holes, although some wooden shutters miraculously remained. Climbing the coral-pink stone stairs, they came to a courtyard, floored with planks that had been recently added.

"The buildings look a little rickety," Boone said, when he looked inside. The pink interior walls were covered in graffiti and the floors appeared questionable.

"Let's climb the tower, then," María said. "The view is what I wanted, anyway."

The spiral staircase was extremely narrow, with small steps and no handrails, but they made their way up with care and soon reached the windows at the highest point on the island.

The actual beacon was higher, but Boone didn't trust the ladder that led to it.

Klein Curaçao was only a mile and a half long and a half mile across, so they could see all of the island from coast to coast. The upper windows faced east and west and afforded a great view of the beach they'd just left, as well as the rough seas and ragged limestone shore on the opposite side. As Gus had said, there was a large section of an oil tanker rusting away in the shallows, and Boone spotted a smaller wooden yacht lying on its side to the north of the larger wreck.

Boone had left his smartphone back on the catamaran, but María took hers out and snapped several pictures from the windows.

"Can we visit those wrecks?" María asked.

"Sure. One sec—lemme check in with Tomás."

"I can call him."

"Not out here, you can't. No cell service." Boone went to the western window and trained the binoculars he'd brought on the observation tower by the beach palapas. He wasn't surprised to find the bodyguard staring at him through his own binos. Tomás spotted Boone looking at him and stretched his arms to the sides, waving them up and down. Then he beckoned, making an exaggerated "come back" gesture. Finally, he pumped his arm to the north, pointing three times toward the fishing huts and the dock there. Boone squinted in that direction and spotted a familiar boat tied up at the dock.

So? They were fishermen after all, he thought. That dock was where fishermen would rest or clean their catch. He was about to reassure Tomás, when a whisper of suspicion tickled his thoughts. When he was young, his mother had always said he seemed to possess some sort of sixth sense, and he listened to it now.

Boone raised his binoculars to get a closer look. He spotted two men on the pier by the boat. *Where is the third?* Looking into the cluster of little fishing huts, he spotted the glint of a reflection at an open window and remembered seeing something similar in the cockpit of their boat when it had been fishing. After a moment, there was motion inside the hut, and Boone could make out the third man, also with a pair of binoculars. He appeared to be looking to the south, toward the daytrippers on the beach.

"Shit."

"What is it?" María asked.

Boone didn't answer, shifting his view back to the fishing boat itself. He couldn't tell the make of the three engines, but they looked like they were well cared for. Then something else caught his eye. Lying on the deck of the boat was a bundle of something, wrapped in beach towels. Protruding from one end of the towels was the unmistakable barrel of an AK-47 assault rifle.

Back in Tennessee, he'd gone shooting with Fred at a range up the road from the fix-it shop, and while Boone wasn't a "gun guy" by any stretch of the imagination, he *was* mechanically inclined. The owner of the range had let them fire his AK, and looking at the business end of the weapon sticking out of the towels, he recognized the distinctive gas-piston chamber mounted above the barrel, as well as the oversized front sight.

"María... we need to go. Now. Head down the stairs, I'll be right behind you."

"Are we in danger?"

"Not yet. Please, go... I'll explain in a minute." He trained the binos on the observation tower and found Tomás looking back at him. He lowered the glasses and made exaggerated hand signals, pointing at himself, then made his fingers "walk" before pointing at Tomás. Then he tapped his dive watch and held up five fingers. Finally, he raised an "OK" sign. Hopefully, the man would get the gist: *I am walking back to you. Five minutes. Okay?*

Tomás returned the "OK" gesture. Boone debated trying to signal about the guns, but decided against it. The observation tower was less than half the elevation of the lighthouse, so he'd bet the bodyguard couldn't see into the bottom of the "fishing" boat. If Tomás overreacted before Boone and María got back, they might tip their hand.

Boone went quickly down the stairs and joined María in the courtyard.

"What on earth is going on?"

"Your brother might not be so paranoid after all," Boone said. "We need to walk back to the beach, but we need to do it calmly, smiling all the way." As they started back, Boone explained what he had seen. María, to her credit, kept her reactions muted, although that changed when Boone said, "Your family is cartel, aren't they?"

María whirled to look at him, then aimed her sunglasses at the ground as they continued to walk toward the beach at a brisk pace. "I did not know how to tell you. But I *should* have!"

"No argument from me."

"But... that is not *my* life, Boone!" she pleaded.

"Look... not the time or the place. These guys... they're probably from a rival family. That Maxi guy, from the restaurant. My guess, they're after you and your sisters to give them some leverage."

"Then why haven't they attacked us already?"

"Because there are about ten leisure craft lying at anchor. A lot of eyewitnesses and radios. Probably several sat phones. No,

I bet they're waiting for us to leave, then they'll come after us at sea."

"Why didn't they do that when we were on our way out here?"

"The day trip boats all tend to leave for Klein at roughly the same time... we saw quite a few on the way over. That's still a lot of eyeballs and radios. But the return to Curaçao tends to be staggered. Some boats leave early, some stay until late afternoon. They'd be more likely to catch us out of sight of another boat if they waited. And they've got enough horsepower to be long gone before the Coast Guard shows up."

"So, what do we do?"

"I'm still working that out," Boone said.

Back at the beach, Boone and María took Tomás, Gustav, and Mark aside, out of sight of the fishing shacks. After Boone explained the situation, he said, "Listen, we can't look like we're alerted, or they may decide they have to act now, regardless of witnesses. Innocent people could get hurt. Gus, you've got a sat phone, right?"

"Yes."

"Good. Our 'friends' over there may be monitoring the VHF emergency channels, so use the sat to call for the cavalry."

"There's usually only one Dutch Caribbean Coast Guard cutter in Curaçao," Gustav said. "And we don't know where she is... so it might take a while for her to get here."

"And I bet that boat there is faster," Boone surmised. "But they can get a chopper out here. Or one of their smaller fast boats. Heck, maybe Bonaire's got a cutter that's closer—we're not far from that island. Just make sure they know they may be facing three men armed with assault rifles."

"Okay. I will go aboard and make the call."

"Tomás, stay up in the observation tower until we're almost ready to go. I have no doubt those guys know who you are, and as long as you're up there, they won't think we're leaving."

"María, go speak to your sisters and their friends. Suggest it's time for a dip in the ocean. We're going to need them to be near the bow steps, so everyone can pile aboard fast. Mark, can you start getting the boat ready to go... without looking like you are?"

"Will do," he replied.

"But leave the dinghy there on the beach. It'll add to the appearance that we're not leaving any time soon, but also... I'll need it later."

"Why?" María asked. "What are you going to do?"

"A little something to slow them down."

TWENTY-TWO

"Are you mental?" Aboard the *Green Flash*, Mark stared at Boone like he'd lost his mind.

"Not really," Boone said. "Looking at all our options, I think it's the best one." He slid another two-pounder onto his weight belt and looked across the water, estimating the distance and running a few calculations. He wished he had his freediver fins, but that wasn't something he carted around when crewing for *Green Flash*; the extra-large snorkeling fins he kept aboard would have to do. "The dock they're at is about two hundred meters away... four Olympic swimming pools. With snorkeling fins, going slow and steady so I don't burn up my air... I can probably make that with only a couple visits to the surface. Although this will slow me down." Boone patted the coil of nylon dock line that lay beside him on the bench.

"How long will it take you to get there?" Gustav asked.

"At top speed, two or three minutes. But dragging that with me... and swimming a bit slower to conserve air... probably more like five or six." He stopped speaking, then shook his head. "Only problem is, if I swim straight at the dock and they spot me, the jig will be up. I'm going to angle out to deeper water a bit, then swim parallel to the shore. When I'm close enough to make it to the dock in one breath, I'll make the final run completely underwater."

Boone did some quick calculations; he figured his detour would add about a hundred more meters to the distance. "Let's say, eight minutes after I start, be ready to go. Once I reach the pier, I'll need a minute or two more, then I'll flash you an 'OK' sign... so keep an eye on the stern of their boat. Once I give you the go ahead, hustle everyone up the steps and get underway. I'll catch up if I can. Otherwise, I'll hitch a ride with one of your competitors."

"As long as you don't start working for them." Gustav said with a grin.

"No worries there. Zimmy's cooking is too good. What did the Coast Guard say?"

"Well..." The Dutchman bit his lip. "They might've thought it was a hoax call. When I told them who I was, they were able to check with the office and verify we were out here. Still... since there hasn't been an actual attack yet..."

"Yeah, I was afraid of that," Boone said.

"But they said they'll send the cutter, since it was scheduled to go to sea anyway. I asked them what the speed was, and they said twenty-six knots. Depending on how long it takes them to get underway, we might meet it at the halfway point."

"Okay. Good. Let's do this."

Boone glanced toward the north, then went around to the starboard side of the catamaran, where he would be out of sight from the fishing huts. Donning his mask and fins and clipping on the weight belt, he slipped over the side. It was shallow enough there that he could stand with his head above water. Mark stood by with the coil of line while Boone tried to relax and do his breathe-up, preparing his body for a long breath-hold. He spared a glance along the bow and saw María in the shallows, watching him. She'd wanted to come aboard when he'd explained what he was going to do, but Boone reiterated the need to keep up appearances that the group wasn't leaving anytime soon.

Boone refocused his thoughts, continuing his preparation. Once he was ready, he started the stopwatch function on his dive watch, then held up a hand toward the cat.

Mark gripped the railing and leaned over the side, giving Boone the coil of line. "Best of luck, mate."

Boone didn't reply as he slipped beneath the surface and dropped to the sand. He glanced up at the underside of the catamaran's dual hulls, then swam at a forty-five-degree angle toward deeper water, noting the slope of the sandy bottom. He kept his kicks slow and steady and pressed the coil of line against his chest to minimize drag. A minute later, when he figured he was in about twenty feet of water, he turned and swam parallel to shore.

He had traveled for nearly three minutes when the urge to breathe required a visit to the surface. Maintaining his kicks, he ascended. When his mask cleared the water, he quickly took his bearings. Boone had always had an excellent sense of direction and the dock was almost where he thought it would be. Kicking gently, he turned his head and took a long, slow intake of breath, careful to angle his head away from the wave action.

Lungs filled, he angled toward the bottom and tucked the coil of line against his chest once more, doing his best to remain hydrodynamic. Without a proper breathe-up, he only managed two minutes for this stretch. Again, he ascended for air and to eyeball where he was. If he was right, he would now be close enough to make the run to the pier.

Raising his mask above the water, he found he was within striking distance. The boat was on the south side of the pier, bow toward shore. He could see one of the men on the pier, smoking a cigarette. The other two were not in sight, so he assumed they'd both be in the shade of one of the fishing huts. The man on the pier wasn't looking his way, so Boone took the time to pack a little extra air into his lungs before locking his eyes on the pier and descending to the bottom. He swam straight toward where he believed the back of the boat was, staying as close to the bottom as possible. Soon, the outermost pilings of the pier came into view. Next, the props of the trip outboards appeared. Those were his target.

Reaching the stern of the boat, Boone laid the coil on the shallow bottom and quietly raised his head above the water, listening. He could hear men's voices, but they were too distant; likely the two men he hadn't been able to see. He took a moment to relax his mind and body, drew in a lungful of air, then dropped down.

Back in Tennessee, Boone had seen boats whose props had been fouled by getting tangled in a line. Often it wasn't that big a deal; you cut your engine when you felt the vibration and dealt with the issue. But he had something a little more extensive in mind.

Retrieving the dock line, he proceeded to uncoil it, then took the ends over to the nearest pier piling. The line had loops at both ends, and he wrapped it twice around, then fed an end through one of the loops and pulled it tight. He then proceeded to wrap the rest of the line around the propellers, two coils around each, going down the line until he reached the end. He still had some left over and was about to go back along the propellers again when he felt the boat shift. Thumps were audible on the hull.

One of them just got aboard. The boarding didn't seem rushed or hurried, but nevertheless, Boone backed away from the propellers, then slowly kicked along the bottom to a position under the pier. Rising to the surface beside the piling he'd attached the line to, he replenished his air and listened.

The man aboard was whistling, and then the crackle of a VHF radio came on. Boone could hear the man flipping through some channels, presumably monitoring traffic for any distress calls. Boone breathed a sigh of relief when the radio was flicked off. The boat rocked a bit, then footsteps sounded on the wooden planks above Boone's head.

"Nada en los canales de emergencia," he called out, his voice raised but lacking any urgency.

A voice replied back, too distant for Boone to make out over the lapping of the waves. He waited another moment, then ducked under and returned to the stern to tangle the rest of the line in the propellers, ending with the remaining loop, which he then hung on a blade on the nearest prop for good measure. Satisfied, he carefully lifted his head above water, preparing to give the signal.

For a brief second, he debated grabbing the bundle of guns and taking them out to the reef, but he had no way of knowing whether the men in the shack now had them. He looked at his watch and saw that the whole swim-and-sabotage outing had taken nearly ten minutes, so the *Green Flash* should be ready to make a run for it. He could just make out Tomás up in the tower, no doubt looking right at him. He prepared himself for one last breath-hold, then arranged his fingers into an "OK" sign and pumped his hand three times.

The bodyguard leaned over the edge of the observation

tower, calling out to the bathers below. At the distant beach, in the shallows, Boone saw María, her sisters and other guests suddenly making for the bow steps on the cat. The reaction from the "fishermen" was immediate.

"Ellas se van!"

"Sube al barco! Rápido!"

Boone heard footsteps pounding on the pier and dove for the bottom, swimming straight south toward the beached dinghy, no longer bothering to head for deeper water and kicking for all he was worth. By the time he needed air, he was certain his little trick would be consuming all of their attention.

As his lungs started to burn, he heard the low rumble of the outboards starting up. About six seconds later there was a loud series of thunks, then the engine noises abruptly stopped. Boone's face lit up with a closed-lip smile as he kicked for another thirty seconds, then angled toward shore and beached himself, turning faceup to strip off his fins. Gasping for air, pulled his mask down around his neck and looked toward the pier. The "fishing" boat was now angled away from the dock, its bow pointed to the southwest. Two of the men were looking over the stern, and the third had jumped into the water near the outboards. One of them started screaming, and while Boone was no lip-reader, he was fairly certain it was a litany of Spanish obscenities. Glancing in the other direction, he saw that the *Green Flash* was now underway, circling to the south.

Boone got to his feet, fins in hand, and started walking toward the catamaran's beached dinghy. Then the shouts from the pier changed. He affected a casual stroll, but when he glanced over his shoulder, he saw one of the men on the boat pointing at him, rage on his face. Boone broke into a run. As he reached the dinghy, he threw his mask and fins into it and dragged the little boat into the shallows. He looked out to sea and saw the catamaran had completed its turn and was accelerating to the west. Shouts drew his attention, and he saw one of the cartel men dashing up the beach, one hand held at his side. Handgun.

Boone jumped in, fired up the little boat's 3.5 hp engine, and ducked down as he steered for open water, then opened up the throttle. In moments, he managed to get the dinghy up on plane, something he'd never have been able to do with anyone else aboard. Still, the *Green Flash* was capable of about nineteen knots, and he would never be able to catch her if she got up to speed. Looking back toward shore, he spotted the cartel man watching him for a moment before he turned and ran back toward the disabled boat.

The *Green Flash* was getting farther away, and Boone decided he'd follow her for a bit in the hopes that they'd see him and slow down. If that didn't work, then he'd circle back to shore and head to the south side of the island, out of sight of the fishing pier. There, he would wait in the shallows, keeping an eye out for another boat to begin boarding. Hopefully, they'd let him join them.

As luck would have it, Tomás was at the stern with his trusty binoculars. The bodyguard waved and beckoned, and Boone could see the wake on the cat's dual hulls begin to subside. In minutes, he throttled back and coasted up alongside, then tossed his fins aboard, grabbed the railing, and hauled himself up. He wondered if Gus would attempt to retrieve the dinghy, but quickly got his answer when the Dutchman yelled to the captain, "We have him! Go!"

"Thanks, Gus," Boone gasped, as he felt the catamaran surge forward. "Sorry about your dinghy."

"Oh, that's okay... your girlfriend said she'd buy me a new one."

With drug money, Boone thought. "Where is she?"

"Here!" María appeared and hurled herself at Boone, hugging him tight. Boone held her, then pulled back slightly to look down at her. She was without her sunglasses so he could clearly see her eyes this time. "Boone. I'm so sorry."

"Yeah. Me too."

Three weeks later, Boone sat at a picnic table overlooking Saint Michael's Bay. He ate alone, enjoying a cold beer and juicy burger from Niffo Huts, a seaside bar and restaurant around the corner from his home in Boka Sami. Setting the half-eaten burger in the basket, he picked up the Polar beer and took a long sip. The outdoor seating provided spectacular sunset viewing and it looked like it was going to be a good one tonight. While he waited, he thought about how things had ended with María.

The escape from Klein had worked, with the *Green Flash* coming upon the cutter *Panther* just as the eastern tip of Curaçao came into sight. After giving details over the radio, the *Panther* continued on to Klein. Boone later learned from Gustav that the cartel men and the boat were no longer there. Boone wasn't surprised. While his stunt might have damaged a prop or overheated an engine, if even one outboard was still functional, they could have gotten out of Klein—but not fast enough to have caught the catamaran, which had been the whole idea.

Once they were back in cell range, Tomás's phone as well as the phones of the Cabrera sisters exploded with calls and texts. Apparently, the Mesa Cartel had indeed gone after the Cabreras in Medellín. Things were still fluid, but it appeared that

Santiago had come out on top, at least for the moment. It looked like he wanted to "circle the wagons" and María and her sisters had been summoned back to Colombia.

Back in Curaçao, María had asked Boone to join her at her villa for a frank talk, but he had told her that he needed time to think.

"But Santi is sending a plane for us tomorrow!" she had protested.

"Do you *need* to go?" he had asked. "If *that* life isn't *your* life..."

She had shaken her head, then spoke softly, "My family needs me right now. But perhaps, when I return...?"

"We'll cross that bridge when we get to it."

That had been three weeks ago, and to Boone, it felt like a chapter of his life had come to a close. Two weeks ago, he had put out feelers about dive ops on the other ABC Islands—Aruba or Bonaire—as well as the Dutch "SSS" islands: Saba, Statia, and Sint Maarten. The urge for something new tugged at his soul.

Just as the sun dipped below the horizon, painting the sky in oranges and purples, his phone rang. It was Laura with Scuba Dooby Do.

"Hey Laura. You need me tomorrow?"

"No, we're covered. Listen, I'm calling about that thing you asked about? Dive ops looking to hire on other islands?"

Boone set down his beer. "Yeah?"

"Well... I'd hate to see you go, but... there's a brand-new dive op opening up on Bonaire. And they're looking for dive instructors. Plus, they are specifically looking for ones with boat and compressor maintenance skills."

"Sounds perfect. What's it called?"

"Rock Beauty Divers."

PART FIVE

TWENTY-THREE

BONAIRE, DUTCH CARIBBEAN

"You say you have worked in Bonaire before?" Thomas Dupont asked. The Rock Beauty Divers owner had an unusual accent that Boone couldn't place. *Not Dutch... perhaps French?*

"Well, I wasn't working as a divemaster, sir. I was taking a semester here as part of my studies for my degree. We were doing coral reef surveys and studying coral nursery techniques."

"For university, yes?"

"Yes, sir. Marine Science and Biology."

Thomas lowered the résumé Boone had cobbled together. "You have a degree in these things, and you want to be a divemaster?"

"And instructor. Yes, I do. Maybe someday I'll put those degrees to use, but right now I want to see the world and go diving every chance I get."

"Well, you will not dive every day. One day a week, you will have off whether you like it or not. And some days you will do maintenance." He flicked the résumé with a finger, a smile on his face. "Your work repairing engines, this is very useful. Have you ever fixed a compressor?"

"For filling the tanks? Yes, sir. In Curaçao. Several times for several shops."

"Well, if you work for me, you fix *my* machines first, you understand, yes?"

Boone grinned. "Loud and clear, sir."

"*Très bien.*"

"So... am I hired?"

"You are. The starting salary is as we discussed in our emails, but there will be opportunities to improve on that."

"How many divemasters do you have working for you, sir?"

"Including myself, you will make four. We also have a captain, although sometimes I will skipper for the day. We are a small operation. Just the one boat." He gestured out the window over his shoulder.

They were seated in the man's office, situated near the dock. The boat he gestured to, the *Kleine Dancer*, was a 36-foot Dive Special. The dive shop was located beside a lovely complex of condominiums, a five-minute walk to the north of Captain Don's Habitat.

"Any thoughts on accommodations?" Boone asked.

"You have somewhere to stay at the moment, yes?"

"Yes, sir. A bartender from Rum Runners is letting me use her couch."

When Boone had learned he might be coming over here, he had reached out to Penny. He had learned that she was still working as a bartender at Rum Runners, but he had *also* learned that she was no longer single. Fortunately, her boyfriend was a chill guy from Venezuela and the use of her couch hadn't appeared to cause any friction.

"Well, as far as accommodations, the closer to town you are, the more expensive," Thomas explained. "Since we are the northernmost of the dive shops—and Captain Don's and Buddy Dive are north of town, as well—I know that some divemasters have found affordable housing in Rincon."

"That's near the big park, right?"

"Yes. Rincon is the 'other' town on Bonaire. It is to the north and inland, about twenty minutes from here, by car."

"I'll check it out."

Boone's phone plan from Curaçao worked in Bonaire, so he fired up Google Maps and scouted out the route to Rincon. The app suggested a couple of roundabout ways, but there appeared to be a more direct route: a dirt track that split off from the main road just north of the STINAPA headquarters, perfect for a bicycle. Boone's bike was back on Curaçao, of course, waiting to be shipped across, along with his other meager possessions, but Penny's boyfriend had been kind enough to lend him his bicycle.

After cycling over to the Zhung Kong Supermarket across from Rock Beauty Diving, Boone bought a bottle of water that he slipped into the bottle cage on the bike. He then started his stopwatch before continuing northwest along the coast. Very soon, he reached the turnoff. It was readily apparent why the map's directions hadn't suggested it: the road was in rough condition and wouldn't be any fun in a vehicle. Fortunately, on a bike, Boone was able to navigate the ruts and cracks with ease.

The landscape was much as Boone remembered it, with several varieties of cactus, stunted trees, and thorn-bearing bushes lining the dusty track. The interior of Bonaire had more in common with the American southwest than the typical "tropical paradise" you might find in the Leeward Islands of the Northeastern Caribbean.

For the entire length of the shortcut, he didn't pass a soul—unless goats had souls. He came across two groups of them that scattered into the brush upon his approach. The road was completely devoid of civilization: no structures, no telephone poles, no signs. Nothing until the end, where Boone passed a tiny patch of low buildings before reaching an intersection. Turning north, he was again on a stretch of rough road that arced toward Rincon. Then, abruptly, he reached an actual street.

Boone got off his bicycle and leaned it against a sign for Kaya Lourdes; *kaya* meaning street in Papiamentu. He looked at his stopwatch and saw that the entire journey had taken thirty minutes. *Perfect.* He took out the bottle of water and drank half of it. A flash of movement drew his eye, and he spotted a small, yellow warbler on the driver's-side mirror of a parked car. Abruptly, it began fluttering and pecking at the mirror. Boone laughed at the territorial little bird, remembering this behavior from his earlier visit.

Raising his phone, Boone got his bearings on the map and continued north along the road. As he neared an intersection, he spotted a business off to his right. Painted blue and yellow, the wooden building was decorated with emblems for Amstel Bright and Polar. A weathered awning stretched over an outdoor seating area that lay inside waist-high yellow walls. Several sets of patio chairs and tables, all of them empty, were sprinkled about the courtyard. Boone immediately recognized the establishment as a "snack," a type of bar-restaurant popular in the ABC Islands, serving ice-cold beer and cheap eats. *Bit early for lunch, but I could eat,* Boone thought. He turned the corner and coasted to a stop beneath the snack's sign, at which point he burst into laughter.

When Boone was in Bonaire for his semester abroad, he'd visited the national park that encompassed most of the land in the northeast corner of the island. That park was close by and went by the name of Washington-Slagbaai. The name on the snack's sign was "Washington-Snackbaai."

Boone walked his bicycle to the snack and leaned it against the wall beside the entrance. He could hear music coming from a serving window on the right, so he figured someone was inside. Removing his sunglasses, he entered and gave his eyes a chance to adjust. There were two more sets of chairs and tables inside and a counter with some stools, but no one occupied any of them. Back outside, he went to the serving window where he'd heard the music and looked into the kitchen. An ancient boombox sat on a shelf, playing some form of Antillean music, and a large stock pot was on the stove. From the wonderful aroma, he knew something was simmering inside it.

"Hello? Anyone in there?" When no one replied, he dredged up some Papiamentu and called out, *"Bon dia!* Uh... *konta?"*

"He's not answering, is he?"

Boone turned to find a skinny Bonairean entering the courtyard, carrying a sack of onions in one hand and a sack of potatoes in the other. The old man's face was lined and weathered, and his close-cropped hair was almost white. Boone figured his age could be anywhere between fifty and seventy.

"I heard the music," Boone said. "And there's something cooking on the stove."

"That'd be the pumpkin *sopa,*" the man said.

"You know the owner?"

"I certainly hope so, or I'm getting senile faster than I

thought. I'm Martin Petersen, and this is my snack." He held up the bags of produce. "I'd shake your hand, but..."

"Oh, here, let me help."

"Masha danki," Martin said, pressing both sacks to Boone's chest, then walking past him once Boone took them. "Come around back. I'll show you the secret entrance."

It turned out the "secret entrance" was just the back door to the kitchen. Martin pointed to some wooden crates on a low bench; one was empty and the other contained two lonely onions.

"Put the bags in the crates they belong in. If you get it right, I'll let you taste the soup."

Boone laughed, dropping the onion bag with its counterparts and the potatoes in the other.

"Well done. You get some *sopa*." Martin gave the stock pot a stir, then ladled some of the thick soup into a bowl and set it on a counter beside Boone. "Grab yourself a spoon," he said, pointing.

Boone picked up the bowl. "*Danki*. You want me to go outside with it?"

"Why would I want that? Then I'd have to shout. And who knows, I might need those crazy long arms of yours to reach something from the top shelves." He gave Boone a wink, then whistled. "You're a tall one, you are. Looking up at you, I'd guess you were Dutch, but you sure don't sound like it."

"No, I'm American. But... well, I've got some Dutch on my father's side."

"Well, Dutchy, you going to taste my soup, or you just warming your hands with it?"

Boone dipped the spoon in and tried some. It was spectacular, with a creamy consistency like split pea soup, a smoky flavor from what he guessed was added meat, and a great combination of spices. "This is amazing! A little sweet, a little heat."

"The heat's the Madame Jeanette peppers I put in."

"It's delicious." Boone held the bowl in one hand and extended the other. "Boone Fischer."

Martin shook his hand. "Fischer... yeah, that's a Dutch name, all right. What you doing all the way up in Rincon, Dutchy?"

"Actually, I'm looking for somewhere to live. I'm going to be working at a new dive shop, Rock Beauty Divers."

"Oh, yeah... they're the one by the Zhung Kong market." Martin pointed at the potatoes and onions. "Got those from there yesterday, but forgot them in my house. I live across the road."

"So, you know the area?"

Martin laughed. "Oh, I'd say so. Been living in Rincon for near seventy years. My ancestors been here since the Dutch brought them here as slaves to work the salt pans. And my grandfather worked as a day laborer in the two plantations that became Washington-Slagbaai Park. So, young man, I know the area very, very well." He took Boone's bowl out of his hands and set it down. "Come."

Boone followed him out of the kitchen and around to the front of the snack. Stepping into the street, Martin pointed to the left. "See that street over there? That's Kaya Mango. Hang a left, go up the street toward the cemetery... third house on the right is for rent. I know the owners. You like what you see, come back here and we'll call them. And then you can buy a big lunch. You're too skinny for your height, Dutchy."

Back at Rock Beauty Divers, Boone went looking for Thomas Dupont, but there was no one in the office. He saw the *Kleine Dancer* tied up at the pier and there were three people unloading tanks from her. *Well, might as well get started,* Boone thought, as he walked toward the dive boat.

A deeply tanned brunette woman with a ball cap and a Rock Beauty Divers T-shirt called out to him. "You looking for Frenchy?"

"Who?"

"Thomas."

"Oh, that's the accent I heard," Boone said as he reached her. "I wondered if he was French."

"He's not."

"Uh..."

"He's Belgian."

"Then... shouldn't it be Belgy?"

A hearty laugh came from the boat and a bearded man, also wearing a Rock Beauty shirt, stepped to the gunwale.

"You the new guy?"

"Yeah."

The brunette rolled her eyes at him. "We're *all* new, Butch."

"New*est* guy, then."

"Yeah, that'd be me. Boone Fischer."

Pleased to meetcha, Boone," Butch boomed. "I'm Barry... but you can call me Butch." He jerked a thumb back at a man with deeply tanned skin. Unlike the others, he wasn't wearing a crew shirt. "This is Ernesto. He's been captaining for us a few times a week."

Ernesto nodded his head in greeting, then went back to work. The brunette offered a hand and shook with Boone. He was impressed with her grip, and his eyes were drawn to the tattoo of an octopus on the back of her hand, its tentacles twining around her fingers.

"Sidney." She held up her hand and showed off her ink. "And this is Inky. Get it?"

Boone laughed. "Nice. So, what's with Thomas's nickname? I assume it's 'cause he sounds French?"

"You'd think that, but… no. Hang on, Ernesto has to get going, so we need to divvy up the tips. We had American divers, and they were pretty generous."

Boone nodded. While tipping was common and expected in the US, in many parts of the world it was not. There had been many occasions in Curaçao where European divers had not tipped at all; that would be fine if divemasters were well paid, but they generally weren't.

While the crew attended to the tip distribution, Boone eyed the scuba tanks. There were only eight empties and it was the afternoon—which usually meant a single dive—so he figured there had only been six divers aboard. He started shuttling the tanks to the shop, then met Barry and Sidney back at the boat while Ernesto jogged past, heading toward the nearby parking lot.

"He works the dinner shift at Eddy's," Sidney explained. "Damn good cook."

"All right, about Frenchy…" Butch began. "So… this is a Dutch island, right? And Belgium is right by the Netherlands, yeah? First week we're here, some guy from California hears Thomas's accent and asks him where he's from. He says 'Belgium' and this guy makes the mistake of saying 'Oh, so you're practically Dutch.'"

Sidney burst into laughter. "Big mistake. Thomas turns red and starts berating the poor guy, explaining that he's Walloon, and going into this whole diatribe about Flemish Belgians, who live next to the Netherlands, versus Walloon Belgians, who live next to France, and that if anything, he's closer to French."

"It was obviously a sore spot for him," Butch said with a sly smile. "So, naturally, we sunk our teeth into that weakness and started calling him Frenchy the Belgian."

"To his face?" Boone asked.

"Of course!" Butch replied. "Doing it behind his back would be just plain mean. Hey, where you from, Boone?"

"Tennessee by way of Curaçao."

Butch slapped his ample chest. "Nebraska by way of The Bahamas."

"Minnesota," Sidney said. "By way of Minnesota. This is my first divemaster gig."

"Frenchy will be back pretty soon," Butch said. "He ran the divers back to their hotel. Hey, did you find a place to live?"

"As a matter of fact, I did."

TWENTY-FOUR

Two weeks later, Boone was fully moved in. His little house was perfect, and it had the added benefit of a built-in biological alarm clock—or "alarm cock," as Boone started to call him. "King Cock" was the neighborhood rooster, and his idea of dawn was about two hours earlier than Boone's.

At Rock Beauty Divers, Boone quickly got into the groove. He ended up doing a lot more work there than at any individual place he'd worked for in Curaçao, but even with all of the divemastering, certifying new divers, maintenance, and even painting the entire dive shop, Boone found the overall vibe on Bonaire to be far more relaxed.

Gone were the hours spent navigating through Willemstad or driving to distant shore dive sites. Here, he woke up and cycled to work. Then he'd dive two or three dives, put away the gear, and go home.

Shore diving was just as popular in Bonaire as in Curaçao—perhaps, even more so—but working for Rock Beauty, Boone divemastered almost exclusively from the dive boat *Kleine Dancer.*

Once he was in the swing of things, Boone started to go out with the other divemasters to various restaurants in the main town of Kralendijk, as well as hitting up some of the live music at Eddy's, Oscar's Lighthouse, or occasional concerts of local music at the Arawak complex on the "wild side" of Bonaire, not far from Rincon.

Next door to the Arawak was a "land-sailing" racetrack, and Boone availed himself of that a few times, although he had much more fun trying out the windsurfing on Lac Bay in the south. Also operating out of Lac Bay was a unique dive op called East Coast Diving. Boone enjoyed doing some "extracurricular" dives when he was on his own time. These were usually shore dives, but when he heard about the diving on "the wild side," he signed up for a two-tank trip with East Coast. Sidney joined him.

Operating a custom Zodiac dive boat from the piers in Sorobon, the dive op took them into some very choppy water. Mooring was impossible there, so these were exclusively drift dives. Divers were advised not to linger on the surface for too long, unless they wanted to get seasick. Beneath the waves, the sea fans and other soft corals were pitching from side to side, but once the dive group descended along the sloping reef, things calmed down. The site "Turtle City" earned its name, with more hawksbill and green turtles than Boone had ever seen in one place.

Back on land, Boone joined Sidney at her truck and the two of them ditched their wetsuits for shorts and tees. As Boone changed, Sidney gave him a look, raising an eyebrow.

"What?"

"For a skinny guy, you are *ripped*. What's your secret?"

Boone shrugged as he pulled on a T-shirt with the Scuba Dooby Do logo on it. Boone had learned that Sidney preferred women, so he knew she wasn't hitting on him. And truth be told, he felt like he was in the best shape of his life. "I dunno. Diving and hauling scuba tanks all the time probably has something to do with it."

Sidney shook her head. "Nope. I do the same thing. That's not it."

"Well... I do a lot of biking, hiking, yoga... a little rock climbing in Washington-Slagbaai. And capoeira."

"Cap-a-what now?"

"It's a martial art from Brazil. Gets the blood pumping, that's for sure. I practice every morning, but I haven't found anyone to spar with here."

"Wait a minute... is that the thing where you jump around and spin and kick a lot? Somersaults and handstands and all that?"

Boone laughed. "Sounds about right."

"Get in the truck."

***

"I was getting some lionfish tacos at the Cactus Blue food truck down on Donkey Beach," Sidney explained. "Over by the Corporal Meiss dive site?"

"Been there. Delicious."

"Right? Anyway, I'm sitting on a rock, stuffing my face in the shade of that huge divi-divi tree, when I see these two guys fighting. Except... it looked less like a fight and more like a dance. Pretty sure it was that thing you said. They came over to the food truck for some fruit juice afterwards and I talked to them. One of them was a cook at that Brazilian restaurant in

Kralendijk. The one around the corner from Fort Oranje and the cruise piers?"

Boone smiled and checked his watch. "I could eat."

The restaurant wasn't open yet, so they killed a little time in the shops in Kralendijk. An hour later, they were seated at a table with caipirinha cocktails in hand and Sidney asked the waiter if they could talk to the "capoeira cook." The waiter laughed.

"That would be Lucas. It's still early... I'll grab him now before it gets busy."

A few minutes later, a tanned young man with hair cropped close to his scalp came out of the kitchen. He had a grin on his face. "Capoeira cook... I like that!" He took one look at Boone and pointed at him. "You want to spar."

"I do. How'd you know?"

"I saw you practicing one morning on Te Amo beach."

"Wish you'd come and said hello," Boone said.

"I would have, but I was on my way to pick up my brother at the airport." After they all introduced themselves, Lucas asked, "What is your style? Regional? Angola? Contemporânea?"

"I didn't have any formal schooling, so... probably a little of each."

A group of customers entered the dining area and Lucas signaled the waiter. "Listen, I need to get back to the grill, but I would very much like to spar if our schedules permit." He called out to the waiter as he started back to the kitchen, "Andre, I have no pen; give them my number, would you?"

"Well, that worked out well," Sidney said.

"You wanna join me?"

"Do I have to get kicked in the face or anything?"

"Not if you do it right."

"Um... pass. But you boys have fun."

It turned out that Lucas was an exceptional sparring partner. Once or twice a week, they'd work out in a flat area near the parking lot by the Harbour Village Marina. If Boone got an early enough start, they might head to one of the beaches near the airport.

Lucas was *fast*; much faster than Boone. Boone's long arms and legs gave him an advantage in reach, but the young Brazilian's speed was uncanny. Back in Miami, Boone had won most of his sparring matches with his friends from Barbados, but against Lucas, it took every ounce of energy and focus he could muster just to keep up. For every match Boone won, he lost two. Though it wasn't really about winning or losing and there wasn't a referee standing there handing out points... when you'd been beaten, you knew.

One day, Lucas showed him some strategies for one of the most famous kicks in capoeira, the *meia-lua de compasso*, or compass crescent. Known as the "king of kicks," the maneuver was extremely difficult to master, requiring the capoeirista to turn his back on his opponent for a brief second as he spun and dipped his head and torso down, acquired the target by looking back through his legs, then planted one foot and whipped the other in a high arc as the spin was completed.

The momentum this kick achieved was extreme, sending the kicker's heel crashing into the opponent's head. Or at least, that was the idea. Getting it to connect required a great deal of precision. Boone was already quite good at the compass crescent kick. In the dusty backyard of his little Rincon home, he would occasionally hang gallon jugs of sand from the sturdy branches of a gumbo limbo tree, using them as targets. But a jug of sand wasn't the same as an opposing fighter who didn't fancy the idea of taking a foot to the face.

"You need to think of the *meia-lua* as a combination sequence," Lucas explained. "Yes, your opponent may very well dodge or block such a bold move... so you let that happen and continue the spin. Continue the attack. And count on the second kick to do the deed."

"Well, yeah... I often do several in a row..."

"Yes, but focus your *intent* that the second one is your true attack. Use the first to get your opponent to commit to a defensive move, then strike with your follow-on before he can reset. And you can vary the target of the second strike. If you go for the head with the first, you can aim the following one for the ribs."

In addition to his weekly sparring with Lucas, Boone engaged in near-daily sparring with Martin Petersen, albeit of a friendly and verbal variety. The old man had taken a shine to Boone and schooled the young man in *krioyo* cooking. Boone had enjoyed local Creole food in Curaçao, and he thought Martin's was as good as any he'd had.

"Seriously, Martin, you could open up a swanky restaurant down in Kralendijk with cooking like this."

"Why would I want to do that, Dutchy? Here, I can roll out of bed, brush my teeth, and cross the street to the kitchen. This snack of mine... it may not be a fancy restaurant, but for me, it's like cooking at home. Now, cut up that green papaya. Gonna use it in the *kabritu stoba*."

Boone often found himself wrangled into helping in the kitchen with the old man razzing him much of the time. Often, the teasing dealt with Boone's height or build.

"I swear, you don't put some meat on your bones, you going to blow away with the trade winds."

"Tell you what... you want me to eat more, then make those breakfast *pastechi* I asked for."

"Check the cooler."

Boone looked and found a drawer of uncooked pastechi wrapped in parchment paper. "You made them?"

"All they need is a dip in the fryer. I filled them with eggs, cheese, and a little chorizo. I'll fry some up tomorrow morning, so tell your divemaster friends."

"Will do!"

The pastechi was an Antillean version of an empanada, and Martin had made only three varieties: beef, chicken, and cheese. But Boone had first talked the old man into creating a vegetarian version with some of the ingredients from his spicy pumpkin soup. When that proved popular, he had urged Martin to make something portable and breakfast-y for early risers on the go, and had recommended the creation of a "breakfast pastechi."

"You better eat two or three, skinny Dutchy."

"Martin, you're skinnier than me!"

"True. But I compensate with my big personality. You? Well... you better eat more." He took a spoon and stirred the goat stew. Stifling a grin, he added, "You look like a cactus fence post."

Boone laughed. "Hey, you have any orders to make a new cactus fence?"

"You still want to help build one? Building a *kura di yatu* is hot and prickly work."

Cactus fences were a common sight on Bonaire, particularly in the rural areas. The island had large numbers of wild donkeys and goats and these fences were often used to protect plants or livestock, although they were equally effective at keeping out trespassers of the human variety. Using straight "posts" of the local species of Yatu cactus, the plant was threaded into a framework of wire netting using a pair of carved sticks—one curved, one forked—to maneuver the spiny components into place. The cut Yatu would take root quickly and most fences would last longer than the person who made them. Martin was one of the few locals on the island who still built them the traditional way, claiming to have learned the method from his grandfather.

"Yeah, next time you build one, bring me along."

"Well, okay... but you'll have to make your own *Chi ku Cha*."

Boone smiled. Martin had a way of forcing him to learn Papiamentu. "The sticks, right?"

Martin nodded as he dug through some spices for the stew. "Chi is the female stick and Cha is the male. I'll show you where to get the wood to make them. I don't like other people touching mine. My *Chi ku Cha* came from my father, God rest his soul, and they belong to the family."

"Fair enough."

Martin was about to shake some allspice berries into a mortar and pestle, but he paused. "What about your family? You don't ever mention them. What do they think of you being down here?"

"Well... I guess... short answer is, my mother isn't too pleased I'm in these islands and my father... well, I have no idea *what* he thinks. I haven't talked to him since I was eleven."

"Why for?"

Boone sighed. "Well, the answer to that question is the same as why my mom would probably prefer if I were somewhere else. He cheated on her in Aruba." Boone stopped slicing the green papaya to avoid slicing off a fingertip. "They met in

Aruba one year... had me... got married in Aruba the next summer... and then..." Boone trailed off.

"Then he cheated on her... what... ten or eleven years later?"

Boone snorted a scornful laugh. "I suspect he cheated on a lot of women for a long, *long* time. That last one was just the one where Mom caught him." He picked up the knife again, put it down. "He was in the Dutch Navy. That's why he wasn't around most of the time. Of course, that was likely bullshit, too."

"You hate him?"

Boone looked Martin in the eyes. "I think I did. But now... I hardly think of him."

Martin sucked his teeth and shook his head as he went back to his own chopping and dicing. "Dutchy, you don't need to be honest with me, but at least be honest with yourself."

Later that night, back in his house on Kaya Mango, Boone dug through his belongings to look for the rock with the painted eye that he'd been awarded for learning to swim. At first, he was strangely pleased when he couldn't find it, but an hour later he rose from his bed and searched for it again. Finally, he gave up and went to sleep.

TWENTY-FIVE

By the summer of 2016, Boone had dived nearly every dive site in Bonaire. Visiting divers often asked him which site was his favorite and he found his answer changed from month to month. Currently, he would give his vote to Karpata, a northern site not far from the border of the Washington-Slagbaai park.

Bonaire's waters weren't known for having many large animals, so Boone became quite adept at spotting smaller critters for his divers, keeping an eye out for frogfish, seahorses, and especially nudibranchs, a group of soft-bodied mollusks. Despite being brightly colored, "nudies" were very hard to spot, given how tiny they were.

Another creature Boone liked to look for was the shame-faced crab, a small crustacean that held its claws flush against its mouth in such a way that it appeared to "hide" its face. A local naturalist, Jerry Ligon, had told Boone about them, and about how the shame-faced crabs would often pair up with a small peacock flounder in a symbiotic relationship. Tragically, Jerry had passed away the previous year. Another recent loss for Bonaire was Captain Don Stewart, who had weighed anchor in 2014 while Boone was in Curaçao.

On Friday, August 19, Boone took a group of three divers—a husband and wife and their teenage son—on a night dive on the house reef for the Hamlet Oasis, "Cliff." Frenchy the Belgian joined them, which was a rare occurrence. Returning to the shore, as they rinsed their gear in the glow of the dock lights, the family recalled with excitement all of the sights they had seen. The son had never night-dived before, and was the most vocal.

"I want to do a dive like that every night we're here!" the teenager declared.

"Well, if you thought that was *magnifique*, then you should see the ostracods," Frenchy suggested.

"Oh, yeah, if you can, you should!" Boone chimed in. "And the full moon was yesterday. How long are you staying?"

"Another week," the teen's father answered.

"Perfect," Boone said.

"Wait, what are ostracods?" the teenager asked.

"They are tiny crustaceans, no larger than a millimeter," Frenchy explained. "They spawn several days after a full moon —I have found that five days is best, but it can vary."

"This happens forty to forty-five minutes after sunset," Boone said. "And those little buggers put on a magical light-show like nothing you've ever seen. They use a form of bioluminescence."

"Like fireflies?" the mother asked.

"Yep."

"Can we do it, Dad?" the kid pleaded.

"Sure. Boat dive? Shore?"

"I prefer from the shore," Frenchy said. "But not here. Too much light. Gather by the shop next Tuesday an hour before sunset and we will drive north." He turned to Boone. "And text Sidney and Butch to check their schedules. If they are free, they will want to join us."

The following Tuesday, the visiting divers piled into Frenchy's SUV and Butch's Jeep and the two vehicles traveled north with Frenchy in the lead. He turned toward the coast, passing the STINAPA headquarters and the Oil Slick dive site, then turned onto the "tourist's road" that ran along the coast as the sun dipped toward the horizon. Ahead, there wasn't a streetlight in sight.

"I want to take us to Jeff Davis Memorial," Frenchy said. "But if there are already cars there, I may go farther to Weber's Joy or 1,000 Steps. But after that, the road becomes one way, and we'd be stuck on a long, long drive, all the way to Rincon and back to town from there."

Fortunately, the parking lot for Jeff Davis was empty and they pulled in and brought their gear across the road and down to the water. A rough, stone platform with some steps that were just managing to maintain their purpose led down to a shore composed of jumbled chunks of coral and rocks.

"Watch your step," Sidney warned. "Turned my ankle first week I was here."

"And I had to pick up your slack," Butch teased.

"Sundown is at 6:48," Frenchy said. "If we are in the water by then, we will have plenty of time to make our way to the reef."

"There's no rush," Boone emphasized. "They start their performance at ten minutes before nautical twilight. Which I had to look up, of course," he added with a laugh. "It's 7:35. But they may start a little early, so we'll try to be in position fifteen minutes before that. At about thirty feet, we'll level off. Take your time to get your buoyancy just right. Once the event begins, I guarantee that lightshow is all you'll be thinking about."

"And here's the most important thing," Sidney stressed. "No lights, unless absolutely necessary. We'll use them getting in, but once we're on approach to the reef, we'll go dark and let our eyes adjust. And once we're in place at about thirty feet of depth, don't even light up your gauges if you can help it."

"Obviously, if anyone has any problems, that takes priority," Boone said. "But the current has been minimal, and we'll be at thirty feet, so everyone will have plenty of air."

"Keep your eyes on the gorgonians," Frenchy said. "You might know them as sea fans. The ostracods often cluster near those."

Frenchy set a single green glowstick on the top of the steps, to give them a reference point when they returned: when the dive was over, it would be pitch black on the shore. The Belgian then informed the group that Boone would lead the dive. Once everyone was geared up, they gathered in the shallows, then made their way to the reef as the sun set.

Even without dive lights, the corals were visible. The divers got into position and Boone assessed the buoyancy of the family; everyone seemed to be hovering in a good spot. He looked at the dim glow of his Aquinus dive watch before pulling his wetsuit sleeve over it. *Ten minutes or so until showtime.*

Ten minutes of simply waiting for something to happen—without light, without clocks—could seem like an eternity. Boone had joined Sidney and Butch for an ostracod dive shortly after he had arrived in Bonaire, and he remembered the wait.

He also remembered that at some point, he thought they might be punking him, and that this might be the marine version of a snipe hunt. Hazing the new guy. But then, the lights had started up. Just as they did now.

It began with a glow here, a glow there... infrequent enough that an observer might wonder if they were just seeing what their mind wanted them to see. But then, the tiny pinpoints of light began to resolve into vertical strings of embers, floating amongst the gorgonians. Within a minute, Boone's entire field of vision was filled with dotted lines of ethereal phosphorescence, creating an otherworldly sight unlike anything Boone had ever experienced. It was almost like finding oneself on the inside of a Christmas tree, festooned with fairy lights.

The light show lasted for almost half an hour, although time had lost much of its meaning when the last of the sparks of light faded into darkness. Boone waited a full minute before turning on his light. He raised a hand in an "OK" sign and illuminated it, then swept it from side to side. Dive lights ignited all around him as everyone lit up, returning the signal, indicating that everyone was good. The teenager's "OK" sign pumped forward and back, indicating he was more than okay, he was stoked!

The group had agreed to continue with a leisurely night dive for another twenty minutes or so, and they continued against the current, spotting a free-swimming moray and an octopus out and about. And then, like in so many night dives in Bonaire, a huge tarpon showed up, hoping to munch on any hapless creature that might be illuminated in a dive light for too long. Boone decided this newcomer's arrival was as good a reason as any to end the dive and start back toward shore. As they reached the shallows, the green glowstick was just visible.

Once on shore, the divers burst into exuberant descriptions

of their experience. Boone smiled and looked up at the night sky, lit with its own pinpoints of light. This far from manmade light sources, the Milky Way traced a wide swath across the sky. And then... a shooting star. The last remnants of that year's Perseid meteor shower made an appearance.

Couldn't ask for a more perfect night.

TWENTY-SIX

Boone decided that he'd like to end this perfect night with a visit to Martin's snack. Grab an ice-cold beer, maybe a pastechi or three. If some of the neighbors were there playing All Fours, he might join them. The old English card game was particularly popular in Trinidad and Tobago and had found its way to Bonaire. It had a lot of rules, but Boone thought he was getting the hang of it.

After rinsing the gear, stowing the tanks, and helping Frenchy close up the shop, he bade the others good night, switched on his bicycle headlight, and began the twenty-minute ride to Rincon. While cycling along the back road, his headlight and the stars overhead were the only illumination for much of the trip.

As he arrived near the little crossroads by the snack, he could hear music playing. Boone had upgraded Martin's old boombox—which had an actual cassette player in it—with a pair of Bluetooth speakers, and had showed the old man how to sync them to his phone. As he drew closer, he heard another sound: raised voices. And not the happy, celebratory kind. The smash of a bottle breaking spurred Boone to pedal faster.

As he turned the corner, the courtyard came into view. A local woman Boone recognized from a nearby street was sitting at a table, weeping. Standing beside the table was a man Boone had seen before, often drunk. He was ranting and raving, with most of his aggression raining down on the woman. Martin was standing a few feet away, arms outstretched, playing the peacemaker, trying to calm the man down without raising his voice. Boone noticed a broken beer bottle at Martin's feet, the shards of glass still glistening from the beer.

Boone coasted his bike to a stop, letting it fall against the low border wall as he quickly approached. For a brief instant he debated ditching his athletic shoes—he always fought better barefoot—but the broken glass decided him against it. He was now close enough to see the man's eyes, and it was instantly clear that he was under the influence of more than a beer. The man's fast, twitching gaze flicked between the woman and Martin.

It happened fast. The raving lunatic stepped into Martin and shoved him hard, sending the skinny old man sprawling on the ground, where he cried out as he landed in the remnants of the beer bottle. Boone felt a surge of rage and his vision seemed to tunnel in on the attacker. He ran to the courtyard just as the man brought a folding knife from his side. He snapped it into place, but when he stepped forward with the blade, he found a tall, lanky young man standing in his way.

Boone instinctively went into a *ginga* step, which seemed to confuse the knife-wielder for a second, but then the man came for him. Boone acted without thought. Dodging to the side as the man stabbed, Boone crouched and spun rapidly, snapping a *meia-lua de compasso* kick, intending to drive him back. He planned to continue the spin into a leg sweep, and once he had the attacker down, he could lock him up in a jiu-jitsu hold.

But the man didn't make any effort to block or evade the kick. The heel of Boone's foot slammed into the side of his temple, and he went limp, the knife falling from his hands as the force of the kick sent him into a table and chairs beside the restaurant. The cheap patio furniture upended, and he crumpled into a heap, unconscious or worse.

The woman, who had been sitting in shock, with tears running down her face, cried out and went down on her knees beside the fallen man. Boone mirrored the motion, crouching beside Martin.

"Are you all right? You're bleeding!"

The old man looked at his palm and forearm and sucked his teeth, dismissing the wound. "Just broken glass. Done worse in the kitchen with my knives."

Boone turned and picked up the man's knife. He was about to hurl it up onto the roof, but instead tossed it through the open door into the snack. The surge of adrenaline and anger was fading, and he realized the knife might be needed as evidence.

"You killed him!"

"I don't think I did," Boone said, although he wasn't completely certain. He rose and went over to them.

"Don't touch him!"

"I know first aid, ma'am... please let me check him."

She moved aside and sat in the sand as Boone checked the man's vitals. He was breathing but his pulse seemed weak.

"He's alive."

"Oh, *danki Dios*," she gasped. "Maurice is *mi dushi*... my sweetheart."

"Listen, is Maurice on something?"

She nodded her head reluctantly. "I don't know what."

"Uh, Martin..."

"Police and ambulance," the old man grunted as he struggled to his feet and took his phone from his pocket. Overhead, the speakers continued to pump out a tropical beat, but the night went silent as Martin tapped his screen, killing the music.

"And can you get me a bag of frozen peas and a dish towel?" Boone requested. "Pretty sure I gave this guy a concussion."

Twenty minutes later, a patrol car from the Dutch Caribbean Police Force arrived. This was a surprisingly fast response time, so Boone figured they must have already been nearby. Two officers got out. One attended to the still-unconscious attacker, cuffing him just in case. Martin had explained what had happened, and if the man was on some form of drug that was causing psychotic behavior, the officers didn't want to take any chances.

The younger of the two policemen, a constable, approached Martin and Boone. "Ambulance is ten minutes away," he said, sizing up Boone, then taking out a pad and applying the tip of a pen to it. After he took Boone's name and information, he asked, "You the one who hit him?"

"Yes, sir."

"What you hit him with?"

"My foot."

The constable looked up from his pad. "You kicked him?"

"Yes, sir."

"You kicked him a half hour ago, and he still out? Must've kicked him pretty hard."

"I didn't intend to... but I'm pretty sure I connected with his temple, which is a vulnerable spot." Boone sighed. "I should have tried to disarm him, but I wasn't thinking too clearly."

"Lucky you didn't kill him."

If I'd been barefoot—hit him with a naked heel—I might well have, Boone thought. His athletic shoe had likely softened the impact.

Martin looked at the man's badge. "Constable... Winklaar. You related to James Winklaar? Owns the barbershop?"

"Yes, that's my uncle."

"Oh, yeah, your cousin is a policeman, too!" Martin said. "Listen, constable... Boone probably saved my life. Maurice has got a temper when he's just plain drunk. And he was more than drunk."

"Drugs."

"Sure seemed like it," Boone said. "And his girlfriend implied he was on something."

"Martin, you told the dispatcher there was a knife..."

"Boone threw it into the store after the fight. I didn't touch it, so it's in there somewhere."

The ambulance arrived and Maurice was placed on a collapsible stretcher. The woman climbed in with one of the paramedics, who closed the rear doors. Constable Winklaar asked Boone and Martin a few more questions, then placed his pad in his pocket.

"The girlfriend confirmed your statements, by the way. I'd like you both to come by the station tomorrow. We may have more questions."

"Hey, uh... Constable. You have my number." He gestured toward the departing ambulance. "If you find out how he's doing, will you text me?"

Winklaar nodded and he and his partner left. Boone stood in the dirt road, listening to the sounds of the night.

"You want a beer?" Martin asked.

"Not really."

"I'm having a beer. Have a beer."

"Okay."

Martin went to the door, flipping the sign in the window to CLOSED. Boone righted the tables and chairs, then went inside for a dustpan and broom. He was sweeping up the broken glass when Martin came back with two ice-cold Polars. "The glass'll keep. Sit down."

Boone set the glass-filled dustpan aside, then joined Martin at a table. The old man pressed a bottle into Boone's hand and then clinked it with his own. They drank in silence for a time, then Boone spoke.

"I coulda killed that guy, Martin."

"He coulda killed *me*."

"I wouldn't have let that happen." Boone shook his head. "I should've done things differently."

"Once the goat is out, don't stand there wishing for a fence. Go get the damn goat."

Boone's beer paused on its way to his lips. "I thought the fences were to keep the goats *out*."

"Well, *now* they are, most of the time. But that was something my grandfather used to say. Back then, a lot of people kept goats for the stew pot."

Boone took a sip, set his beer down. Stared at the bottle. "How's your hand and arm?" he finally asked.

"Fine." The old man looked at the bandages the paramedic had put on, focusing on his palm. "Not the most convenient place for a cut."

Boone's phone dinged and he dug it out of a pocket to look at the text, then set the phone down on the table

"What?" Martin asked.

"Skull fracture."

"Oh." After a few more minutes sipping beers in silence, Martin said, "You are a good person, Boone Fischer." When Boone didn't reply, the old man got up and went inside the snack, returning with another pair of beers.

"Martin, I don't think I need another."

"Oh, I think you do. Besides, you got the day off tomorrow."

"I do? Oh... right. I do."

"All that talk of fences and goats got me thinking... you carve your fence-making sticks? Your *Chi ku Cha?*

"Yeah. Did 'em like you told me."

"You still want to help with a cactus fence?"

"We're supposed to go to the police station."

"I know. I need a roll of wire from town anyway. Police first, fence after."

"You've got a bandage on your palm."

"That's why I need a second set of hands."

Boone thought for a moment. "Maybe. Tell you what—let me sleep on it. When that damn rooster wakes the neighborhood at King Cock o'clock, I'll text you."

"Fair." Martin slid one of the beers toward Boone and clinked it with his. "You do that crazy glowing shrimp dive you was telling me about?"

Boone smiled. "Ostracods. It was amazing. "I've done four of those dives now and it's just as breathtaking every single time."

Martin smiled and sat back in his chair. "Why don't you tell me about it?"

TWENTY-SEVEN

Boone managed to sleep better than expected, probably due to the adrenaline of an intense day followed by a two-beer chaser. When King Cock announced his importance to the pre-dawn morning, Boone simply texted Martin: "I'm in."

The visit to the police station was uneventful and brief. Maurice was stable and the swelling was under control. The drug tests hadn't yet come back but doctors suspected methamphetamine. After a brief stop at the Kooyman building materials store, Martin got into the truck and slapped a pair of work gloves against Boone's chest.

"These are the biggest they had. Hope they fit."

They drove northwest along the backside of Bonaire toward Rincon. At one point, Martin pulled over to the side and grabbed a trash bag from the back of the cab. "Help me pick up these plastic bottles and cans."

Boone stepped out and assisted with the impromptu roadside cleanup. Like many places in the world, Bonaire had its share of litterbugs. "This is cool of you, Martin. You carry a trash bag around for this?"

The old man grinned. "I need this junk for something."

"For the fence?"

"No, you *lolo*, for something else. You'll see."

Back in Rincon, they took one of the dirt roads that left the north side of town and ran into the scraggly scrub on the way to the coast. Halfway there, Martin turned off on a dirt track that was far rougher than any Boone had been on before.

"This is where we harvest the Yatu," Martin said, pulling over to the side of the road and backing his truck into the scrub. He pointed to an area that was thick with tall pillars of cactus. "Grab a machete and your sticks. I'll line the cargo bed with the tarp."

An hour later, they had the cargo bed loaded with Yatu cactus segments, cut to about five feet in length. Boone had done most of the cutting and he and Martin had used their *Chi ku Cha* to place them on the tarp. Back in the truck, they bounced and jounced their way back to the road and Martin continued along it to another dirt track that led into the brush.

"This is my friend's ranch. He asked me to build a small fence for some produce he wants to grow."

After backing the truck up to the area they'd be working in, Martin and Boone dragged the tarp onto the ground from the cargo bed, cactus and all. Once they had the wire fencing up, the segments of Yatu were inserted, half angled in, half angled out, with each cactus leaning in toward the top in an alternating pattern. The Y-shaped stick was placed against the cactus and the curved stick was looped around and held against the Y, acting much like a set of fireplace tongs.

The day was hot, and the two of them went through a lot of water, but once Boone got the hang of the procedure, the work went quickly. Thanks to the special sticks and the work gloves, he was surprised to find that he had very few pricks by the end of it.

"Okay! That's done," Martin announced. He looked up at the sky. "And it's not too late... go get the trash bag and the backpack that's under my seat."

Boone did so, then followed Martin into a remote area of the property. They came to a series of posts in the ground, at which point Martin beckoned to Boone to bring the trash bag over. He took a plastic bottle out and stooped, digging the mouth of it in the sand until it was about a third full, then placed it on a post.

"The wind'll blow them over if you don't weight them. Fill some up and put 'em on the posts."

"What are we doing?"

"You'll see soon enough."

Boone already had a sneaking suspicion, and when Martin opened the backpack, it was confirmed. Inside were two blocky handguns and several magazines. Boone wasn't sure what exact model these were, but he'd seen plenty of Glocks before at the shooting range in Kingston.

"Martin... are you telling me you took two loaded handguns to a police station parking lot?"

"They aren't loaded yet. Besides, the police weren't going to come out and question my truck."

Bonaire had extremely strict gun laws, and he suspected these weren't licensed. "Why on earth do you have these?"

"A few years ago, I had a problem with some gang members hassling me." Martin walked back toward a large, flat rock and set the backpack down on it. "Well, I say 'gang,' but it was more like a bunch of kids who didn't have nothin' better to do. Friend of mine sold me these. Turned out I never needed 'em.

Police sorted those kids out so these have been sitting in a drawer."

Martin loaded each pistol with a magazine and set them gently on the rock. "Last night... well, I suppose seeing a knife pointed in my direction reminded me I had these. You shoot?"

"A little. Been a while."

"Well... help me blow holes in these plastic bottles. They been giving me the evil eye."

Boone didn't mention his run-in at the snack to his fellow divemasters, and he certainly didn't mention Martin's illicit firearms. Back at work the next day, he was eager to stick a reg in his mouth and let the ocean wash away thoughts of the fight: the feel of his heel striking the side of Maurice's head... the image of the man going boneless and crashing to the ground... the fear that he might be dead. Boone skipped his capoeira workout for obvious reasons, telling his sparring mate Lucas that he was taking a short hiatus.

The weeks passed, and life settled back into a routine, although that routine was interrupted in late September, when a tropical storm began to brew to the east. Aruba, Bonaire, and Curaçao were outside of the "hurricane belt," and storms were very infrequent, but this one looked like it was headed their way. On September 28, a tropical storm watch was issued for Bonaire and residents were advised to board up and stock up. There were long lines at supermarkets and gas stations, reminding Boone of how it sometimes got in Tennessee when there was a chance of an inch of snow in the forecast. Next door in Curaçao, the government went so far as to postpone an upcoming election.

Boone offered to help Martin board up the snack, but the old man had waved away the offer, insisting it wouldn't amount to anything. Rincon was far from the coast and the most he planned to do was bring in the chairs, tables, and Boone's fancy speakers.

At Rock Beauty Divers there was plenty to do. The shop didn't yet have shutters, so Boone, Sidney, and Butch helped Frenchy put up some plywood. The winds weren't expected to be catastrophic, and the storm would likely be on the north side of the island, so they decided against bringing the boat in, leaving it at the offshore mooring.

The following day, preparations were complete. Frenchy lived nearby in a sturdy house and offered to have everyone over for dinner and a game of poker while they waited out the storm. If the power went out for an extended period, Frenchy might lose the lobster tails he'd been saving in the freezer, so best to go ahead and enjoy them now. By the late afternoon, Matthew was a strong tropical storm, but was on course to pass by the ABC Islands to their north. Nevertheless, the prospect of hunkering down with good food, good drinks, and good friends was too tempting to pass up, even if everyone would likely be perfectly safe in their own beds.

After a delicious meal of Caribbean lobster and steaks, the group gathered around a table and played poker. While money was collected and chips distributed, Boone sized everyone up. Frenchy bragged about how much he had won playing black-jack in the casino in the Divi Flamingo, and Butch claimed he was the poker king in college. Sidney smiled quietly as she arranged her cards. *She'll be the one to watch out for,* Boone thought.

Unfortunately for everyone else at the table, Boone had an uncanny knack for reading people, and if a player bluffed or was holding a high hand, he'd know it nine times out of ten. He wasn't familiar with all the rules of some of the fancy variations some tables liked to dabble in, but if it was five-card draw, seven-card stud, or Texas hold 'em, Boone would always walk away richer than when he sat down.

At about nine o'clock, when the winds were at their peak and Boone was dragging yet another pile of chips from the center of the table to the piles in front of him, Frenchy the Belgian had had enough.

"*Mon dieu!* I swear, Boone Fischer... you must consort with dark powers. I have never seen you fall for a bluff! Not once."

Boone smiled. "Sidney almost got me."

"Yeah, right," Sidney muttered, although she had the second largest cache of chips, so the mutter didn't hold too much resentment.

Boone rose and stretched. "I'm gonna sit the next one out. Want to check the storm track."

"Don't you go taking pity on us," Butch declared. "Get your ass back in that chair so I can win my chips back!"

"I'll be back for the round after. And I'll bring fresh beers."

"Now you're talking," Butch said, shuffling the deck for a new round.

Boone was still getting cell service, which was a good sign. He checked the track and saw that Matthew was now a hurricane, albeit a weak one. Sustained winds of 75 mph meant it had just barely qualified.

He had just looped the necks of four bottles of Belgian beers in his long fingers when a cry of despair rose from the poker table. Boone arrived just as Sidney gathered the pot to herself. She looked up at him with a grin.

"Boone, if you want to sit out another hand, I won't be offended."

TWENTY-EIGHT

urricane Matthew was mostly a rain event, with some
street flooding. The eye had been nearly 150 miles away
to the north, but the counterclockwise rotation had brought
some swells into the "crook of the hook," where many of the
dive sites were. Rock Beauty volunteered their services to
STINAPA, as well as the Reef Renewal Foundation, going out to
assess damage to coral and sponges at several sites. Reef
Renewal was an independent organization that had been operating for a few years and had some extremely successful coral
nursery and reef renewal programs running. Frenchy saw it as
giving back to a group that would do much to help the diving
industry in Bonaire in the years to come.

Below thirty feet in depth, the reef was largely untouched.
In shallower waters, a lot of sand had been shifted, and about a
quarter of the coral showed some damage. Overall, Bonaire had
fared well. Of far greater concern to the diving community was
the influx of cruise ships. The island had been spared their
intrusion for a long time, but the first one had arrived in

Bonaire just before Boone had. Now, there were quite a few more, and two cruise ships could be accommodated at the piers. There were already rumblings of the need for a "one ship at a time" rule, to preserve the sleepy nature of Bonaire, as well as to protect its reefs.

The holiday season arrived and not for the first time, Boone felt guilty for not buying a plane ticket and visiting his mother, but she seemed to be quite happy with the fellow she was seeing. Apparently, he would be taking her to Biltmore Estate in North Carolina for a Christmas mini vacation. The holidays were one of the busiest times in the Caribbean, and it was all-hands-on-deck at Rock Beauty Divers.

In the waning months of the 2017 high season, Sidney announced that she would be leaving them soon. She had accepted an offer in Cayman Brac and would be departing at the end of April. And truth to tell, Boone, too, had been feeling the urge to see more of the world, and had put out a few feelers recently.

"I hope that's enough time to find someone, Frenchy," Sidney said.

"I'll survive, *ma chérie*. I'll post to some of the scuba forums today. And Emilio over at Habitat was looking for some additional subbing work. We'll be fine... so long as no one else sneaks away..." He gave Boone and Butch meaningful looks.

Boone cleared his throat. "Uh... full disclosure... I did talk to someone. Early days, but..."

"Tell me," Frenchy insisted.

"I've been messaging a Dutch divemaster in Saba named Anders. He's been looking for a change. He and I were talking about... I guess you'd call it a swap."

"You take his place, he takes yours?" Frenchy asked.

"That's the idea. And I could take over his rental lease there and he takes mine in Rincon. But like I said, early days. We were just tossing ideas around."

"Well, if any of those tosses becomes a catch and hold, you will let me know, yes?"

"You have my word."

Later that day, Boone, Sidney, and Butch were out on the *Kleine Dancer* with a group of divers from the States. During the surface interval, Boone sat beside Sidney on the flybridge.

"Cayman Brac, eh?"

"Saba, eh?" she countered.

"Yeah, I've been feeling a bit of wanderlust bubbling up."

"Same here. I wanted to try something different," she said, then she chuckled. "Although I think your choice is way, way more different than mine. Saba is a frikkin' mountain!"

"And covered in green," Boone said. "It'll be a bit of an adjustment, going from this desert to that place. Rain forests up high, I hear. And a lot of sharks. Don't get me wrong, I love the life here, but sometimes you want some bigger fish."

Back on shore, Frenchy came out of the office to help change out the tanks in preparation for the afternoon dive.

"You put out a call for a new divemaster, Frenchy?" Sidney asked.

"I cast my hook," he said. "Now we see if I get a nibble."

"Try to get one that sucks at poker, okay?" Butch said.

On a late-April morning, Boone was sitting on the edge of the dock beside the *Kleine Dancer* enjoying the breeze on his face when Frenchy came down from the parking lot. He had just taken Sidney to the airport.

"I'm missing Sidney already," Boone said.

"I as well, but the good news is, I just found a replacement!"

Boone stood and stretched. "I thought we already had someone?"

"They bailed at the last minute," Frenchy said. "Family emergency, they said. But last night, I received a message from a new candidate. She sent a video as a résumé and she was absolutely delightful. So very funny! And she is already here in Bonaire! I don't know how she knew there was an opening, but I am not complaining. She has excellent references."

"Where's she from?"

"I don't know... England... maybe Australia. Very thick accent, but incredibly charming."

Just then, Boone's phone rang and he glanced at it. "It's the owner of Scuba Dooby Do over in Curaçao."

"Ah, I remember, you worked for them... with the funny van, yes?"

"That's the one."

"You take that. I need to prepare some paperwork for our new hire."

Boone tapped the screen. "Hey, Laura! How's the Marine Machine?"

"Bearable, now that we fixed the air conditioner," she replied with a laugh. "Listen, do you remember that man with the funny mustache? Noah? We certified his daughter."

"Oh, yeah! Big Dutch guy. I remember him."

"Well, he contacted me out of the blue, looking for you."

"Yeah?"

"When we came in from diving Double Reef, he mentioned he was in the Dutch navy and you asked him about a Dirk Fischer?"

Boone had almost forgotten. "Uh... yeah, I guess I did."

"Well, Noah said he heard the name the other day and remembered you asking. He found out something and wanted to talk to you. Can I give him your number?"

Boone hesitated before he replied, "Sure."

A few hours later, Boone was filling tanks when his international calling app rang with a call from the Netherlands. He left the noisy fill room to answer.

"This is Boone Fischer."

"Boone, this is Noah. I hear you switched islands."

"I did indeed."

"Listen, I'll be brief, because I have to leave for a meeting, but I wanted to call you while I was still near my desk. Back in Curaçao, you asked if I knew or had served with a Diederik Fischer. And that he would be about my age."

"I did. But you said you didn't know him."

"I don't. But... the other day I was at a bar with some of my old navy friends, and the name Diederik Fischer came up... although my friend Hendrik called him Dirk."

"Okay...."

"Boone... is this man your father?"

Boone was silent for a moment.

"Are you still there?"

"I'm here. Yes, my father went by Dirk. But I don't know if this person that your friend mentioned is him."

"I think he is. May I ask... when did you last see him?"

"August 2000. My mom divorced him not long after."

"Well, apparently Dirk Fischer had served with Hendrik until Dirk left the service in early 1999."

Boone tried not to grind his teeth. So, his father had been out of the service for almost a year and a half before that final trip to Aruba. Boone's memory dredged up an image of his father's long hair on that trip, a clue that hadn't registered with an eleven-year-old still worshiping his father.

"But the reason Dirk was the topic of conversation was because he had been sent to prison for bigamy. It is illegal here... punishable by up to six years. Apparently, his wife in Amsterdam didn't know that he was already married to someone in the United States, but when the American wife divorced him, I guess that got back to her. She divorced him too, of course. Anyway, Dirk Fischer had fathered two children with her and apparently, he'd had a son with the American wife."

"Her name is Jenny."

"So... that *was* you."

Boone swallowed. "I suspect so."

"I'm sorry, I'm sure this is difficult to hear."

"S'okay. Happened a long time ago."

"Yes... well... I could see if I can get an address or phone number for him...?"

"No." There was no hesitation before Boone's reply, although there was silence on Noah's end. "As I said, it was a long time ago," Boone said. "And my mother is happier now."

"I understand."

"But... the other family... the wife... if you happen to find a number for her...?"

"Of course. I will try."

"Thanks, Noah. I gotta go." Boone hung up.

———

The following morning, Boone rose with the rooster. Once dressed, he grabbed the work gloves Martin had gotten him and shoved them into the pockets of his cargo shorts. Then, mounting his bike, he turned on its headlight and headed out, passing the dark shape of Martin's snack. This early in the morning, Martin would likely still be in bed—although he might be lying awake, cursing the vocal stylings of King Cock.

Boone headed west out of town, intending to travel the long way round and cycle through the southern part of Washington-Slagbaai Park past Goto Meer, an inland salt lake known for its flamingos. Pedaling hard, he pushed himself until he could feel his heart pounding. As he cycled south, he passed the eyesore oil refinery, then turned west along the coast.

If Noah turned up a phone number for the "other" family, Boone wasn't sure if he would do anything with it. And he wasn't sure if he should tell his mother anything about the phone call with Noah. She had a right to know, but he feared what might happen if she tried to contact his father. One thing he was certain of: he didn't want Dirk Fischer anywhere near his mother ever again.

Reaching the Karpata shore dive site, the coastal road turned one-way the wrong way, so Boone cut north until he reached a back road to continue his journey to Rock Beauty Divers. He wanted to get there early and lose himself in work. He'd been meaning to clean the underside of the boat, and this was as good a time as any.

When he arrived at the dive shop, he unlocked the equipment room, grabbed a scraper and the keys to the *Kleine Dancer*, then took everything down to the empty pier. He dug the work gloves out of his pockets and dropped them beside the scraper, then stripped to his swimsuit. Sponge Bob and Patrick were on hiatus, and he was back to basic red swim shorts. While there was a dinghy available, Boone ignored it as he often did, instead diving into the ocean to swim out to the dive boat at its mooring. Bringing it in just as the sun's upper edge breached the horizon, he tied up and stepped across to the dock.

While many dive op employees used a scuba tank to do the hull cleaning, Boone saw the activity as a way to practice his breath holds. Donning the work gloves, he grabbed the scraper and jumped in beside the *Kleine Dancer*. After a breathe-up, he ducked under the hull and began to scrape at barnacles and the thin coating of algae, surrendering his thoughts to the work at hand.

He wasn't sure how long he'd been at it when he decided to take a break and surfaced at the bow, figuring he'd get a tiny bit of a workout into his morning. He tossed the scraper aboard, then reached up to grip the bow line and raised himself within reach of the gunwale. Once he'd grabbed hold, he did a pull-up and hauled himself onto the bow of the dive boat. Breathing hard and dripping salt water, he was startled by a feminine voice coming from the dock.

"You know there's a ladder at the back, yeah?"

The accent was thick, sounding almost Cockney to Boone's American ears. He turned and found himself looking down at a young blonde in her twenties wearing a lime-green tank top, yellow shorts, and flip-flops. Fit and curvy, she was exceedingly petite, probably no more than five feet in height. Her shining hair was tied in braids that draped over her tanned shoulders. Even though the sun was still quite low in the sky, she sported an enormous pair of bright green sunglasses perched atop a button nose. The shades completely obscured her eyes, but Boone suspected they were shining with amusement, based on the crooked smile that was dimpling one cheek.

Boone realized he was staring. "Uh... hi."

The crooked smile shifted, and perfect upper teeth bit a plump lower lip. Then the girl's body posture shifted. "And a hearty hello to you, good sir." She pointed at the boat. "There were a few times I wasn't sure you were coming up."

"Oh... yeah. I was just cleaning the hull. Figured I'd practice breath-holding while I did it."

The crooked smile returned. "You do realize there's an entire stash of scuba tanks over there, yeah?"

Boone grinned, then looked toward the shop and feigned surprise. "Well, whattaya know? Thanks, helpful stranger."

"Happy to help, dripping-wet stranger. You done mucking about under there?"

"Uh, yeah."

"Good. I need the ha'penny tour."

"Oh. Okay..." Boone went amidships and stepped across to the dock. Now that he was beside her, he noted her face was barely to the level of his chest. "Are you looking to dive with us? We don't open until eight."

The blonde's smile grew, lighting up her face. She lifted her chin to look up at him. "Well, as a matter of fact, I *am* looking to dive with you." She raised her huge sunglasses and balanced them above her forehead. Wide, green eyes gazed up at him, sparkling with mirth. "I'm the new hire."

"Oh! Sorry. Wow, you're here early."

A tan shoulder shrugged. "So are you. You Frenchy? You don't sound French."

"No... I'm Boone."

"Pleased to meet you, Boone. I'm Emily."

Keep reading for The Afterword, for an inside peek at what was based on fact, and what was made up... but first:

· · ·

If you enjoyed this book, please take a moment to visit Amazon and provide a short review; every reader's voice is extremely important for the life of a book or series.

Want to see what happened next? (well... three months later, to be precise) Then be sure to check out Book One of The Deep Series:

DEEP SHADOW

And if you'd like advance notice of Boone and Emily's next adventures, head on over to

WWW.NICKSULLIVAN.NET

where you can sign up for my mailing list. If you're like me, you hate spam, so rest assured I'll email rarely. Be the first to know when my next book is available!

FOLLOW ME ON BOOKBUB to get an alert whenever I have a new release, preorder, or discount! And it will bring me joy. The more followers I have, the more powerful I become!

And check out other authors who set their tales on the water, near the water, or under the tropical sun at

WWW.TROPICALAUTHORS.COM

And now... on to The Afterword!

AFTERWORD

All of us can remember an event that played an outsized role in shaping who we are. And with a little thought, another event... and another. Some positive, some downright terrible. Life's journey stretches back in time like a road paved with days, weeks, and years, and that road is filled with these seminal moments. And then there are the people we've met along the way: an inspirational teacher, a friend who turned unfriendly, or a first love.

When I started *Deep Shadow* back in 2017, I had an inkling of who Boone was. After all, we shared a few traits—none physical, alas—and we came from the same part of the world. And, of course, we both loved diving. But as I wrote The Deep Series, Boone became less and less like me and more and more like himself. There was a point, midway between *Deep Focus* and *Deep Hex*, where I thought, "Wouldn't it be nice to go back and see what happened to create the Boone we meet in The Deep Series? And Emily, too!" Although, she'll have to wait her turn. You may be surprised to learn that I am, in fact, *not* a 4'11"

243

British woman in her twenties. Em's prequel book will require extra research.

After completing *Deep Hex*, I put some thought into how I might tackle Boone's origin story, and one of the first steps was to sit down and read through every single book in the series, making notes about every bit of backstory that Boone—and Emily—revealed. I ended up with a large document full of information: schooling, pets, earlier loves, hobbies, places they had visited before Bonaire, and lots of tidbits about family. Quite a few of these were things I had completely forgotten! I separated out the Boone from the Emily, then shifted things around so that the information was in some semblance of chronological order.

This provided the bones I would build the story on top of, beginning with a rough year-by-year calendar. I realized that most readers wouldn't want to spend a great deal of time with Baby Boone sitting in a highchair, eating strained peas and carrots. Almost immediately, I decided that this book had to start with one of the most momentous events in Boone's life: learning to dive. This happened to coincide with another major event: his parents' divorce. Throughout the series, Boone has always been fairly close-lipped about what exactly happened between his parents, but I had long ago decided that his absentee father was absent for a reason, and it wasn't an honorable one. Once I had sculpted those two formative events, it was time to watch Boone grow up.

One of the challenges I faced was that Boone's childhood occurred within a time period that wasn't during my own. So, when it came time to, say... explain how an eleven-year-old Boone would learn about freediving in 2000, naturally my modern brain thought, "Oh, he'd watch videos on YouTube." Well, I quickly realized YouTube wasn't launched until 2005!

And cell phones: they are such a part of our lives now, but it would be highly unlikely for eleven-year-old Boone to have one in 2000. I didn't get mine until 1998, and I remember some of my buddies didn't yet have one. I actually found it—my old Samsung—and used that to model Dirk's phone. And I use Google Maps constantly when I go to islands for dive trips, but when this book starts, I realized he'd be doing what I did on my first trip to Bonaire in 2000: print maps out from MapQuest. Google Maps wasn't really around until 2005... and not on phones until 2006. Needless to say, every time I had Boone use some form of mundane tech that we now take for granted, I paused to research if it existed in the year I was currently writing about.

I had originally planned for this to be a novella. But as is often the case, the story went where it wanted to go. When the dust settled, I had a novel that was about the same length as *Deep Roots*. I realize this book is quite different from the other books in the series and I hope you all enjoyed it! I have two solid ideas for Book Seven in the series, and I'm eager to get started on that one. Emily will get her turn at some point in the future, but as this trip down Boone-memory lane took longer than expected, I'll be shifting gears to return to the main storyline.

And now we come to the part of my books that I very much enjoy: I'll reveal where some of the elements of the plot came from and separate fact from fiction.

Boone's Family and Kingston, TN: I had a phenomenal childhood with the greatest Mom and Dad, and Boone's parents bear zero resemblance to my own. As for Kingston, it's down the road from where I grew up in Oak Ridge, TN. The decision to have Boone come from the smaller town of Kingston goes back to *Deep Shadow*. I wanted Boone to grow up in a much smaller town than Oak Ridge, and one with a *lot* of water around. The Clinch River is very much a part of Kingston —I still have fond memories of watching the 2017 eclipse there, from a friend's riverfront backyard. But Boone would need to visit Oak Ridge for a few things...

Oak Ridge, TN: Yes, that pool is there and it is *huge*. At the time it was built, it was the largest pool in the southeast. Yes, I swam up under that dock. No, I didn't enjoy it as thoroughly as Boone did. And no, I wasn't a lifeguard; I worked in the concessions stand. But I did take advanced swimming lessons there, and I also took swimming lessons in the indoor pool I mention in the book. And yes... I studied jiu-jitsu in that same complex, although it wasn't Brazilian JJ and I only made it to green belt. And finally, Big Ed's Pizza had to make an appearance; that was *the* place to go when I was in high school. But let me return to the topic of swimming lessons.

The rock with the painted eye: When I was very young, my parents took me to a neighbor's house that had a pool, and that's where I learned to swim. And yes, for graduation, if a kid reached the bottom and grabbed a painted rock, they got to keep it. It's faded now, but I still have it.

Aruba: I've never been. And I have no idea what businesses were there in 2000, so I made up the hotel and dive op. I found a lot of information on the Pedernales dive site, and that seemed to be a perfect open water cert dive. Fun fact: the Creole language of the ABC Islands is called Papiamento in Aruba and Papiamentu in Bonaire and Curaçao.

Boone learning to dive: Like Boone, snorkeling was my gateway drug to scuba diving. For Boone, it was in Aruba, but for me it was in Barbados. I remember snorkeling for so long, my young back was sunburned to a crisp. One area where Boone's story and mine match is *when* the diving starts. A quick thank-you to Roger Josselyn of PADI for helping with the time-line of what the age and depth limits were for the Junior Open Water certification in 2000.

I did my first dives in 1999 (a PADI Discover Scuba Diving course in Statia, with Golden Rock Diving), and I got my actual certification in 2000... just like Boone! But unlike Boone, I got my certification from NAUI (shifting to PADI when I took my Advanced Courses) and my open water dives were not in the idyllic, tropical waters of the Caribbean. While a gravel quarry in Pennsylvania was an option, for whatever insane reason, we chose instead to do our open water cert in the Reynolds Channel of Far Rockaway, not far from JFK Airport. I remember whipping currents (you did *not* let go of the training cage) and near-zero viz. Crawling down a line along beds of mussels, a horseshoe crab paid me a visit—in this book, I had Fred mention a snapping turtle instead. And when we came up, a fisherman snagged my buddy's wetsuit with his hook. His dive knife made short work of the line—I still remember the fisherman begging "No-no-no-no!" Don't feel too bad for the fisherman; I recently talked to the instructor who trained me on that dive, and he said they sometimes aimed at the bubbles for laughs.

The aquarium: When I wrote *Deep Shadow*, I had decided that Boone would have worked as a diver at an aquarium, because his hometown was smack-dab between two of the best in the southeast: The Tennessee Aquarium in Chattanooga and the Ripley's Aquarium of the Smokies in Gatlinburg, Tennessee. I had been to both, but I decided on Ripley's for a number of reasons. I'm glad I did!

First, a *huge* thank-you to the staff of Ripley's Aquarium of the Smokies. I met with the dive safety officer, presentation divers, aquarists, marine veterinarian, the director of husbandry, and more. Mike, Frank, Shayne (from Oak Ridge!) and especially Jay... everyone made me feel incredibly welcome, and I was given a detailed look behind the curtain of a massive undertaking. I was there for over six hours, and by the end of it I had pages and pages of notes and gigabytes of photos and videos to sift through. I met some of the younger divers during a lunch break, and could easily see Boone there. Now... what was real, and what did I fudge a bit?

The procedures of day-to-day activities for the divers I tried to keep as accurate as possible. Cleaning and feeding are probably the most time-intensive portion of a diver's day. The triggerfish with the pacifier and the skimmer guard full of Binkies from parents holding up their kids... I *wish* I was that creative, but that came from interviews. The vinegar and meat tenderizer: on my walkthrough, I took a picture of a first aid station. Yep... that's real. The jar with the pennies found in the tanks and filters... okay, I made that up.

Sally the sea turtle sneaking up on divers? I saw that happen. She's a sweety—I fed her some bok choy. And she did come from the Seaquarium on Virginia Key, right next to the campus where I had always said Boone went to college... that was a complete coincidence. Sally was a rescue, but one thing I didn't put into the book was the manner of the rescue. Apparently, a family had taken a baby turtle from an island in the Caribbean and smuggled it back on the airplane to be a pet. Well, that turned out about the way you'd expect. A steadily growing Sally was given to the Seaquarium and rehabilitated. Unlikely to survive in the wild, she found a new home in Gatlinburg, and has been the queen of the aquarium ever since her arrival.

Finally, there were a few times where I had to "cheat" to include things that would not have been there at the same time as Boone. While I don't spell it out, Boone would have been working at the aquarium in 2007. There wasn't yet a glass bottom boat there, but I thought that was a fun item to include. And the sawfish breeding program had not yet begun, but the Aquarium of the Smokies is one of several aquariums that are participating in captive breeding programs in partnership with several conservation organizations and government agencies. Currently, of the five sawfish species, two are endangered and three are critically endangered. While there would not have been a sawfish in a tank when Boone was there, I felt they deserved a mention.

And finally... mermaids. If you've read The Deep Series, you will know that a certain British blonde is obsessed with them, so when I learned that the aquarium had mermaid shows, well... I *had* to include that. Full disclosure, the mermaids didn't find their way to Gatlinburg until 2016, but how could I not have Boone hanging out with a mermaid? So... the mermaid show: while some shows use a hookah, in Gatlinburg the mermaids are freedivers—another nice connection with Boone Fischer. The shows involve two mermaids and a safety diver... and yes, they do a "Breakfast with a Mermaid" function. And the lube? When I was doing the tour and saw some sitting there where the mermaids suit up, its practical purpose was very quickly explained to me. I rather enjoyed Faye/Finny... and maybe she'll show up again someday. Perhaps working for "Greg the Divemaster" of Scuba Radio at one of their diving convention appearances!

Search and Rescue: This was an area that I had planned to do more with, but it quickly became clear that I would be doing the practice a disservice, trying to "shoehorn" it into the plot. I decided to include a little about it as a way to create a bond with Boone and one of his surrogate "father figures," and that seemed to be the best way to do it justice. My sincere thanks to one of my favorite professors from college, Dan Backlund, who is a search-and-rescue diver with the Franklin County Rescue Squad and a certified Master Underwater Criminal Investigator. If I ever bring Boone back to Tennessee, I'll be calling on his expertise again! The area where I placed that fictional search is quite real and is a popular place to swim and picnic.

University of Miami: I had established that Boone attended this college back in *Shadow*, and I had planned to have him attend with an athletic scholarship; otherwise, one of the books would probably have to be *Deep Debt*. A swimming scholarship was the obvious choice. Alas, the men's swimming program ended in 2000, so I had to go the cross-country route. U of M is consistently in the top list of colleges with Marine Science degrees and with the Rosenstiel campus being on an island, it seemed like the perfect place for Boone, particularly with its proximity to The Bahamas and the Florida Keys.

Semester abroad in Bonaire: In *Deep Shadow*, I had said that Boone had taken a semester abroad here, so that had to happen. When I visited in 2006, I got to meet Phillipe Cousteau Jr. and Captain Don Stewart at Dive into Adventure Bonaire, held at Captain Don's Habitat. This does not match up with Boone's semester chronologically, but it was close enough. My favorite memory was a moment in the Q&A when I raised my hand and Cap'n Don appeared to point at me, but when I stood and opened my mouth, he waved his hand and said "No, no... not you... the pretty girl," and pointed to the woman behind me.

And speaking of pretty girls, "Penny," the freckled Irish lass who mans the bar at Rum Runners, appears in *Deep Shadow*, and while I never said so, I'd always had it in my mind that she and Boone had had a dalliance at some point. One amusing bit of backstory that I didn't initially intend: her working in an aquarium. I chose for Penny to be from County Kerry because my father had some ancestors from there, and then I chose the town of "Dingle" because I thought the name was amusing. And when I dropped into the town on Google Maps, there it was: Dingle Oceanworld Aquarium.

One item that may have caught your eye: the lionfish and the cork buoy markers. This is indeed something that was used when they first started showing up—*right* before Boone would have arrived. But by the time I visited with a Ziploc of wine corks, I was told "Oh... no, we stopped using the corks a long time ago." On my first visit to Bonaire, there wasn't a single lionfish to be seen. On my latest trip in 2023, I saw the largest lionfish I have ever seen in *any* island.

Curaçao: I visited there in July/August 2023 (my first time). I plan to base an entire book in Curaçao in the future, but for this prequel I wanted to hit some of the highlights. *Masha danki* (thank you) to Laura Van Loon, a divemaster/instructor in Curaçao, who took me on a tour of some of her favorite dive sites and was kind enough to sit down with me for some lengthy Q&A sessions. A reader of the series told me to check her out, because she looked like how this reader pictured Emily. Go visit her page on Instagram (Laura.Van.Loon). Additional thanks to Pursy, a cab driver my hotel recommended, who took me on a tour of many neighborhoods and drove me up to Fort Nassau and the restaurant up there.

With Boone's time on the island taking place from roughly 2012-2015, I didn't know what businesses were around, and decided to make some up. Curaçao is a lot larger than Bonaire, and many of the shore dive sites are quite far apart, so I thought I'd be clever and have a dive op that has a bus that takes groups to the shore dive spots. I figured I'd just call it the

Scuba Bus... and have it painted red with white stripes. Well, when I opened up a Google Street View of the Tugboat Beach site (looking for a place for Boone to practice capoeira), what did I find but an old school bus, painted like a dive flag! And yes... it's called Scuba Bus. Okay, fine, I'll call it the Dive Bus. Nope, there's one of those, too! And that's why I went all out with the Scuba Dooby Do and the Marine Machine. Fortunately, that nutty idea wasn't taken.

I dove several sites during my visit, and at Double Reef there was a huge warship docked close by. It turned out it was British—more on that later—but I figured I'd put a Dutch warship there when Boone is with Noah, to have another connection to Dirk Fischer. And his daughter, Anika? She's actually from a later book, and tells Boone he certified her in Curaçao. I did not dive the *Superior Producer*, but Pursy told me all about the time it sank and the citizens went out to "rescue" the cargo.

Willemstad is an amazing place! The floating market was very cool, and I figured I'd use that setting as the one-and-only time Boone visits the Punda during the book. Another landmark, the Queen Juliana pontoon bridge, is beautiful at night, and I got stuck on it when it opened before I had finished crossing. While I waited beside the locked gate, I heard a strong British accent beside me and struck up a conversation with a young man. Turned out he was a sailor from the HMS *Dauntless*, a Type 45 destroyer of the Royal Navy... and *that* was the ship I had seen at Double Reef.

María Cabrera: In *Deep Shadow*, I established that Boone had a year-and-a-half relationship with a woman named María, "a beauty from Colombia." The catamaran cruise I placed her on is loosely based on a real company, but I decided to fictionalize it, as well as the deep-sea fishing gig. In *Shadow*, I had established both of those as Boone's non-diving side hustles before he came to Bonaire.

The final chapters in Bonaire: Much of what happens in the last chapters of the book is culled from the backstory in *Deep Shadow*: Boone choosing Rincon, his friendship with Martin, sending a knife-wielder to the hospital, shooting Glocks in the desert, and Frenchy the Belgian of Rock Beauty Divers. But I figured I'd need to add some things beyond what we know from *Shadow*.

Here, I want to give a huge shout out and thank you to Nicholas Harvey—a.k.a. Brit Nick—and his wife Cheryl Rains Harvey, for inviting me down to Bonaire and putting me up. We dove together, ate together, and most importantly... saw the ostracods together! The night dive I describe is very close to what I experienced. I used data from my Shearwater Teric dive computer to lock down some of the timing, although I had to change the sunset times a bit, because the August full moon in 2016 was seventeen days later than the one we dove after in 2023. That was a phenomenal experience, and it made me wish I'd dived with the glowworms when I had been in South Caicos. Incidentally, if you'd like to see how Brit Nick handled the ostracod dive with his characters, go check out *Lighthouse Point*. AJ Bailey is normally a Cayman Islands gal, but she spends that book in Bonaire.

In 2018, I stayed with another author, Tricia O'Malley, and she took me to dive the wild side with East Bay Diving. It was amazing and completely unlike the diving on the lee side, so I checked with their owners and determined they were around at the time Boone would have been there. It provided a nice interlude that led to Boone meeting his capoeira sparring buddy.

A big thank you to *The Bonaire Reporter* for their detailed

2009 article about cactus fences. I also found several wonderful videos on YouTube about it. If you'd like to check them out, look for "Building the Cactus Fence." As an added benefit, there is a lot of Papiamentu to listen to in those videos. I had established in *Shadow* that Martin was one of a few who made these fences, and given what an iconic sight they are in Bonaire, I wanted to include a scene about them.

And that's it for my "where did these plot points come from" section. On to the rest of the acknowledgements!

My thanks to all of my friends at Tropical Authors. I had a great time hanging out with many of you in St. Pete in September 2023. If you're interested in beach reads set by the ocean, under the sea, on boats, islands, and coastlines, be sure to sign up for the Tropical Authors newsletter for lots of deals from your favorite tropical authors.

Thank you to all of my beta readers: John Brady, Drew Mutch, Bob Hickerson, Dan Backlund, Patrick Newman, Deg Priest, Mike Ramsey, Malcolm Sullivan, Jason Hebert, David Margolis, Joan Zale, Mark Aldrich, and Gary Cox. Most of you have extraordinary backgrounds in diving, boating, and writing, and I depend on you to "keep me honest" on the technical side of things while making great suggestions on elements of the story.

A big thank you to Shayne Rutherford of Wicked Good Book Covers for creating another gem. This one is a bit different from my usual covers, which is befitting a story that is quite different from the rest of the series. Additional thanks to John Brady for helping me "fix the hair" on the diver on the cover. Hair is hard! And yes, the swim trunks in the stock photo amused me, so I added a scene where Faye gifts them to Boone.

Thank you to Marsha Zinberg of The Write Touch, my stalwart editor, who had her work cut out for her with a book that was almost a collection of linked short stories. Your thoughts were invaluable and helped give *Boone* a more coherent shape. And I think some of your lessons on grammar and punctuation are starting to stick.

Thank you to Gretchen Tannert Douglas and Forest Olivier for sniffing out those pesky typos. I swear, sometimes I think there is some form of Typo Gremlin creating errors that weren't there before! My thanks to my dive buddy Karl Cleveland for his work on my DeepNovels.com website, giving it a clean and polished look.

And finally, as always, thank you to my readers—and my audiobook listeners. I hope you enjoyed this trip down Backstory Lane. I'll be returning to the main timeline of The Deep Series shortly. And Boone and Emily will need a new boat! Any suggestions?

Until next time, stay safe, stay sane... and keep seeking the sun.

ABOUT THE AUTHOR

Born in East Tennessee, Nick Sullivan has spent most of his adult life as an actor in New York City working in television, film, theater, and audiobooks. After narrating hundreds of titles over the last couple of decades, he decided to write his own. Nick is an avid scuba diver, and his travels to numerous islands throughout the Caribbean have inspired The Deep Series.

For a completely different kind of book, you can find Nick Sullivan's first novel at:
www.zombiebigfoot.com

Made in United States
Orlando, FL
29 May 2024

47326447R00162